Eye of the Eagle

by

Sharon Buchbinder

The Hotel LaBelle Series
Book 3

Eye of the Eagle

Contact Information: info@thewildrosepress.com

Cover Art by *Rae Monet, Inc. Design*

The Wild Rose Press, Inc.
PO Box 708
Adams Basin, NY 14410-0708
Visit us at www.thewildrosepress.com

Publishing History
First Fantasy Rose Edition, 2018
Print ISBN 978-1-5092-2356-5
Digital ISBN 978-1-5092-2357-2

The Hotel Labelle Series, Book 3
Published in the United States of America

His heart stuttered, and heat flushed his face. "You sure you're still ready to see me—in the *daylight*?"

She frowned and pursed her lips. "Do I look like someone afraid of taking on a challenge?"

"No. You look like a kick-ass heroine named Thunder Heart, and I would be honored and privileged to share your bed."

"You promised me flying lessons."

"And you shall have them. Now, where did we leave off?"

She stood, placed her hands on the sides of his chair, and leaned in for a long passionate kiss.

He closed his eyes and gave her a preview, taking her with him in his memories, soaring over the hotel, and then swirling and swooping down to the river to grab a fat flopping trout in his talons.

She pulled back, breaking the connection, blue eyes wide, her full red lips agape. "Amazing. I want more."

"Advanced flying lessons require both of us to be naked—and in bed, as close as two people can get."

Phoebe stood back. "What are you waiting for? Let's get going."

He chuckled. "Well, you are my boss. I don't want anyone to say you coerced me or I forced you. Do we need to put this in writing?"

She tilted her head and gave him a puzzled look.

"A legal document perhaps? I, Phoebe Wagner, hereby enter into consensual sex freely and without coercion with one Bert Blackfeather…"

She stomped her foot. "Give me your phone."

He handed her his cell.

Praise for Sharon Buchbinder

"Sharon Buchbinder plunges readers into a high-paced tale with intriguing paranormal elements that fit perfectly into the landscape of *EYE OF THE EAGLE*. Be prepared to read into the night because Buchbinder grabs you with characters you can't help but love, or hate, and pulls every heartstring to the last page."

~*Nancy C. Weeks, author of the Shadows and Light series and The D'Azzo Family series*

~*~

"Sharon Buchbinder seamlessly blends intriguing, sexy characters and fast-paced suspense in a page-turner you won't be able to put down until the end."

~*Sharon Saracino, Author, The Earthbound Series*

~*~

"Ms. Buchbinder weaves ancient secrets and modern mysteries into a beautifully written story that will keep you turning the pages."

~*USA Today Bestselling Author, Roz Lee*

Dedication

This book is dedicated with love to my first reader,
title inspirer, and husband, Dale,
and to our son, Joshua, our daughter-in-law, Elyse,
and our grandson, Dexter.
They remind me every day that family ties bind
with love and priceless memories
—and that bond should never be ripped apart.

~*~

It is also dedicated to my tireless and supportive editor,
Amanda Barnett, who is my book midwife,
helping to bring my book babies into the world.

~*~

And to Sharon Saracino,
my funny and fun critique partner and friend.
She helps me see the humor in all things
in the writing life
and other parts of my sometimes crazy world.

Author's Note

Anyone who has read my previous novels knows that before I begin to write, I conduct extensive research and steep myself in the materials. This approach enables me to speak through the characters and narrative with rich and correct content. I also rely on subject matter experts and readers from diverse disciplines and cultural backgrounds who provide corrections and feedback to me before I submit a story for consideration for publication.

I would be remiss if I did not thank my readers here, starting with my ever-patient husband, Dale Buchbinder, who read every single draft of the story. My deep gratitude goes to the following people for their expertise and feedback: Cheryl Bosse, Julie Bourne, Joshua and Elyse Buchbinder, Toni Chiazza Diblasi, Hal Dorin, Karen and Ken Giek, Ernest and Toni Goetling, Joy John, Nellie Mercer, Sharon Saracino, Sonia Vitale-Richardson, Nancy Weeks, and Susan Willis. Big hugs to my brilliant editor and book midwife, Amanda Barnett, who assists with the birth of my book babies.

Three of my readers were sensitivity readers, i.e., writers and readers who read works of fiction or other writings with a view toward accurate representation of groups of people and for "bias, racism, or unintentional stereotypes" ("What the heck is sensitivity reading?" Marks, 2018). One reader is a graduate of Gallaudet University, the only university founded by an Act of Congress with a charter signed by President Abraham Lincoln "specifically designed to serve deaf and hard-of-hearing students" ("Fast facts," Gallaudet.edu). The other two readers are disability experts, one of whom is also an advocate of accurate representation of Lesbian, Gay, Bi-Sexual, Transgender, and Queer (LGBTQ) individuals. I deferred to my sensitivity readers on all matters of representation, tone, and language. Any errors or misinterpretations of their generous guidance are solely mine.

The National Center for Missing and Exploited Children (NCMEC) is the central resource for families whose children go missing. A multifaceted issue, in order of likelihood, children run or wander away or can be abducted by family members or non-family members. Thanks to the courage and advocacy of parents and family members who have lived through the nightmare of a missing child, we now have more resources on hand than ever before. In addition to local, state, and federal agencies, nonprofit organizations like NCMEC have a place in the pantheon of establishments that are ready to leap to a family's assistance when the call no one wants to make comes in. For a comprehensive listing of these organizations and to learn how to prepare for the unthinkable, go to http://www.missingkids.com/home

Due to the persistence, curiosity, and warmth of Frank B. Linderman, the world has a written history of the Absaalooke, or Crow Nation, a traditionally oral culture. If you have not read his work and are interested in Native American stories, biographies, and autobiographies. I recommend beginning with *Pretty Shield: Medicine Woman of the Crows*. The Crow have a long tradition of stories involving Little-people who are supposed to have special powers, including super-human strength. A number of authors have noted the parallels between faeries, elves, and little-people of other cultures and those of the Crow people. If you are interested in Chief Plenty-Coups' first-hand story of his encounter with the Pryor Mountain Little-people, I recommend you read Linderman's *Plenty-Coups: Chief of the Crows.*

The Magnitsky Act, formally known as the Russia and Moldova Jackson—Vanik Repeal and Sergei Magnitsky Rule of Law Accountability Act of 2012, is the result of Bill Browder's tireless efforts to punish Russian officials who were responsible for the death of tax lawyer Sergei Magnitsky. After Magnitsky revealed massive thefts from the Russian people by corrupt officials, he was arrested, imprisoned, tortured, denied medical care, and, ultimately, beaten to death. The act, commonly referred to as "Russian sanctions," prevents known Russian torturers and murderers from obtaining U.S. Visas and freezes their assets in American banks, businesses, and properties. These assets run into billions of dollars. In retaliation to the Magnitsky Act, the Russian government prohibited Americans from adopting Russian orphans. The phrase "Russian adoptions" is code for "Russian sanctions," i.e., the Magnitsky Act. If you want to have a better understanding of the culture and criminal operations of these corrupt Russians, I highly recommend Bill Browder's *Red Notice*. It is non-fiction, but reads like a crime novel.

Our intelligence agencies and their employees are unsung heroes and heroines. Whether working for the Central Intelligence Agency, or the Federal Bureau of Investigation, the National Security Agency, the Department of Homeland Security, the work can be tedious and mundane—and highly classified. Loose lips do sink ships and kill people. Those who work in the field undercover must be protected from exposure. Otherwise, they and their families are at risk of harm. Since the Cold War we have been in a technology race for intelligence gathering, including spies with psychic abilities. If you are interested in spies and the craft of spying, including the gadgets, I recommend reading *Spycraft: The Secret History of the CIA's Spytechs, from Communism to Al-Qaeda*, by Robert Wallace and H. Keith Melton and *Agent 110: An American Spymaster and the German Resistance in WWII* by Scott Miller.

The Central Intelligence Agency's work with psychic spies, remote viewing, and the infamous MK ULTRA behavioral modification program is well documented. Disbanded for ethical reasons, the full text of the *Project MKULTRA, the CIA's Program on Research in Behavioral Modification 1977 Joint Hearing Before the Select Committee on Intelligence and the Subcommittee on Health and Scientific Research of the Committee on Human Resources United States Senate, Ninety-Fifth Congress, First Session, August 3, 1977* is available online and as a reprint from the collection of the University of Michigan Library. If you are interested in learning more about this unusual chapter in our intelligence agency's history, I recommend the following: "Paranormal Activity: CIA Dimension" by Jim Popkin, in the November 11, 2015 issue of *Newsweek*; *The Men Who Stare at Goats* by Jon Ronson (also adapted to film), and *The Search for the Manchurian Candidate: The CIA and Mind Control, The Secret History of the*

Behavioral Sciences by John Marks. There are some who believe the CIA's more unusually talented people have moved to the Homeland Security Agency. Who knows? Maybe the Anomaly Defense Division I created in 2015 is alive and well under another name!

The hero of this book lost his legs in Iraq, our country's longest and most expensive war at an estimated *three trillion dollars*. The impact of this war continues to be borne by our veterans and their families. In 2013, the Veteran's Administration stopped reporting the number of wounded soldiers because the number was unthinkable: one million volunteers injured or maimed in the line of duty. If you are interested in learning more about this, I recommend reading *The Trillion Dollar War: The True Cost of the Iraq Conflict* by Joseph E. Stiglitz and Linda J. Bilmes.

Deaf Studies programs are available in almost every major university in the United States. If you are interested in learning more about American Sign Language, deaf history, and culture, there are many good books available. I recommend *The Deaf Community in America: History in the Making* by Melvia M. Nomeland and Ronald E. Nomeland, *Forbidden Signs: American Culture and the Campaign Against Sign Language* by Douglas C. Baynton, *Signs of Resistance: American Deaf Cultural History, 1900 to World War II*, by Susan Burch, *Deaf History Unveiled: Interpretations from the New Scholarship* by John Vickery Van Cleve, and the website, Signing Savvy, which has a wonderful supply of information for those who are interested. Your Sign Language Resource. https://www.signingsavvy.com

Of all my books, the heroine in this story is my

most personal. Phoebe Wagner is based on my grandmother, Bessie T. Engelman, who gave me unconditional love when I needed it most. Born in 1881, my grandmother contracted spinal meningitis at sixteen months of age and lost her hearing. She was a resident at what is now the Kentucky School for the Deaf in Danville, Kentucky from age seven to twenty-one. An educated and strong woman, she moved to Washington, D.C., where she worked for a Congressman addressing envelopes with her beautiful penmanship. She met my grandfather, Carl Rhodes, on a blind date. A wild man on a motorcycle, Carl was born deaf, became a ward of the Department of the Interior, and attended Kendall School, which is housed on the campus of Gallaudet University in Washington, D.C. Disobeying her wealthy Kentucky family, my grandmother married her "bad boy" and raised six hearing children in Washington, D.C., where my grandfather worked for the U.S. Botanical Gardens and the White House. Every day I thank my grandmother for defying her parents, for marrying my grandfather, and for showing me the most important of all abilities: persistence, hope, compassion, and love. I know she is my guardian angel, always looking out for me and my family.

I hope you enjoy the story. If you are interested in additional sources I used to research this novel, I would be happy to send you my list of references. Just email me at: sharonbellbuchbinder@gmail.com

Happy reading!

Prologue

Hotel LaBelle, Billings, Montana

Crouched behind a stand of bushes across the river from the Victorian mansion, the stranger surveyed his surroundings to ensure he wasn't observed by a late-night visitor. He did his best work under the cover of night when people slept, secure in their dreams. By day, the place buzzed with people coming and going. By night, the pace slowed, as if the hotel took deep breaths and drifted into slumber, resting and recovering for the next sunrise. The shadows served as his allies, hiding his peculiarity from the locals. Night embraced him like a lover, keeping his secrets. Tonight, in the preternatural pause before the incoming storm, all was quiet, except for the call of an owl and the squeaks of nocturnal creatures. *Predator and prey.*

He'd waited a long time for this special child. With the specific family background he wanted, she was exactly what he needed. It would take time, but he could wait. Patience was one of the things he excelled at. That and taking children away from their homes. He had honed his skills, perfected his technique. But the timing was off and he needed to lay low. No need to arouse suspicion. As he always did, he'd blend in. Beneath the surface, in the shadows, keeping his ear to the ground. Listening, listening, and listening for that one sound that told him the instant had come. When the sign appeared to him, he would be prepared, and no one would be the wiser until it was too late, and the little girl with the wild red hair and large blue eyes was in his possession. Soon, very soon, she would be his.

****

Bright-eyed and bushy tailed, as her husband would say, Tallulah Stewart slipped into the kitchen, flipped the switch for the coffee pot, and began to prep breakfast for her guests. As she sliced the homemade cinnamon bread, she smiled at the thought of the still sleeping Lucius, blissfully unaware of her activities. Ever since her darling daughter came into the world, Tallulah had become a morning lark and Lucius a night owl. With a twenty-four hour a day business like Hotel LaBelle, it was good they alternated shifts. No need for both of them to be exhausted. A huge bolt of lightning flashed, bathing the kitchen in bright light. Moments after, thunder shook the hotel. *That was close.*

Thank God Miriam takes after her father and sleeps through everything.

A frisson shimmied down her back.

Miriam. Something was wrong with Miriam.

Dread bloomed in her chest, and she struggled to breathe. Knife falling out of her numb hand, Tallulah ran to her child's room.

Shadows draped the space over her daughter's nest. Pillows and stuffed animals tilted at all angles and a small lump burrowed deep in the blankets. Tallulah let out a long sigh of relief. Hot or cold, that girl loved her blankets, the more the merrier. Active, even in her sleep, Miriam had been an early walker *and* climber. Despite parental efforts at containment, from eleven months of age on, each morning the little gymnast had been found on the other side of the bars of the crib. They had surrendered and converted the crib to a toddler bed. Tallulah tip-toed next to her precious bundle, gently slid a quilt back—and screamed.

Chapter One

Washington, D.C.
Homeland Security Headquarters

Bert Blackfeather stared at the email on his screen, re-read it for the tenth time, and shook his head in disbelief. A political appointee—a woman with absolutely *no* background in Homeland Security or any other intelligence matters—was now his new boss, the Under Secretary for Management. *Unbelievable.* Third in command of the Department of Homeland Security (DHS), assistant and advisor to the Secretary and Under Secretary on all administrative, financial, and personnel matters—and not a *blessed* thing in her bio indicated she was fit for the position—except the fact that her mother was the highest-ranking member of the U.S. Senate Select Committee on Intelligence.

Not that he disliked Senator Ruth Wagner. She asked good questions, some so penetrating he wondered if she had a few psychic powers of her own. Her willingness to reach across the aisle and her impeccable integrity meant she accomplished more than many of her male colleagues who had served in the role. Senator Wagner's husband, a member of the senior leadership team of the U.S. State Department, had died in a mysterious boating accident on the Chesapeake Bay. His unoccupied twenty-two-foot power boat had run aground on Tilghman Island, and the Coast Guard recovered his body two days later. The Medical Examiner said he died from drowning in brackish water, combined with hypothermia. Arguing that the bay was salt, not fresh or brackish water, rumor had it the senator had demanded the case be reopened, but neither the Talbot County Police, the Maryland State Police, nor a private investigator could find evidence of wrongful death. Case closed, Ruth Wagner soldiered on, raising her daughter on her own, without the live-in help she could have well afforded. If Senator Wagner had been the political appointee, he would have been fine with the placement. But accept her unqualified daughter as his equal, much less his superior?

Never.

The previous Under Secretary's management style had been much more hands off, seldom interfering with his division—unless he ran over budget. This one, on the other hand—can you say micro-manager? Already, without even *asking* him if he wanted to do it, with not so much as an email, the new Under Secretary had appointed him to the intra-agency and inter-agency committee to combat human trafficking, the Blue Campaign.

He had attended one session in person and found nothing of substantive value for him to contribute or learn. Besides, he had no desire to sit in face-to-face meetings while his wet-behind-the-ears boss sat with the head honchos in the enormous meeting room. In this case, maintaining a low profile was his best strategy. Rather than wasting his time watching the other directors and assistant directors vie for her attention, he chose to attend the monthly meeting by conference call.

At least that way, he could get some work done and say "Bert Blackfeather, Director of the Anomaly Defense Division" when the chair asked who beeped in on the call. No one ever questioned him not attending the meeting in person, one of the few perks of being in a wheelchair. Most people had little understanding of what he could or could not do. He allowed them to assume his disability kept him away from the face-to-face meetings—not his lack of interest in the committee.

It wasn't as if he didn't care about human trafficking. He did. *Passionately.* DHS was doing good work—between the committee meetings—not *during* them. The Anomaly Defense Division, however, had more than enough on its plate pursuing leads on terrorist plots. If Immigration and Customs Enforcement (ICE) or the other divisions needed his help, they knew where to find him, even if they didn't know exactly what he and his agents did. That information was on a need-to-know basis. And *they* didn't need to know.

Irritated, he shrugged his shoulders, opened the fists he'd unconsciously been squeezing, and shook his arms to release the tension. He should have gone to the gym this morning. Thirty-three laps in the pool, some bench presses, pull-ups, biceps curls, and he'd be loose and relaxed.

Maybe.

His eyes strayed to the computer monitor again. A stunning champagne blonde smiled at him from the photo. Maybe he read the announcement too fast. He prided himself in considering all the facts before making a judgment. He took a deep breath, and re-read the email in the hopes he had missed *some* indication of her management expertise:

Born and raised in Washington, DC, Phoebe Wagner attended Gallaudet University and obtained a B.A. in International Studies. Ms. Wagner continued her education at Georgetown Law and earned a JD, specializing in International and Comparative Law. A fierce advocate for deaf children, she won a coveted Fulbright Scholarship to conduct research on economic disparities at the Mexican Institute for the Deaf in Mexico City. Ms. Wagner is excited about the opportunity to apply her international expertise and diversity initiatives as part of her role as Under Secretary. When not volunteering her time as a legal consultant for the Deaf Community, Ms. Wagner can be found walking her miniature dachshund, horse-back riding, or practicing her martial arts.

"International expertise and diversity initiatives? Is she going to have us sitting around in sensitivity training sessions, asking us to reveal our deepest, darkest prejudices," he wondered out loud. "Fat chance."

Rolling his wheelchair to the dust streaked window overlooking the parking lot of the Nebraska Avenue complex, Bert stared down at the cars moving in and out and wondered which luxury vehicle belonged to the new Under Secretary.

A knock pulled him out of his reverie. He wasn't expecting anyone. He moved his chair to behind the desk and folded his hands—his "official" pose. "Come in."

The door opened and two women walked in, the first an attractive African American woman with salt and pepper hair, the second a breathtaking blonde.

"Mr. Blackfeather, I'm Jean Johnson, and I'm a member of the DHS team of Interpreters for Under Secretary Wagner," the first woman announced, positioning herself so the tall woman at her side could see her easily. She signed as she spoke. "I will speak when interpreting for Ms. Wagner and sign when interpreting for you, Mr. Blackfeather. Everything said in our conversations will be kept confidential. Also, I have a top-secret security clearance, should you need to discuss such matters. I will be using the first person, but you should keep your focus on Ms. Wagner, and not on me. This signal—" she held her hand up like a traffic cop, "—means I'd like you to pause so I can keep up with the interpretation. Everything said in this room will be interpreted. There are no side conversations with me, this is your conversation with Ms. Wagner."

Phew. Had the room temperature risen ten degrees? Or was it him?

Bert tugged at his suddenly too tight shirt collar. The photograph did *not* do her justice. Ms. Phoebe Wagner was even more beautiful in person than on the computer screen. Tall, lean, and leggy, dressed in a navy-blue pants suit and a white blouse accented with a black pearl necklace, she looked like she belonged on a catwalk in Milan, not in a rundown building with windows in desperate need of cleaning. Long, dark lashes framed sky-blue eyes, and the cut of her hair accented her perfectly symmetrical face, as if gilding the lily. He held her gaze a beat too long and a flush crept up her cheeks. Adjusting her pearls, she straightened her back, and shifted the oversized purse on her shoulder—which began to shake and bark. A

Eye of the Eagle

long-haired red dachshund's head popped over the edge of the bag, startling Bert into laughter.

"Does your dog go with you everywhere?" he signed in American Sign Language, or ASL. "Or just to meet your new employees?"

Surprise crossing her face, she smiled and signed, "Everywhere. Her name is Bisou." She made the ASL sign for the letter *b* and waved it back and forth like a dog's wagging tail, her descriptive sign.

"Well, hello, Bisou," Bert signed and spoke. "How many signs does she know?"

Do not stare at her. Focus on the dog, not her full red lips. She's your boss. Your unqualified, unprepared, politically appointed new boss.

"The last time I counted, one-hundred." Frowning, she pushed her hair behind her ear, revealing dangling pearl earrings and a neck like a swan's, long and graceful. She signed to Jean. "You didn't tell me he could sign."

Jean shrugged and shook her head. "I didn't know."

"You never know what talents are hidden in the Anomaly Defense Division." Bert motioned to his visitor chairs. "Have a seat. Please. What would you like to know about this unit?" The truth would probably send her running. Unless she was like her tough-as-nails mother, which he doubted. Living in D.C., he'd seen lots of beautiful women like her before. Haughty. Cold. Born with a silver spoon in her mouth.

She was nothing like his dearly departed, down-to-earth fiancée, Susan. Nothing. Except, maybe a little around the lips. And maybe the way she played with her hair. And her long, lovely neck. Otherwise, Susan and

Ms. Wagner had nothing in common.

"What does the Anomaly Defense Division do? I couldn't find any paperwork describing its mission." Her gaze locked on his. "What's its charge? Really."

Time to get this attractive nuisance out of his office and his life—for good.

"There's nothing available because this Division performs improbable functions considered by many to be impossible. If an eager senator like your mother were to get her hands on documents describing what we do, there would be more questions than answers."

A frown furrowed her brow, and her full lips pulled down, ruining her flawless face. "My mother has nothing to do with this conversation."

"Okay." *This is going well. Not.* "Are you familiar with the history of the use of psychics and parapsychology by our government?" Eyes narrowed, she turned to Jean, sparks practically flying off her fingers as she signed. "Is this some sort of joke on the new kid? If it is, I'm not laughing."

The interpreter shook her head. "I have no idea what he's talking about."

Bert waited until the Under Secretary looked at him again. "Not a joke. History—but it's not really in the past." He paused. "In the seventies, the CIA had a program to see if certain paranormal methods would have intelligence applications. One of these activities was remote viewing. Researchers would ask someone to envision a place or object which a sender would be looking at. In other experiments, they would put a photograph into an envelope and ask the person to describe the picture. In addition to remote viewers, they had other people with paranormal abilities. You name the talent, they had someone with it." He paused. Had she flinched when he said the last part? "Is there something wrong? You look like you want to ask me a question."

"No." She shook her head, and rubbed her little dog's floppy ears. The dog grinned at him as if sharing a secret. "Please go on."

"The program continued for about twenty years. A large evaluation study found the results were positive. However, while the statistics were good, the intelligence wasn't detailed enough for practical uses in the field. The military picked up where the CIA left off. As far as the world was concerned, the Army, Air Force, and Defense Intelligence Agency discontinued their psychic soldier units a decade later. However, what really happened is they all went underground."

She leaned forward. "And?"

"After 9-11, based on the top-secret recommendations of the Senate Intelligence Committee and the House Committee on Homeland Security, those units were consolidated and moved under the Department you now manage."

You're in over your head, pretty lady. No one would fault you if you resigned. Then we could go for coffee. Or dinner. Whoa! Knock it off, man. She's your boss.

She studied him with a thoughtful expression. "You mean you're psychic?"

He shook his head. "Not me. But many of our Special Agents are—and much more."

She fell back into the chair. "I don't know what to say. This is most unexpected. I need time to process this." Glancing at Jean, who looked as if she'd had the

11

wind knocked out of her also, she signed. "Jean looks like she could use a break." She turned her probing gaze back to Bert. "I want a complete inventory of your agents' talents, by end of business day Monday. Since today is Friday, it's plenty of time to pull it together."

He bit his lower lip. *An inventory?* Were his agents in cans stored on shelves, waiting to be taken down and counted?

Bert tried to make a joke. "Is there something in particular you're looking for? Lost keys perhaps?"

A line creased between her eyes. "I *never* lose my keys. I'm here to do a job, Director Blackfeather. As Under Secretary of Management for the Department of Homeland Security, I'm accountable for billions of dollars. I take my responsibilities seriously. Every division—not just yours—is being asked to provide me with details of what I won't see in the financial statements. The accountant's footnotes, if you will."

Rising, his new boss extended her hand and waited for him to return the gesture.

One beat. Two beats. Reluctantly, he reached out, accepting his small defeat. *Maybe she's more like her mother than I thought.*

She clasped his big hand with her smaller one— and an electromagnetic charge pulsed between them. The hairs on the back of his neck stood up—and downy feathers began to poke at his collar. Her gaze bore into him, her mouth opened in an *o*, and her large blue eyes widened. After holding his hand for a length of time *most* people considered polite, she jerked out of his grasp, stared at her palm and then back at him as if momentarily stunned.

First time he'd ever had *that* kind of effect on a

woman. And the first time a woman had ever had *that* kind of effect on him.

"Something wrong?" he signed. "You okay?"

The Under Secretary brushed her hair away from her face. "I'm fine." A slight tremble in her hand belied her assurance—but she continued, "One more question."

His cell phone blared. The song indicated someone was calling from Hotel LaBelle, either Lucius or Tallulah. That wasn't like them. They never called him during the day. He was busy and so were they. The country western music stopped after three rings, then started up with a second call, the song sounding more plaintive with each passing moment.

"I'm sorry. I have to take this."

"I'll wait." She clutched her bag with the bouncing Bisou, tilted her head, and fixed him with a thoughtful gaze.

He pressed the talk button and put the phone to his ear. "Bert Blackfeather."

On the other end of the line, someone sobbed, and Lucius spoke, his voice rough. "Bert—it's our baby girl, Miriam. She's gone. Out of her room. We were right upstairs. No idea what happened." He broke down. "We need your help. Someone grabbed her, Bert. Took her right out from under our noses."

Phoebe watched Bert's handsome face melt from an all business expression, into one of concern and almost palpable fear. Whatever the call was about, whoever it was from, it was bad news. And he didn't rattle easily, she could tell, and not just from her conversation with him. When they shook hands, the power and depth of the psychic link shook her. An

13

empath, she experienced his most emotionally laden memories in a gut-wrenching burst. She'd almost doubled over in pain when they hit her.

It began as a normal day in his life as an Army Judge Advocate General, or JAG. His commanding officer, or CO, had asked him to come with him to an offsite interrogation to serve as legal counsel. A detainee suspected of masterminding the murder of a sheikh who had been friendly to U.S. troops was being held by the Iraqi in a remote area in the foothills. When they arrived at the outskirts of the village—just a few houses, really—Bert told his CO the place looked deserted. No kids playing in the square, no women drawing water from the ancient well, not even a goat— the national animal of Iraq—chewing its cud at the end of a tether. He opened the door of the armored vehicle, set one foot on the ground—and the world exploded in a flash of light, scorching heat—and pain. In the distance he heard screaming, realized it was him, and passed out. He woke up in a helicopter. Dazed, vision blurred, he looked down. Where his legs should have been, were shredded pants—and two bloody stumps. He lost consciousness and woke up in a field hospital, surrounded by moaning men.

Sucker punched, she marveled how this man was still alive, much less psychologically intact. Just as she began to jerk out of his firm grasp to escape the anguish of his memories, a sense of peace rolled over her. She glanced at his hand and instead of fingers, the tip of a wing appeared, and she trembled at the soft brush of feathers. The vision disappeared, leaving her shaken— and intrigued. Although she'd had many empathic experiences before and used her talent to do her own *background checks* on people, not once had she come away with such a sense of intimacy—and a bone-jarring attraction. The combination of the vision of his war injuries, the images of feathers, and the soft caresses on her hand shook her to the core, leaving her mind—and her body in a state of confusion. She struggled to regain control of her senses, and prayed her expression didn't betray her.

Bert set his smart phone on the desk. "I have to leave immediately," he signed. "I have an emergency. I'm sorry, your report will have to wait."

Phoebe glanced at Jean. "Don't you have an assistant who can do it for you?"

"No one has this information but me. The lives of my agents depend on keeping their secrets. They are all over the country—and the world." He rolled his wheelchair from behind the desk. "Now, if you'll please excuse me." He nodded at the door. "I must go. Now."

Was he hiding something? She dared not use her empathic conduit into his mind. A physical connection, another skin-to-skin contact at this point in the conversation would be completely inappropriate, not to mention dangerous to her composure.

Blocking his exit, Phoebe signed, "Why are you running away from me?"

"It's personal." He frowned. "Don't you have Under Secretary duties to attend to?"

"What's more important than your job?" The moment the words flew off her fingers, she regretted her harsh tone. On the other hand, she was his boss, and he worked for Homeland Security. Weren't these people supposed to put their country before their personal lives?

Something cold glinted in his obsidian eyes. Internally she shrank from his glare. She'd gone too far. Externally she shifted her stance and lifted her chin as if daring him to strike back.

Bert leaned back, anger reflected in his thin lips and jerky hand movements. "My niece has disappeared—taken out of her room." He paused. "This is much more important than my job. I need to catch the next flight to Billings, Montana to be with my family. If you want my resignation, you'll have it."

Phoebe's stomach plummeted. *Shit. Shit. Shit.* What had she done? Her mother was wrong. She wasn't *perfect* for this position. She was terrible. If only she'd stood up to her mother, like she had when she insisted on going to Gallaudet instead of an Ivy League school. Her mother had approved of her choice of law school, but not a Fulbright Scholarship in crime-ridden, smog-choked, overcrowded Mexico City.

Dear God in Heaven. Mexico City.

If Bert could read her mind, he'd see how big of a failure she really was. Mexico City had been a disaster—but only she was aware of how enormous a fiasco it had been. And how devastating. Claiming health reasons, she ended the Fulbright early and came home in a profound state of depression. She'd been unable to even consider applying for jobs. What child advocacy agency would want someone incapable of protecting an at-risk child? Phoebe hadn't shared the reason for her abrupt departure from the study with her mother by text or email. However, her mother intuited a tragedy had occurred. Using her own methods, she had dragged the story out of her daughter, consoled her, and then badgered her to get back into the fray, to fight for other children. Phoebe ached just thinking about working with kids. She couldn't do it. *Never again.*

She'd only allowed her relentless mother to coerce her into this political appointment because she was tired of fighting. When the Under Secretary position became vacant, Phoebe's mother made it her mission to secure the job for her daughter, arguing it was high time for the Deaf Community to have greater representation. Although uncomfortable with being *The Deaf Representative in D.C.,* she couldn't refuse the role. Out of loyalty to her mother, a fierce pride in her deaf identity, and love of her country, she took the job. Today Phoebe wore the position like an ill-fitting suit— and to make matters worse, she had just bullied a key employee, the director of a top-secret division, no less, into offering his resignation.

Great work, Phoebe. She *had* to make this right.

"I'm so sorry. I had no idea," she signed. "Please don't quit. Let me make it up to you. I'll come with you. On my own time, unofficially, off the clock. I have my own resources—connections in the Intelligence Community and the State Department, not just in this agency. I can help."

"Not necessary. The Yellowstone County Sheriff's department and local FBI are on the scene. This is a private kidnapping. Not something you or the federal government should be involved in. I have lots of vacation time saved up."

"I insist on going with you." If she could help rescue this child, would that balance the scale of justice? No. It wouldn't bring Angela back, but maybe doing *something,* knowing she hadn't simply sat on the sidelines when there was something she could do, would give her some kind of solace. She had never expected to be thrust into a situation where she could help another endangered child—not here in this management role. This was an opportunity to redeem herself, if not in the world's eyes, then in her own.

"Thanks, but no thanks." His jaw twitched. "I'm sure you're needed here."

Phoebe shook her head. This was not going well. Summoning up her legal prowess, she decided to pursue the argument from a different angle.

National security.

"You just told me the lives of your agents depend on your discretion. You're the only person who knows every single agent in the division. Would you agree your information would be highly attractive to a malicious foreign power?"

He rubbed his chin and nodded. "Yes, I would agree with that assessment."

"Would you agree your family is the most important thing in your life?"

He shifted in his streamlined wheelchair and looked everywhere but at her. Heart thudding in her throat, she waited what seemed an eternity for his response.

His gaze finally returned to hers. He nodded. "Family first."

"So, how do you know for a fact this event has nothing to do with the extremely important secrets you carry in your brain?" He shrugged and looked away. *Rude and obstinate.* Phoebe wasn't taking no for an answer. She tapped his hand, forcing him to look at her—and triggered a feathery feeling again. "*You* may be the real target. Someone could have kidnapped the child to lure you into a trap."

He stroked his chin. "I hadn't considered that possibility."

A thrill ran up her spine, and she ducked her head to hide a quick smile of victory behind a curtain of hair.

"I see from your bio you can ride," he said.

She nodded, wondering where this was going.

"If you come with me, you'll be put on a horse and sent out to search along with every other volunteer in the community. Out there, I'm the boss. If you can't follow instructions, you'll be useless."

A frisson of excitement pierced her backbone. Phoebe's heart skipped a beat, and her breath came just a tad too fast. This was it. She was going. Thank God it was Friday. She couldn't wait to get home and pack. "I will do whatever I can to help. I swear. I can—" Stopping herself before revealing more, she glanced at Jean. The interpreter might hold a top-secret security clearance, but this was *not* the time for Phoebe to reveal her gifts. "—be ready in an hour."

He's not the only one with secrets. I have a few of my own.

Chapter Two

Baltimore-Washington International Thurgood Marshall Airport, Baltimore, Maryland

The only flight to Billings left at five in the evening, giving Bert time to wrap things up at the office, go home, and pack. He arrived at the departure gate two hours ahead of the anticipated take-off, found an outlet, and plugged in his laptop. The Internet, rich and random, revealed a wealth of information about Under Secretary Phoebe Wagner. Even in the absence of a social media presence—an oddity in this day and age—the media articles about her rise to her current role reinforced his first impression of a well-off, arrogant woman. Beyond her father's accidental death during her childhood, just as he expected, from play-dates to prep school, she had never experienced life outside her privileged bubble.

He glanced up from reading just in time to see his new boss make an entrance to the waiting area for the departure gate. Male and female heads swiveled as she passed, her stiletto heels clicking on the hard surface of the airport floors. With her smoked sunglasses, long hair, black flare leg pants, a thigh length black leather jacket, and a crimson vee-necked blouse that matched her lipstick, Phoebe appeared to be heading to a fashion show—not a search and rescue mission. Pulling a small black travel bag and shouldering a zippered mesh carrier, she strode onto the gray carpet, spotted Bert, and made a beeline to his side. Mouth open, eyes bugging, the gate agent tried to speak, but words failed the star-struck young man.

Bert took pity on him, signed hello to Phoebe and said, "She's with me." He could have sworn someone whispered, "Lucky him!" but perhaps he imagined it. No, this was not the woman he was looking for. In fact he was not looking for a woman at all. No one could ever measure up to Susan Foxtail—especially not this blue blood. Ms. Wagner was the polar opposite of the warm, kind, giving woman who had helped him crawl out of his post-traumatic stress disorder and pity party by forcing him to focus on what he still had in his life—not what was gone. How could this woman—no matter how well-meaning—ever measure up to Susan?

Bert closed his laptop as Phoebe glided into the blue cushioned seat next to him, and slid her expensive shades up to the top of her head. The woman made *everything* a fashion accessory.

He pointed at her rolling bag and the soft dog kennel and signed, "You travel light."

Eyeing him as if he was the village idiot, she replied, "I checked another piece."

"This is just a long weekend trip for you, correct?" He could put up with her on his home turf for a weekend. Past three days, as the saying went, fish and guests began to stink. "Friday through Sunday?"

"Yes." She unzipped the top of the pet carrier, and Bisou's head popped out, the little canine's mouth open in a doggy grin.

At least her dog's cute. "Nice smile. Will she be

okay on the trip?"

"World traveler. Been to ten different countries and fluent in five dog languages."

Did she just make a joke?

As if reading his mind, she smiled and brushed her fists atop each other. "Joke."

"Oh-ho!" He slapped his thigh. "Got me." Did he see a crack in the Ice Queen's frosty exterior? *Interesting.* Maybe she was more human than he first thought.

She grew solemn. "Any news?"

He shook his head. "Sheriff and FBI are searching. Father glued to phone, waiting for ransom call. Mother medicated." Knowing Tallulah as he did, he doubted she took the tranquilizers willingly. The FBI agent told him she kept repeating, "Ugly little man, ugly little man" without elaborating, and getting more and more distressed. Why hadn't Tallulah been able to see Miriam? The child was joined to her mother at the hip. Tallulah was one of his best agents. Frenzied and frantic, she must have burned out her remote viewer skills searching for her daughter. Something or someone must have interfered with her vision. Maybe the new boss was onto something. Perhaps a malicious actor with his or her own psychic talents *was* at work here. "Sheriff's deputies dragging river."

"River." Her face drooped. "Sad for parents."

Another fissure? Or good acting? Then he recalled her father's boating accident. *Ouch.* Of course drowning would resonate with her. *Shame on me.* Time to build some bridges. Try to make this new professional relationship work. Most people loved to talk about their proudest accomplishments.

"I understand Fulbright Scholarships are very competitive. Brave of you to go to a strange country and work there for a year. What did you do in Mexico?"

She froze. For two complete heartbeats, she stared at him without blinking, then shook her head and flashed a megawatt smile.

Was that real or meant to throw him off balance? Either way, the effect was the same. He was dazzled, and drawn to her smile like a moth to a flame. She was beautiful. Stunning when she smiled. *Not like Susan.* But, still, she had a way about her, one a *weaker* man would find hard to resist. Not him. He was made of sterner stuff and could separate phonies from real people. He leaned back in his seat. No sir, he was not going to be captivated by this prep school beauty's well-rehearsed act. They didn't call those places *charm schools* for nothing.

Phoebe signed. "You first. Tell me why you know how to sign. Deaf family members?"

The gate agent's voice crackled overhead. "Anyone who needs assistance with boarding or is accompanying someone who needs assistance, please line up in front of the jet way."

Saved by the bell.

He signed, "Time to line up."

She pointed at the boarding screen, waved her ticket, and wrinkled her nose in disgust. "Group C."

"No. You come with me. Group A plus." A good thing about being in a wheelchair, no one ever challenged Bert's need for an early boarding pass, for a seat in the front row, or for a parking place. "I told them you're with me."

The airline's motto appeared to be *Hurry up and*

wait because they still had an hour before take-off. The gate agent went down the queue of a dozen people and checked each ticket, verifying their blue boarding sleeves.

As they settled down to wait—again—her perfume floated past him. *Gardenia.* He bet it was the expensive British one. Susan had loved that fragrance—and cried when he bought her the extravagant three-hundred-dollar bottle. She was worth every penny. He would have bought her a truckload if she had asked for it, but the relationship, not gifts, were what mattered to her.

Phoebe waved her hand in front of his face. "Would you hold Bisou on your lap until we board?"

"These little dogs look adorable, but I know they were bred to flush out badgers and other burrowing animals. They're feisty." *Like you.* "Will she bite me?"

Phoebe smiled. "Only if you threaten me. She's very protective."

"In that case." He nodded and accepted the dog. The little red dachshund turned three times, settled onto his lap, and went to sleep.

Phoebe smiled. "You're a dog person."

"Wait until you meet my sister, Emma. She's the real dog person. A dog and horse whisperer." At Phoebe's puzzled expression, he added, "She trains them."

Understanding flooded her face. "Like the movie."

He nodded. "Better."

Phoebe returned to her original line of inquiry. "Where did you learn to sign?"

"At Walter Reed Hospital." *When I was learning to live again.*

She tapped her closed finger tips together. "More."

"After Iraq, I spent a long time in the rehab unit." He paused for a minute, then pointed at his thighs. "I lost my legs below the knees. The guy in the next bed lost his hearing. He was angry. Wouldn't look at the therapist, kept yelling at her to go away." He was one pissed off dude. Not that Bert blamed him. Jamming Joe had been a guitarist—a *good* one on his way up—before being deployed. After the explosion, not only did he lose his hearing, he lost his passion for living. Most days the musician fought with the staff. Other days he curled into a fetal position, his back to the world.

"What happened?"

"I told him if he learned ASL, I'd hook him up with some of the best drummers in the country."

"Yes, many famous deaf drummers."

"He didn't know—I did because of our annual Crow Fair. Drummers—deaf and hearing—come from all over the country. He told me I had to learn ASL with him." He grinned. "Teacher said I was a natural."

"You are good. Who do you practice signing with now?"

A reasonable question. ASL was a language. And, like any language, if you don't use it, you lose it. "I work with deaf kids on the reservation. We have Indian Hand Signs, but it's not the same as ASL."

"Nice. I can teach you more signs. Less finger spelling. Help you go faster, teach kids, too."

She was right. He could use some practice with more signs. Finger spelling took time and effort. "Happy to learn." *Maybe he could teach her to loosen up a little. On second thought, why bother? People like her don't change.* His turn to ask a question.

"Tell me about your Fulbright," Bert pressed.

Phoebe held up a manicured finger, pulled a water bottle out of the front pouch of her rolling bag, and sipped.

Could she stall any longer? She was like a safe. He'd acted as legal counsel during interviews with hardened Taliban members who had been easier to squeeze for information than Phoebe. This was normal social conversation. He could only imagine how tight she'd be with Homeland's secrets. He wondered if her mother had trained her from a young age or if this was a newly acquired skill. Either way, he was impressed. Maybe, he *could* trust her with a few things. Nothing big to start with. Small stuff, to test her.

He waited until she placed the bottle back in the bag. "Why Mexico?"

"Long story." She took a deep breath and began to sign. "Not many schools for deaf children. Public support only goes to sixth grade. Then—nothing—unless you are wealthy or have help getting into places like the School for Language Difficulties." Splaying her fingers, she pulled both her hands down in front of on her face, making the sign for *sad*.

"No education, no jobs. Best many deaf people can do is earn three dollars a day cleaning hotels." She made a disgusted expression. "Or beg with alphabet cards—and make twelve dollars a day."

Bert was familiar with the alphabet cards. *Learn to communicate with the Deaf!* or *I am Deaf! Please help.* Even in the U.S. there were those using the same tactics at train stations, bus stops, and on city streets. It was impossible to tell how many of the panhandlers were really deaf, pretending to be deaf to gain sympathy and con people out of money, or coerced into doing this by a human trafficking ring.

He nodded. "Yes, I've seen those."

She continued. "I worked at the Mexican Institute for the Deaf, collecting what little data was available on the effects of education on the deaf community. Since I was a lawyer, even though I couldn't practice in Mexico, I assisted families with applications for grants to special education schools. Many could not read or write."

"So, you are quadrilingual? ASL, English, Spanish and Spanish, and Mexican Sign Language, too?"

She laughed. "Bisou, too!"

Bert waved his hand over his face. "Wow!"

A blush crept up Phoebe's fair skin, and she turned her face away.

Perhaps she wouldn't be quite as awful as he feared. Glancing at his phone, he prayed for a text announcing Miriam's rescue. Nothing. He'd looked a hundred times in the last hour. He should know better by now. Lucius or someone would call him if there was good news. Helpless rage bubbled in his chest. He wanted to take to the skies, find the bastard who did this to his niece, and rip his face off with his talons. The back of his hands pebbled, a sign of an impending eruption of feathers.

Shit. Settle down.

Nothing could be done from thousands of miles away. Despite what others thought, patience was not one of his virtues. When he became angry and agitated, his old brain—the instinctive portion designed for survival—brought out his eagle. Outside of the family, many people remarked on how calm he remained under pressure. What they didn't know was if he allowed his

27

emotions to take control, he would morph into one of the largest birds of prey known in the US. Growing up, his grandmother had shown him how to control his primal flight-or-fight response. Calling on the Great Creator, Bert closed his eyes, took ten deep, slow breaths and envisioned himself in a canoe, rocking slowly on the gentle waves of the Yellowstone River. With each mental rock, he patted the doxie's head. As if sensing his tension, her tail thumped on his chest in time with his exhalations. His heart rate slowed, a sense of peace washed over him, and he blinked. Was happy-go-lucky Bisou a therapy dog?

The gate agent's voice boomed. "Early boarding passengers may now proceed onto the jet way."

They were on the first step of the journey to rescue Miriam. He prayed they still had time.

****

One of the first things Phoebe had admired about Bert was his graceful movements. His wheelchair, a model most often used by Paralympians, was an extension of his body. He glided around his office as if he was an ice skater. When she connected with him on the visceral level, she recognized his courage and resilience. In addition, not only had he overcome his own great loss, he had helped another man learn to live again. No small feat. Bisou liking him was an added bonus. As soon as she had lifted the dachshund out of Bert's hands, the little dog had passed joyful feelings—tail wagging at a hundred miles an hour—to Phoebe. Giggling, she stuffed the happy pooch into the bag and waited to board the plane behind Bert. After transferring himself into his front row seat, behind the bulkhead, he waved away his wheelchair. It was obvious he worked out. Under his polo shirt and navy blue blazer, his hands hinted at his upper body strength. He didn't even break a sweat when he transferred from one seat to the other. She placed her rolling bag into the overhead compartment, slid Bisou's carrier into the designated take-off space, dropped into her seat directly behind Bert, and closed her eyes.

With her having a pet onboard, she had to be where she could push his crate under a seat. But maybe it was better she couldn't sit beside Bert. It would make talking harder.

Her mind raced like a hamster in a wheel, going back over the conversation. *Careful, Phoebe.* You almost told him what happened. She couldn't even bring herself to think about what happened in Mexico City, much less share it with her subordinate. Handsome, charming, and exuding masculine pheromones that made her wish she'd met him in another way, Bert Blackfeather was one-hundred percent off-limits. The rules were quite explicit on romance between an employee and his boss. *Nope. Nyet. No. Never.* And if it happened, someone had to go. End of story. She wouldn't mind getting out of this job—but she would *never* want to risk embarrassing her mother.

Phoebe mentally ticked off all the ways she didn't fit. She was the only deaf political appointee in Homeland. Her education and experience had nothing to do with intelligence work. Except for her law degree and her expertise in international matters, she was out of her league with these spymasters. No matter how well-intentioned, her mother had erred in getting her this political plum. Phoebe didn't belong here. Mother doesn't always know best. For once in her life, Senator Ruth Wagner was wrong. A larger than life personality, Mom pushed Phoebe to be smarter, stronger, tougher, every day. Depending on the hour, Phoebe alternated between admiring, loving, and being angry at the woman. She knew where her mother came from, how she got to be the way she was, but understanding her mother didn't make life easier for Phoebe.

A child of a deaf adult, a CODA, Mom had been raised by her deaf mother and father to fight for her rights and the rights of others. A graduate of Kentucky School for the Deaf who moved to Washington, D.C. to work as data entry clerk, Grandma met and married a mailman on a blind date set up by mutual friends. Observing and experiencing many barriers to opportunities for her and her husband, Grandma became a one-woman letter writing machine. She tore local, state, and federal representatives into pieces, closing each letter with "I pray you make the right decision, not the easy one." Mom told Phoebe a few beleaguered staffers had even called the house and begged her to ask her mother to stop the fire and brimstone letters. Relentless, Grandma never let the pressure up until she passed away in her sleep, happy to have contributed to the fight for deaf rights—and proud of her daughter, the young, newly married senator from Virginia.

Despite a strong family history of civic engagement, this job was *wrong* for her. She wasn't *anything* like her mother. Her mother thrived on politics and invited the media spotlight. She was all about transparency in government—up to a point. When it came to state secrets, Mom was a vault. And so was the attractive, strong-willed man sitting ahead of her. When they arrived in Billings, the first thing she would do is set up a meeting with the missing child's parents and try to get a feel for them—and their loyalties. Friends, family, co-workers—given the right motives—rewards, punishment, blackmail—*anyone* could be a foreign agent. She scribbled a note, reached forward, tapped Bert on the arm, and passed him a folded piece of paper.

Sharon Buchbinder

Chapter Three

Billings, Montana

Bert jolted awake when the plane bounced onto the tarmac. He raised his arm to squint at his watch. The rescue mission clock had started ticking when Tallulah found Miriam's bed empty. Unfortunately, the wait time and the flight took a chunk out of the golden forty-eight hours, the time window in which it was optimal to find missing children. They had to find Miriam in the next two days. If not, they could assume it was no longer a search and rescue, but something horribly worse—a recovery mission.

The local law enforcement officers, or LEOs, would have conducted the initial response investigative checklist: completing the intake report from Lucius and Tallulah, obtaining details about Miriam—photos, clothing she was wearing at the time of abduction, medications, searching Miriam's room, and taking photos, as well as preserving any evidence they found. In addition to an Amber Alert, all law enforcement communication channels would broadcast the case and flyers with her photo and a phone number for a tip hotline would be printed and distributed. Within two hours of receiving the report of Miriam's abduction, the child's information would have been entered into NCIC, the FBI's National Crime Information Center.

Background checks would be conducted on anyone who had ever had contact with Miriam. Any employees, guests, suppliers, or contractors with a history of disputes, conflicts, or altercations with the hotel and its owners would be put under a microscope. The sex-offender rolls would be painstakingly reviewed to see if anyone in the registry had a history with the hotel, the family, or the child. No slimy rocks would be left unturned.

In a city or town, the neighborhood and vehicles would be canvassed. However, the Hotel LaBelle was an hour away from the closest city, and the closest neighbor, a cattle rancher, was across the Yellowstone River—ten miles away. The vehicles at the hotel would have been searched first, along with any outbuildings, animal burrows, or other enclosed spaces. Bert's mind spun thinking about all the detailed response plans unfurling while they traveled to Montana. As soon as he could slip away unnoticed, he'd let his anger out, release his eagle, and search the remote areas from the sky. He wiped his palms over his face, shook his head, and put his hand in his pocket to retrieve his phone and take it out of airplane mode. Instead of the mobile, he found the crumpled note from Phoebe and opened it.

"I'm willing to do anything I can to help you get your niece back. I promise."

A lovely thought, well meant he was sure, but how the hell could a city slicker help him on a search like this? Sic her ferocious dachshund on Tallulah's pug or Bronco's bobcat? He shook his head. *Lordy, I hope this weekend goes by fast—and Miriam comes home faster.*

The plane coasted up to the jet way and the overhead bell chimed. "We know you have choices.

Thank you for flying American JetStream. Whether coming for a visit or returning home, we hope you have a pleasant day in beautiful Billings, Montana, where the current temperature is thirty-two degrees and the full moon is shining on the plains."

Bert called Hotel LaBelle and watched the other passengers deplane. "This is Bert Blackfeather." He didn't recognize the voice on the other end of the line. "Who's this?"

"FBI Special Agent Jake Wilson."

"Did the sheriff call you in?"

"Yes. The age of the child warranted mobilizing the Child Abduction Rapid Deployment—or CARD—team."

He established his bona fides with the special agent, introducing himself as a family member and the Director of the Anomaly Defense Division of Homeland Security. "We should be at the hotel in an hour or so. We need to deplane and get our bags."

"We have millions of acres to cover out here," the FBI Agent said. "*Please* tell me you brought someone good at tracking?"

"Umm, not exactly." Out of habit, Bert lowered his voice, although he knew Phoebe could not hear him. "It's my boss. Under Secretary Wagner."

"Senator Wagner's daughter? You're kidding."

"Wish I was." He craned his neck around the seat and waved at Phoebe. She flashed a dazzling smile and neglected parts of his body came to attention. "She insisted on coming." *Against my better judgement.*

Wilson blew out a long breath. "I'll be damned. Isn't she deaf?"

"Correct."

"Well, how in the hell is she going to be of any use on this case?"

"Just because someone is deaf doesn't mean they're incompetent." It came out a bit sharper than intended, but really, he had to nip this crap in the bud.

"Point taken. Even so. What exactly *will* she be doing?"

He wasn't really sure himself. Why had she insisted on coming? Didn't she have other things to attend to? He couldn't disrespect his boss to this man, or tell him she was doing this on her personal time. It was up to her to disclose her reasons. He decided to go the plausible excuse route. She was doing her job. Sort of.

"She's new, so my guess is she's trying to learn who does what and how. Not like it's all in a manual somewhere. I guess you could call it a ride along." *A high stakes one.*

"Good luck." Wilson's voice dropped to a conspiratorial whisper. "Having a suit in the field with you can throw a cramp in your style, if you know what I mean."

He forced a laugh. "Oh, ho! I sure do." No shifting into an eagle with her around. "Hey, can I speak with Lucius, please?"

"Sure, hold on." Footsteps trailed in the distance and then back.

"Bert?" Lucius' voice cracked. "Thank God you're here. I'm half out of my mind with worry. Tallulah is having hallucinations—we had to sedate her. I hated to do it, but she was in overdrive." He choked on the last words. "I'm worried I'll lose her, too."

"I came as soon as I could. Wish the flight had

been shorter." He paused. "Gonna need two rooms. One for me and one for my boss. She insisted on coming."

"Okay, sure, whatever you need. Just get here soon. Please?"

"We're on our way." He pressed the off button. *Poor guy.* Normally laid-back and easy-going, Lucius was the eye of the storm at boisterous family gatherings. Never had the man been so unglued. Whoever took Miriam, he'd better hope Bert didn't get to him first. Balling his hands into fists, he tried to smooth down the unbidden bumps on his knuckles. His talons ached to rip free, and his thighs cramped beneath his pants. This was not the time to set his eagle free. Not yet. *Save it for the bad guy.*

The skycap delivered his wheel chair. He thanked the airline employee and transferred into it, looping the strap of his laptop bag around his neck. They needed to get to the luggage area where visitors could view statues of bighorn sheep and horses reinterpreted by local artists. Then they'd need to find their driver, one of the local companies. Get to the hotel, find out where they were in the search and rescue process—

A muscular male flight attendant interrupted his thoughts. "Would you like some assistance sir?"

"I'm fine, thanks." He turned and pointed at Phoebe. "Could you check on the lady with the dog, please? She's my boss. I don't want to lose her."

Rolling bag at her feet, Phoebe waved and smiled brightly. How could she look so perky at this hour? Unlike him, she must have had a great nap on the flight. On her shoulder, the dog carrier lurched, swayed, and yipped. *Someone else was up and at 'em.* Despite his fatigue and weak attempts to repel her magnetic personality, he grinned and waved back. Hard to resist her smile. *Dammit, man. She's your boss.*

They made their way into the airport, and came to the Welcome to Billings sign next to the *Picture yourself here* bear photo. At the podium near the exit, a young man in a TSA uniform ogled Phoebe. Maybe he'd seen her on the Homeland website? Or maybe it was because she was beautiful.

Bert cleared his throat. "Excuse me, young man." He pointed to the other side of the entrance. "Is this the way to baggage?"

The kid shot him a sour look. "Yeah."

Mission accomplished.

Phoebe waved and signed to Bert. "Bisou needs a rest room—me, too!"

"Pets go out the door by the baggage claim area. People rest rooms down there, too." He motioned for her to go. "Don't worry. The driver texted me. He's at the carousel and will help us with our bags."

"My bag is red." She pointed to her blouse. "Like this." Dragging her bag behind, Phoebe turned and raced toward the pet relief area.

The carousel area was practically deserted by the time he arrived. A short man in a Yellowstone County Deputy Sheriff's gray and black uniform stood by the luggage belt with his arms crossed over his chest, his gaze fixed on the two lonely bags—one black, one crimson—riding the circuit.

"Tommy Otterlegs! What a nice surprise. What are you doing here?"

A member of the Crow Nation, Tommy had been a burr in his sister Emma's saddle—until he finally accepted she was in love with Bronco and would never fall for him. A hard lesson, one he took with grace, or so Emma told him. He'd always liked Tommy. Yes, he was like a bantam rooster scratching the dirt for a fight, but he meant well. Now that he and Wanda, a cute little red-headed deputy who also worked in the Yellowstone County Sheriff's Office, were engaged, he'd become much happier.

"I told your driver to go get the car and I'd keep an eye out for you." He lifted his chin toward the carousel. "One of those yours?"

"Both of them."

Tommy lips quirked. "I never took you for a guy who was into red bags, Bert. Want to tell me about it?"

"Belongs to my boss."

Pushing her bag at her side, the dog's carrier draped over the handle, Phoebe crossed the space from the ladies' room, with Bisou hanging over her arm. Stilettos clicking, she headed straight to Bert, handed him the dog, and made for the carousel.

Tommy stared at Phoebe, the dog, and back to Phoebe. He mouthed, "Your boss?"

Bert laughed. "Oh, ho! Better not let Wanda see you look at another woman that way. Your fiancée knows how to handle a gun."

Tommy glared at Bert, puffed up his chest, and strutted over to the conveyor belt. "May I help you, ma'am?"

She yanked the red bag off the belt and backed into the short man who stared at Bert's boss with his mouth agape.

Bert snorted. "You can get my bag, Tommy. It's the only one left."

One eye on Phoebe, Tommy shot a glare at Bert

and did as he was told.

"Thanks, Tommy." He waved at Phoebe and signed, "Come over here and I'll introduce you. "Under Secretary Wagner, this is Deputy Sheriff Tommy Otterlegs." This time Bert signed and spoke out loud at the same time.

"Off duty." She signed. "Call me Phoebe."

Tommy's eyes grew larger. "Wagner? As in Senator Wagner?"

Bert continued to sign and talk, keeping Phoebe in the conversation. She was *not* an object to be discussed.

"Her daughter." Amused by his friend's gob smacked expression, he added. "Who knew we'd get a celebrity in little old Billings, right Tommy?"

"Got that right." Otterlegs shook his head. "Let's get your bags out to the SUV. I'm driving a cruiser. I'll meet you at the hotel and tell you what we found out when we canvassed the Cheyenne and Crow reservations."

****

Bouncing along in the black SUV, Phoebe wondered how she'd be received by the rest of the team and the family of the missing child. While she was pretty certain the local authorities would use polygraph tests on the parents—at least that's what she'd read somewhere—after Mexico, she intended to use her own lie detector method. She planned to probe the parents, the immediate family—and anyone else involved in this case—even if the intense emotions took a toll on her physically. Back in Mexico Angela's parents hadn't given any hint of a change of plans—not a clue—but then again before the tragedy she hadn't had any physical contact with the family in a month. Not a handshake, not a hug, nothing. Touching Angela's arm the only impressions she had received were those of the girl's excitement about her new school.

She should have known.

Everyone in the tiny eight-person Mexican Institute for the Deaf had known how hard Phoebe had worked to convince Angela's parents to take their daughter to the School for Language Difficulties for an evaluation. After the results of the tests had shown Angela would definitely benefit from their services, Phoebe had moved heaven and earth to convince the administrators to waive the school's monthly fees.

If Angela didn't get in, her special education would stop at sixth grade. From seventh grade on, no public schools would accommodate her. Without private schools, educational and occupational opportunities diminished accordingly. Most of Mexican society viewed deaf people as incompetent and treated them with disdain. With two deaf parents whose jobs were cleaning hotels for three dollars a day and no way up, this was a dream come true for Angela.

How had she missed the warning signs, the parents' mood changes? They'd been hard to convince, but eventually they had decided it was best for Angela's future. Phoebe's own excitement at Angela's bright new opportunity must have clouded her vision. A spotlight highlighting a blue and white carved wooden sign denoting the entrance to the Hotel LaBelle pulled Phoebe away from her thoughts. The vehicle turned onto a long, blacktopped driveway and up ahead, a Victorian mansion with a large wrap-around porch came into view. It looked as if it belonged in a historic neighborhood on the shores of the Potomac instead of out here in the middle of nowhere.

Sitting next to her, Bert turned on the dome light and signed, "We're here. That's the father." Finger spelling Lucius Stewart, he indicated the man on the porch was a distant cousin who rejoined the Crow tribe almost three years ago. "Lucius and his wife worked like dogs to update and restore the hotel."

"I look forward to seeing it in the daylight."

Bert glanced at his watch. "Won't be long. Sunrise is coming pretty soon."

The driver pulled the vehicle in front of the steps and shut off the engine. The passenger door flew open, and a lanky man with a large old-fashioned mustache reached in and grabbed Phoebe's hand. A tornado of sights, sounds, and feelings slammed into her like a body blow, taking her breath away. Head reeling, she took deep breaths and attempted to sort out the impressions. Jumbled and jumping around between days, hours, years, and centuries, it was hard to get any specific date or times. A kaleidoscope of images whirled into her mind like a runaway Ferris wheel. A blur of old-fashioned clothing, a beautiful young Native American woman, a modern woman with long unruly blonde hair, a red-haired toddler, an elderly Native American woman holding a stick with a feather at the tip—all tumbled along a whitewater river of emotional connections. Behind it all, a clock loomed, the hands pointed at the number twenty-four, the number of hours elapsed since the abduction. Under it all a constant beacon of fear emitted one message—hurry, hurry, hurry, save my baby, save my baby, save my baby.

Chapter Four

Hotel LaBelle, Billings, Montana

When he rolled into the door of the hotel, a large cast of characters, in and out of uniform, greeted Bert. Many were old friends, but a few faces were new. All were engrossed in tasks, busy at work. Some looked up and met his gaze as he entered the foyer, some with nods of hello, and others with a quick wave. Stacks of MISSING CHILD flyers lay atop the mahogany registration desk along with notepads. Three women he didn't recognize worked the phones, speaking in calm tones and taking notes. Large white boards with bulleted lists hid the lobby walls, covering the carvings of the deer, fish, and waterways. Hal Wiley, one of his best friends from high school and the Yellowstone County Sheriff, broke free from a cluster of uniforms standing at a white board, strode over to Bert, and placed his hand on his shoulder.

"I'm so sorry you had to fly out for this. A terrible reason to come home." Hal looked up at the ceiling, and his voice grew hoarse. "Everyone's taking this hard. I want you to know we're doing everything we can to find Miriam. Tallulah, Lucius, Emma, and Bronco passed the polygraph tests. Figured we'd do immediate family and friends first and work our way out. We brought in a psychologist to work with the parents," he paused. "Tallulah's taking it real hard."

"Thanks, Hal. I know you and your men are on top of this." He glanced around. "I see you decided to make this the Command Center."

Hal nodded. "Normally we don't like to use the home, but this is a unique situation. Lots of rooms for interviews. The dining room makes a good meeting space." He pointed to a group of men huddled around a laptop, speaking in low tones, and making notes on paper and smart phones. "Lots of space in the lobby for whiteboards for timelines and search plans. The hotel has multiple phone lines, so we ran the hotline number to here. Brought in specially trained communications operators. They know how to screen and assess the data coming in. We anticipate a lot of crackpots calling, asking for ransom, offering private investigation services—even psychics."

Bert shook his head. "Everyone wants their fifteen minutes of fame."

Hal opened his mouth to reply and shrieking erupted as if a banshee had been released from the depths of hell.

Franny, the fawn pug and resident food hog, danced in front of Bert, wearing a plastic Elizabethan collar, begging to be picked up. "I was wondering where you were. Awful quiet without you." He leaned over and lifted the ball of fur into his lap, grunting as he did so. "What did you do to earn the cone of shame? Stealing food again, my chubby friend?" The bug eyed dog cocked her head and snorted in protest. Placing his fingers inside the protective collar, Bert rubbed her velvety ears. "I know. You're not overweight, you're under tall."

Breathless and sweaty, Tommy Otterlegs entered the foyer dragging Phoebe's red bag behind him. "The driver's getting your bag, Bert. I thought I should help your boss, you know, make a good impression for you."

Hal stared at his deputy, a frown carved on his forehead.

The woman in question strode into the foyer, and all the air was sucked out of the room. The buzz stilled and every man in the room stopped what he was doing and stared at her. It was as if someone had hit the pause button on a police show.

Bert chuckled. Signing and calling out to the assembly, he said, "Everyone, this is Phoebe Wagner. Ms. Wagner, this is everyone."

Heads nodded, the staring ceased, and everybody returned to their tasks, except Tommy, who was standing at attention at her elbow. "Could you ask her if I can do anything else?"

Bert passed along the question.

She shook her head, put the tips of her fingers to her lips and pulled them away, like blowing a kiss.

Tommy turned beet red.

"She said thank you." Bert laughed. "Not I love you."

Tommy returned the sign, surprising Phoebe—and Bert. "See, even *I* know a little sign language."

Phoebe glanced at Bert's lap and smiled. "Playmate for Bisou?"

He nodded and put the pug on the floor. It looked as if a lamp had come to life and sprouted a furry body and legs.

Placing the dog carrier alongside the pug, Phoebe allowed the pooches to sniff each other through the screening. Cone flattened onto the carrier like a small satellite dish, Franny's entire body wriggled right down to her curlicue tail. When both dogs were wagging and dancing at about one hundred miles an hour, she released Bisou. The doxie shot out like a rocket, and the little dogs raced around in circles, shrieking and yipping in ecstasy.

"Someone her size," Phoebe signed and turned to the sheriff. "Now who is this man?"

"Hal Wiley," Bert finger spelled his friend's name. "We have been getting in trouble since we were in high school and used to cut classes together."

Hal extended his hand, and Phoebe accepted it. Holding his large hand a few seconds too long, she released him, a thoughtful look on her face.

Quirking a brow, she smiled at Bert. "Playing hooky for fishing?"

"Clearly the sign for reeling in a fish." Hal gave a surprised laugh. "How'd she know?"

Grinning, Bert shrugged and signed, "Must be psychic."

Tommy cleared his throat. "Hal—and Bert—and Ms. Phoebe." He bobbed his head at the senator's daughter. "I wanted to give you the run-down on what they told me on the rez."

Hal made a sweeping motion with his hand. "You've got the floor. Speak up."

"Officers with the Bureau of Indian Affairs on both reservations canvassed the Cheyenne and Crow." Ears turning bright red, Otterlegs continued, "No one on Tribal Lands has seen her."

The sheriff nodded. "They're pretty short-handed in the BIA. Takes a year for someone to get cleared to go on duty. The Crow have ten people to patrol an area the size of Connecticut."

Bert asked, "Are you sure? Not even a rumor on the Indian telegraph?"

Leaning back in his chair and interpreting for Phoebe, Bert explained, "Indian telegraph—word gets around fast on the reservations, everybody knows everyone else. Mothers, aunties, cousins, friends, they all talk."

She nodded. "Like Deaf Community."

"Well, there is one story going around," Tommy faltered. "It's pretty weird. You know, some of the tribal stuff."

"So, are you going to tell us the story or what, Otterlegs?" Hal glowered at the little man. "The clock is ticking."

The stress of the investigation must be getting to him. Hal wasn't normally this sharp with his men. Even though Tommy had tried to make a run for his job a couple of years back, Hal wasn't one to hold a grudge.

"The Crow medicine woman and the Cheyenne medicine man both said Miriam wasn't taken by a man." Tommy frowned. "They said he wasn't human—he was a spirit creature."

"Of course. Why didn't I think of that?" Hal's voice dripped with sarcasm. "It all makes sense now. Miriam Beautiful Stewart, descendant of a Crow Medicine Woman and granddaughter of a Choctaw Medicine Woman was taken by some kind of supernatural being. Sure, it all makes sense. Does he or she have a name? Maybe one we can run through a couple of databases for wack jobs who like to pretend they're not human?"

"No, but they said what he looked like." Otterlegs glared up at his boss, a muscle twitching on the side of his face. "They said look for an ugly little man—if you can see him."

"Hal," Bert interjected, "can we talk?"

Shooing Otterlegs away, Hal passed a hand over his face. "You going to tell me I was too hard on the Beaver?"

"I was gonna say you were too hard on the Otter. Come on, Hal. The guy is just the messenger. Don't shoot him. Besides, Wanda will kick your ass if she finds out you've been picking on her boyfriend."

"I'd better take away her sidearm." Hal shuddered. "This case—it's killing me. It could be my daughter, anyone's child. We're a safe community. Things like this just don't happen here." He patted Bert's shoulder. "Thanks. You're a good friend. I'll find him and apologize." He walked away, shook his head, and repeated, "Ugly little man."

Phoebe asked, "What do you think about this ugly little man story? Is it real?"

"We follow the clues—no matter how strange." He shrugged. "Never heard of a spirit taking a child. Could be someone who thinks he's a spirit. Or is just ugly and short."

Wraithlike, Tallulah floated down the stairs. Wild blonde hair in complete disarray, sunken eyes, she stumbled down the last two steps and stared at Bert. "Is it really you? Or am I dreaming?"

He opened his arms, and she staggered over to him, fell on her knees in front of his chair, laid her head on his lap, and began to sob. Placing his big hands on her shoulders, he said, "I'm here, Tallulah, we're all here.

47

And we are going to hunt for Miriam with everything we've got." A fresh wave of rage threatened to bring out his animal side. He gritted his teeth and suppressed his shape-shifting, cursing the man who did this to his family.

I will find the kidnapper and bring him to justice— or die trying.

****

Tears welled up in Phoebe's eyes. She didn't need Bert to interpret what she had witnessed. The devastated mother's appearance and behaviors spoke volumes. Wanting to give Bert and Tallulah some privacy, she wandered around the first floor. Next to the gleaming wooden stairs, an antique elevator awaited passengers. On the second floor, railings on three sides formed a gallery, and Lucius Stewart stared down at his wife with glassy eyes. She had felt his agony when he pulled her out of the SUV, desperate for help. The pain was intolerable, and she'd been forced to pull away from him, lest she faint from the intensity of the connection—and his story.

Dear God. His story. So many losses.

His mother, his first wife, the child he never held in his arms. A hundred years in limbo. His memories rang true—not a hint of falsehoods or fabrication. How was it possible that he was over a century old or that he thought he was? At some point, she'd have to ask Bert—when he trusted her. Lucius had been redeemed by the very woman who now sobbed in Bert's lap. They'd had a child and the joy at her birth had been exquisite—despite the fact that Lucius had narrowly survived a terrible battle. Now, he feared losing not only Miriam, but Tallulah, too. How much tragedy was a person supposed to be able to bear?

As if in answer to her thoughts, Lucius' gaze moved from his wife to Phoebe, a prayer in his beseeching eyes. *Save my baby.*

She made an *a* with her right hand and circled her aching heart. *Sorry, so sorry.* She swore she would do *something* to make this right. She could not fail again. This time, she'd bring all of her talents to bear, not just her brain. This time, she would succeed. Distancing herself from the pain on Lucius' face, Phoebe's gaze fell on pieces of intricate beadwork in a glass display case. A sign noted the names of the Crow artists who had created them, along with a suggestion to take home a lovely memento of a wonderful vacation in Big Sky Country. This wasn't supposed to be a crime scene. This was supposed to be a vacation getaway. A pleasant escape from work, a holiday from worry. Running her hands along the animals carved into the walls, she found a hallway leading to a huge eat-in kitchen. A gleaming espresso machine caught her eye. As she wondered if she could have some, Lucius came in and pointed to a cup.

She nodded enthusiastically. Soon the heady aroma of dark roasted coffee drifted to her as steam rose from the machine. He squeezed his hand as if milking a cow and smiled at her obvious surprise. He pulled out a notepad and wrote, "We learned baby signs for Miriam. I still remember a few." He signed for eating, and she smiled. Lucius opened the refrigerator and placed hard-boiled eggs, sliced chicken, and a bowl of mixed berries on the large wooden table along with rolls and condiments. The man was grieving, yet he went out of his way to take care of her. Humbled by his kindness, she sank into a chair and wolfed down enough food for two people.

She patted her stomach and signed thank you. Lucius responded with the same sign, "You're welcome." He picked up the pen to write. Set it down. Picked it up again. "I want to show you something."

She cocked her head. This was interesting. What could he possibly want to share with someone who was a complete stranger?

Lucius waved at her to follow him. He led her through a passageway to a door crisscrossed with yellow tape. *Crime scene. Do not enter.* He stood outside the room, his eyes filled with tears. He made a swinging motion with his arms, one on top of the other, his palms up. "My baby."

Phoebe placed her hand on the doorway and an impulse to duck under the X blocking the entry beckoned her to go in. She resisted the urge and stood glued to the doorjamb, images washing over her. Miriam touched this spot on a regular basis, slapping the wood on her way in and out of the room, marking the place as her own. Lucius left, probably overcome with grief. She dropped to her knees, touched the threshold, and a revolving array of images of Miriam and other people going in out of the room rose in her mind. Just as she was about to break the connection, she caught sight of someone who didn't belong.

A shadowy figure the size of a child whispered in Miriam's ear and pointed at the open window. The little girl giggled, and then pushed a child's wooden chair over to the low window sill. She then climbed out into the early morning light. Clambering quickly to follow her was a short dark, ugly, little man.

Phoebe *had* to see where he took Miriam. Standing, she teetered on her spike heels and wished she'd changed her shoes. She couldn't wait. It had been twenty-four hours, and she might lose the trail if she dawdled. Phoebe found the back door in the kitchen and greeted the rising sun. Taking care as she went down the stairs, she held the railing. A mistake. Every man, woman, and child in Billings seemed to have touched it at one time or the other. She lifted her hand and followed the side of the house, finding the child's room within moments. Touching the clapboard beneath the window, she watched as the ugly little man took Miriam's hand and led her through the herb gardens and down a gravel path. Quickening her pace, she leaned down and patted the ground from time to time to confirm her direction. She slid on some sand, righted herself and kept going—right up to the river's edge—where she lost the connection. She had failed again. Choking back a sob of frustration, and berating herself for her stupidity, she picked her way back to the kitchen door where she found a puzzled looking Bert watching her.

"You okay?"

"Yes, of course. Why do you ask?"

"You disappeared. I got concerned. We don't need to lose any more people," he signed. "Especially not a senator's daughter."

Anger bubbled up in her chest. "This has *nothing* to do with my mother."

"Yes, I know. But if anything happens to you, I'll have to answer to her." He drummed his fingers on his thigh. "What made you come out here?"

"No reason." She shrugged. "Just needed some

fresh air."

"Wow. You are a terrible liar."

Her face burned. He was right, of course. She'd never revealed her gifts to anyone but her mother and grandmother. The Anomaly Defense Division had some very special agents with supernatural talents. Even so, would Bert believe her? And if she told him, would he keep her secret?

As she stood with her hands on her hips and glared at Bert, a movement behind him caught her attention. An elderly Native American woman with long black hair woven into two braids wearing a buckskin dress covered in elk teeth raised a hand in greeting.

Phoebe pointed at the woman and signed to Bert. "Who is the woman behind you?"

Bert craned his neck to look around. "What woman? I don't see anyone."

"Native American. Old. Long black hair—"

He put his hand up like a traffic cop. "It's my ancestor, Beautiful Blackfeather."

"Ancestor?" She stared at Bert. "No, not possible. She's right there—"

The woman shimmered, faded, and vanished.

Chapter Five

Hotel LaBelle, Billings, Montana

Bert eyed Phoebe over a cup of coffee, trying to fit this event into his previous appraisal of his boss. Over the course of the last day, his attitude toward her had undergone a shift. Mind you, not an earthquake level disruption, not even something you could see on a seismic graph, but enough to force him to temper his original impressions. At first, his mental framework had placed her squarely into the category of *book smart, but not street wise*. Her education was fine. A lawyer himself, he couldn't argue with how hard she must have worked to pass first the law classes, then the D.C. bar. Unfortunately, when she sashayed into his office, he was instantly reminded of the spoiled brat hotel heiress who had had a short-lived reality show. Phoebe was much prettier and much classier. Plus, she had those pouty lips—his groin tightened in a not safe for work response. *Not now. Jeez.*

She may have come from money and privilege, but she'd had some hard knocks along the way, like the loss of her father at a young age. When Bert's mother died, he'd practically raised Emma. If it hadn't been for their grandmother, they would have bounced from relative to relative—or worse, been placed in a foster home. When he'd gone off to college, then law school and JAG

Corps, he'd been worried about his little sister. But she'd turned out okay—*better* than okay. He wondered if Phoebe and Emma would get along. His sister had loved Susan from the moment they met. Not that he was interested in his boss *that* way. No way, no how, could he even consider this woman from another world as potential dating material. He might as well want to court the moon.

In fact, he'd probably have better luck with the moon than this ice queen. No, they were from opposite sides of the tracks. Nothing happening here, despite her side glances—and those pouty lips—which she was licking right now. Good Lord. This was so unfair. Why couldn't his new boss have been a mousy woman in sensible shoes and a shapeless tweed suit? Why did she have to be so damn sexy?

Why did Beautiful appear to Phoebe? Neither he nor his sister, Emma, could see their ancestor. They could feel her presence, see her move objects—her favorite trick was flipping over a rocking chair on the wraparound porch—but only a few people could *see* her. Phoebe wasn't a remote viewer nor did she appear to be Native American. Or was she? Tallulah didn't look like the stereotypical dark-eyed, black-haired Indian woman either, what with her wild blonde hair and blue eyes. He set his mug down, tapped the table for Phoebe's attention, and signed, "You have any Native American ancestors?"

Wide-eyed, she shook her head. "Why do you ask?"

"The woman you saw, Beautiful Blackfeather, can't be seen by everyone." He tilted his head and squinted at her. "Only people with special gifts."

Her eyebrows shot up. "Your agents?"

Hand in the finger spelling of the letter *A*, he tapped his thumb twice on his lips. "Secret."

"Tell me about Beautiful."

What was the correct way to convey the history of his family to this outsider—who also happened to be his boss? Yes, his division was different, but how did he condense centuries of history? He glanced at the clock. Six in the morning. His neck itched, a sure sign his eagle wanted to be set free. He needed to hit the sky and search for Miriam. In daylight, with his eagle vision, he could see four times better than in his human form. Colors were more vivid—he could see five, not just a human's three basic ones—and his ultraviolet vision enabled him to see urine trails of small animals. At night, on the other hand, his vision diminished greatly and made hunting dangerous.

Silence filled the room. Many of the law enforcement officers had left the hotel to follow up on the sparse leads and roust the usual suspects out of bed before they had the chance to leave town. The kitchen clock ticked, underscoring the passage of time, minutes that could be used searching for Miriam.

Okay, here we go. Condensed version.

He started with Tallulah, telling Phoebe about how she'd been invited by the former hotel owner to help him get the LaBelle back on its feet. Prior to coming to Montana, Tallulah had run a consulting business as a hotel inspector, and had occasionally used her second sight on the sly to help a few of her clients. Tallulah could see Beautiful and served as her interpreter.

"Incredible." Phoebe shook her head. "Others can see her?"

He nodded. "Bronco. My sister's husband. Works for me as a remote viewer. My ancestor likes to play tricks on him—and the rest of us. She's like the teasing cousin who never stops. Loves practical jokes."

"What kind of jokes?"

"Rocks the chairs on the front porch. Turns lights on and off. Taps people on the shoulder or arm. Throws stuffed animals at Tallulah. Makes things disappear and reappear. Leaves small objects as gifts."

"Not jokes. Wants attention. Can people hear her?"

"No. She uses Plains Indian Sign Language to communicate."

"Different from ASL."

"Yes, but I'm told she's a pretty good communicator."

Phoebe looked thoughtful. Funny how her eyes changed colors from glacial blue to sea gray. Again, he wondered about her heritage. *So blonde.* German? Scandinavian?

Bert gave her a moment to adjust to the notion of having a very active spirit on the premises. It was pretty overwhelming—and he hadn't even gotten all the way into Tallulah and Lucius, Bronco, and Emma, or the rest of the special agents.

The sound of a balloon releasing air through a tiny opening swelled into a shriek and yipping. Franny and Bisou raced into the kitchen tumbling over one another, banging into chair legs, and generally whooping it up. Panting, the pug ran to her large water dish, shoved her cone of shame into it, and the mini doxie followed. After splashing water all over the floor, the pug used the collar to push against her metal food dish, making it clear what was always on her mind. The chubby puggy was a mini-vacuum cleaner who required strict supervision, or she'd turn into a giant potato with bug eyes—a pugtato. Bisou trotted over to her owner and put her paws on her legs.

Phoebe clapped her hands, lifted the dog onto her lap, and frowned. Using a paper napkin, she pulled something off Bisou's long neck and slid it across the table to Bert, a questioning look on her face. "What is this?"

He examined the one-strand, beaded Crow necklace and smiled.

"Elk tooth necklace." He slid it back. "A gift for you. From Beautiful."

"Why me?"

"You must have some special talent." He tilted his head and gave her a meaningful look. "Would you like to tell me about it?"

Hands still, she avoided his gaze.

In his experience, patience was the best tool, and something he was running out of fast. He glanced at the clock, sipped his tepid coffee, and waited.

****

Phoebe stared at the necklace. If she picked it up, what would she see? The ivory colored tooth called to be touched. Unable to resist, she picked it up and turned it around in her fingers. She closed her eyes and images flooded her mind—but this time instead of watching pictures on a screen, like a movie, she was *inside* someone.

She looked down at beaded moccasins and brown legs hugging the sides of a horse. Two cowpokes staggered up to her, one in a ratty cowboy hat, filthy denim trousers, and mud encrusted boots who planted himself in front of her blue roan and grabbed at the reins. Another man with a sweat-darkened bandana hanging loose around his throat, and a cigarette hanging out of the corner of his mouth, grabbed at her leg and missed, slapping the roan's flank. He raised a bottle, waved it in her direction, and leered at her. She yanked back on the reins, and the horse danced to one side, then the other, but the cow punchers had her hemmed in. The one with the smoke glared past her with his one good eye, the other hidden behind a black patch.

Phoebe twisted on the horse to see what he was staring at. There in the middle of the dusty street stood Lucius, the man who had grabbed her hand in the SUV, who had made her espresso in this kitchen, and who now grieved for his missing daughter.

She dropped the jewelry, stared at the necklace, and shook like a leaf.

Bert's warm hand fell on hers and strength flowed into her like molten steel. No visions of war or violence attacked her psyche. Instead, immense power, peace, and kindness suffused her, restoring her balance, grounding her. As she gazed into the depths of Bert's dark eyes, his face blurred and shifted into a raptor—and not just any predatory bird. This bird was majestic, proud, and beautiful—a bald eagle. Heart swelling in her chest until she thought it might burst, she sat riveted with enthralled wonder. He lifted his hand, and the vision disappeared.

"I showed you mine." He signed. "Now you show me yours."

Trembling, scarcely able to believe what had happened, she nodded. Of all the people she'd ever met in her life, this man would never betray her secrets. It was time to share her gift with Bert. She prayed this time she'd be able to do the right thing—and help find the missing child.

Taking a deep breath, she began her story—her family's story, really. "Do you know what a birth caul is?"

"You mean a membrane on a baby's face?" He nodded. "We see this sometimes."

She paused for moment to look away from those intriguing eyes, a flutter of anxiety in her stomach. Not only was she revealing her secrets. She was about to reveal her mother's. Yet, if she couldn't trust the man who ran a division full of secrets, who could she trust?

"My grandmother and mother came from a long line of Irish seers, women who prophesied and could see into the future." She pointed at herself. "When I was born, I was the seventh daughter in the family born with the caul, including my mother and grandmother. Each of them gifted. Later, when the doctors determined I was deaf, they tried to convince my mother I needed a CI or a cochlear implant. Mom refused because she worried about what it might do to my developing brain—and my gift."

Bert's gaze never wavered.

"A lot of little things happened early in my life, stuff one could explain away. Proof of my talent came when I was five years old. My mother took me to a holiday party, one of those D.C. events everyone goes to and brings their kids. A Russian diplomat, I can't recall his name, brought wrapped gifts for all the kids and put them under the tree. Each child was to pick out one package—blue for boys, red for girls. Paper flew everywhere. The children were happy. Bears for boys, dolls for girls. Mine had snow-blonde hair, like me. She was beautiful in her red gown and matching sparkly headdress. I ripped it out of the box." She shook her head. "As soon as I touched it, I handed it to my mother."

"Why? What happened?"

"I needed my hands to sign to her, to tell her what I saw. Someone put a metal box inside the doll—and it was watching me. My mother thanked the man and told him I was thrilled. She held onto the doll and we left a little while later. When we arrived home, a black car sat in our driveway. A man in a black suit, white shirt, and black tie stepped out of the car, took the doll and drove away."

Bert finger spelled, "Spy?"

"Yes. Every toy the man brought was bugged." She could tell him many more tales, but they'd be here all day and night. The story of her life. "After that, my mother made sure I received only new toys. No history. No bad memories. As I grew older, I realized when I touched people skin-to-skin, I felt their emotions." Heat crept up her neck to Phoebe's face. "I see their worst and best events, and the feelings attached to those memories."

A sad, slow smile of understanding grew across his handsome face. "At my office. What did you see?"

Tears pricked her eyes. "Bombing. Helicopter. Hospital. Your legs. I'm so sorry."

"Explains why you jumped back as if I shocked you." He nodded. "Yes. A horrible day."

It was such a relief to share her secrets with someone who wouldn't ridicule her. All her life she'd been told, you are special, you have an important role to play. *It's a secret.* He had a secret, too. "The eagle? What is that?" She sat on the edge of her seat. "Tell me."

"Not until you finish." He tapped his fingertips together. "More."

She sighed. "Normally when I touch an object— unlike people—the images are only sharp for up to forty-eight hours. Then they start to fade, like a sun-bleached photograph." She pointed to the necklace. "But when I touched the elk tooth, everything was vivid—it was as if I was the person who wore the necklace, reliving a memory."

He rubbed his chin. "What did you see?"

She described the vision—and Lucius' appearance in what was clearly an old west town. "It was amazing—and scary at the same time. He really is a man from another century."

Bert tilted his head. "Why were you outside?"

"I was following a trail. Got to the river and lost the images. Water doesn't hold memories." At his puzzled expression, she backtracked. "Lucius showed me the baby's room. When he walked away, I placed my hand on the doorjamb. Saw images of Miriam, Tallulah, and Lucius, coming and going. Just normal family activity for the last two days. But when I felt the floor—" She bit her lower lip, worried she'd be taken for a fool—or worse.

He took her hand into his large warm one, and his emotions flowed into her.

Worry. Fear. Anxiety. Compassion. Intense attraction.

At the last one, she flushed and withdrew from his comforting grasp. The attraction was not one-sided. But this was not the time—or the place—and she needed her hands to answer. "I saw who took the child."

Eyes widening, Bert leaned in. "Who?" He pressed. "Was Miriam hurt? Was she crying?"

"No. Smiling. Laughing. Followed him right out the window. Thought it was a game." She closed her eyes. "Like she was playing with another child."

"Where did he take her? Who is he?"

"My mother told me other people don't understand our history. She said I must remember and tell my children."

Bert's brow furrowed.

He thinks I'm rambling.

She rushed to explain, but needed to give him some background first. Otherwise, it wouldn't make sense. "I was raised on bedtime stories about the wee folk in Ireland. They lived in a world similar to humans, but time passed much slower in theirs. Some called them fallen angels, others said they were gods. Everyone said they had special powers. Faeries could shapeshift into anything, any size they wanted. They could become invisible or use glamour to make people see what they wanted them to see. Human midwives, nannies, and healers were their favorites, and they often called on these particular humans to help them give birth. In return they would bestow gifts and favors on humans. They could be great helpers. Or they could be evil, vindictive over the smallest slights, attacking people, killing cows and men, taking women and children to their own world underground. This one did not have evil intentions."

"A faerie took my niece?" Bert's face reddened. "What did he look like?"

"Big ears, long nose, dark clothes. Not a faerie— but like one." She held her hand approximately two feet off the floor. "Just like the deputy said. He's an ugly little man."

Chapter Six

Hotel LaBelle, Billings, Montana

The wind knocked out of him, his anger and his matching urge to fly momentarily pushed aside, Bert sagged in his chair. First Tallulah, then Otterlegs, now Phoebe pointed to the same suspect—an ugly little man. Diminutive people were not out of the realm of the Absaalooke or Crow culture. In fact, they were part of the oral tradition, with one of the best known stories involving one lifting a full-grown bull elk—and carrying it on his back into his own world. Called the Little-people by the Crow, they lived in the Pryor Mountains and were said to have created stone arrow points. Legends said sightings of Little-people were few and far between, not because they didn't exist, but because they *chose* who could see them.

Perhaps one of the most famous stories came from Chief Plenty-Coups. When he was nine, he'd lost a close friend. In Crow tradition, he sliced his arms and bled himself into weakness. Seeking a dream, he wanted to learn how to avenge his friend who was like a brother. After taking a sweat-bath, Plenty-Coups traveled into the Pryor Mountains where he fasted and prayed for a vision. After days and nights of despairing of ever seeing a Helper from the spirit world, he fell asleep. A person calling his name woke him and led him to a lodge where he met the chief of the Little-people who took him in as their own. They gave him advice instead of a medicine bag, telling him to use his powers and to make them work for him. Plenty Coups awoke, his destiny to become a Chief burned into his mind.

Phoebe had seen not only Beautiful, his mischievous ancestor, but also a Little-person. And, Miriam had seen him and followed him out the window. Was he like the Pied Piper? Did he intend to take more children? Or was Miriam the only one he wanted? Had Miriam also seen Beautiful? Many had visited the old Victorian hotel, but few aside from Tallulah, Bronco, and now Phoebe, had seen Beautiful. Clearly, there was a common denominator between his boss and the little girl—but what was it? To his knowledge, unlike Emma's twins, Miriam had shown *no* evidence of paranormal abilities. Or had she?

Just then Tallulah stumbled into the kitchen, still in the same clothes from the night before, her hair in wild disarray. Lucius strode behind his wife, attempting to keep her on an even keel. He grabbed at her hand, and she shook him off.

She stopped in front of Phoebe and stared at her. "We need to talk."

The blonde glanced between Bert and Tallulah, her face a question mark.

Bert signed and spoke, "She wants to talk with you."

Phoebe nodded.

Eyes sunken, nearly incoherent, Tallulah choked out, "Beautiful says you saw who took my baby. Why haven't you *done* something?"

"Tallulah, baby." Lucius placed his palm on her arm. "She just got here, don't you think—"

She whirled on her husband. "Don't. You. Dare." Turning back, she shouted, "Dammit, Bert, why aren't you doing something. You're supposed to be my friend. You're Miriam's uncle for God's sake. Don't you care about her?"

Stunned by the ferocity of Tallulah's verbal lashing, he reminded himself she was running on adrenaline and grief. No mother would be calm in this situation. "The sheriff and the FBI, they're using every resource they have to find Miriam—"

Tallulah was right he did need to do something. He needed to fly. The sun was up and here he was, stuck in an emotional maelstrom.

Phoebe slapped the table, making everyone jump. All eyes turned to her. She was *not* happy.

"I'm sorry. I didn't mean to leave you out of the conversation," Bert signed. "Tallulah is upset and wants to know what you saw."

Phoebe nodded and repeated what she told Bert before, "Ugly little man, playing with Miriam. Climbed out window after him. I lost them at the river."

As if a puppet master had cut the strings, Tallulah sagged and would have hit the floor had Lucius not caught her. Phoebe leaped out of her chair and slid it over for the stricken mother.

Tallulah wailed, "I saw him, too, but I can't see him now. God knows I've tried. He led her to the river—and I lost him, too. I don't know what happened." She placed her head on her forearms, and her shoulders hitched with sobs.

Bert translated for Phoebe, and she nodded.

"Running water interferes with memories. Washes them away."

"Lucius, has Miriam seen Beautiful?" Bert asked in a low voice. "Ever?"

Lucius nodded, "All the time. She's her guardian angel. Ever since Miriam was born, Beautiful has kept watch over her."

Bert rubbed his gritty eyes. "Where was she yesterday? Why wasn't Beautiful here?"

Just as the words floated out of Bert's mouth, Bronco entered the kitchen. "Because great-great-great-great-great grandma was at our house, keeping an eye on our twins."

Bert introduced Bronco to Phoebe, finger spelling his name and then describing how he fit in. "Bronco Winchester is a remote viewer, works for me. I sent him out here last year after my sister, Emma—you know, the horse whisperer—was attacked by a bullet-spewing drone. If not for a wild mare who took the bullets for her, my sister would be dead now." He paused for a moment. "Bronco and Emma pretended to be newlyweds, went undercover to find out who was orchestrating the domestic terror attacks—and exposed a neo-Nazi's plan to attack the capitol of Montana." Bert smiled. "They fell in love, got married, now he's my brother-in-law and the proud father of twins—a girl and a boy, Emily and Adam."

Phoebe extended her hand and Bronco grasped it—and gave a surprised shake of his head. Still holding her hand, Bronco said to Bert, "New agent?"

"Oh-ho!" He signed to Phoebe, "He knows."

Mouth open, she pulled her hand back. "How?"

"You have a vibe about you—different from

Tallulah and Emma. I felt it when you shook my hand. You a remote viewer, too?"

Bert translated as fast as he could, wishing he had learned more signs. *This is exhausting. No wonder interpreters work in teams.*

She shook her head, "No." She paused. "Your childhood. So tragic. I'm so sorry."

The color drained out of Bronco's face. "Empath?"

"And psychometrician." A swell of pride in discovering this new talent filled his chest—and Bert promptly chided himself. It wasn't as if he had anything to do with her gifts. On the other hand, it sure was nice to have found out sooner rather than later. This new boss would understand in ways no other manager would about the importance of his division. "She has a good idea who took Miriam. Tallulah and Otterlegs came back with the same description—an ugly little man, about the same size as a two-year old."

Bronco put his big hand on Lucius' arm. "So sorry, bro'. I'm here to help. Emma's on her way. She had to give Stephanie the instruction manual and the hour-long lecture on how to care for the twins."

Lucius swiped at his eyes. "I'm about to make some killer espresso. Anyone want some?"

Hands went up.

Tallulah roused from her stupor, her voice thick. "A gallon, please. No more drugs. They don't help. Still miserable, but dopey." She placed her hand on Phoebe's and signed, "Sorry."

Phoebe put her hand on top of Tallulah's and closed her eyes. A little sigh escaped her lips, and her shoulders slumped.

Bert worried she'd burn out before the day was

even started. Tapping into that level of anguish was taking its toll on her. He had to do something. Gently, he extracted Tallulah's hand and took it into his own, leaving his dominant hand free to sign.

"Do you recall ever seeing the ugly little man before this incident? If he's what we think he is, he only appears to certain people."

Eyes glazed, Tallulah asked in a low voice. "What do you mean?"

"The description is similar to the Little-people of Pryor Mountains, what we Crow call the Nirumbee."

"Not a human?" Sitting up straighter, Tallulah asked, "Supernatural?"

Bert nodded.

"Never saw him before—nor has Beautiful. I asked her when she came back from Emma's." She gazed past Bert looking at the doorway leading to the child's room. "Wait—there she is now."

Heads turned in the direction where she pointed.

Bronco nodded and waved. "She doesn't look happy."

"She's hand signing to me." Tallulah shook her head. "Lucius, give me some coffee, please, I need to wake up."

"Darlin', your wish is my command." He rushed to the machine and began twisting knobs.

Squinting, Tallulah said, "She says she went to Medicine Mountain, looked for the little man and Miriam. Spoke to the Chief of the Little-people. He swore on his people's lives, they had nothing to do with stealing her."

Bert passed his hand over his face, trying to make sense of everything. Phoebe tapped his arm, and he put his hands down. "Thinking," he signed. "Beautiful said our Little-people didn't take her."

"If not Little-people," Phoebe asked. "Must be someone like them? Faeries?"

"Or something else," Bert replied. "But what the devil would that be?"

He glanced out the window, the sun a bright fireball in the sky. He'd given his boss glimpses of his eagle, but no way was he inviting her to watch his transformation. For one thing, she didn't need any more emotional overload at this time. For another, he had to be naked before shifting. And he was pretty sure that wasn't covered in the employee policy manuals.

****

Reluctantly, Phoebe nodded agreement, fell back in her chair, and tried to absorb everything. He was right. She was exhausted, and not just from the long flight. She'd never been with this many psychics before in her life—not to mention the ubiquitous Beautiful Blackfeather, who was as Bert had told her, pretty good at communicating despite the different hand-signs. Phoebe had been able to follow most of what Beautiful had said, helped along with Bert's tireless interpreting. She felt bad for him, after all, most days she had a team of interpreters. Here she was, off the clock, off the government radar, and possibly out of her mind.

What had she been thinking when she insisted on coming along with Bert? If she was honest with herself, perhaps it wasn't only about proving she could balance the karmic scales of justice for Angela and find peace in her heart at last. Maybe, just maybe, it might have been the fact that the minute she connected with Bert, she had become fixated on finding more ways of spending time with him in an unofficial, non-management role. If she was brutally honest with herself, she'd made it a *mission* to find a way to make him accept her on this trip—even to the point of grasping at straws, like National Security. *Desperate much?*

Her conscience piped up out of nowhere. *For heaven's sake, Phoebe. Fess up. If you'd met him anyway other than as his boss, you would have asked him out. Admit it. He's hot. And he's attracted to you, too.*

With heat creeping up her neck, she tore her eyes away from Bert before he caught her staring at him. It was easy, too easy, to become enthralled with his rugged good looks—with cheekbones that models would kill for, a strong chin, and a mischievous smile that made her knees wobble, she wondered why he wasn't married. When they met, she'd caught a glimpse of a woman in his memories from the hospital, but the connection had been broken. Since then, it seemed as if he'd controlled what he shared with her—like the eagle. What did it mean? She needed to find out—but this was not the time. Just then Lucius handed her a steaming cup of decaf coffee, interrupting her train of thought and bringing her back to reality.

She glanced around the room. Where was everyone? Except for Bert and Lucius, the kitchen had emptied out. Bert waved to someone, and she turned in her seat to see who was there.

An Amazon of a woman with long black hair and a feminine version of Bert's features strode into the kitchen. Wearing a plaid flannel shirt over a T-shirt tucked into her jeans, and metal tipped black cowboy boots, the woman commanded the room. Phoebe had no doubt this was Emma, the famous sister, and that she took control of any situation, any time.

Bert introduced the two women, and Phoebe put out her hand. The connection, while not as jolting as the one she'd had with Bert, was instantaneous and deep. Images of a grizzly bear attack, a gunshot wound to the chest, a massive explosion, fear for Bronco's life, and the joy of the birth of the twins roared into her brain. Reeling from the emotional turbulence, she released Emma's hand, closed her eyes, and pressed her trembling palms to her pounding temples.

Too much, too fast, too many people.

Warm hands fell onto her wrists, and strength flowed into her. Her racing pulsed slowed, and her shaky breaths grew deeper. When she opened her eyes, Bert's worried gaze met hers. He had maneuvered his wheelchair closer, putting himself between Emma and Phoebe.

After waiting a few moments before breaking contact, he signed, "You need to rest. Your bag is in your room. Lucius will give you the key. I want you to go lie down. You can't keep this up. From now on, no handshakes. Okay?"

Hesitating for a second, she nodded. How did he know exactly what she needed? He claimed he wasn't psychic, but he acted like he could read her mind.

"Too much going on here, too many strong emotions, for you to be tapping into everyone. You need to know something about someone, ask me. Okay?"

She thanked him and an enormous feeling of relief washed over her. She didn't have to go it alone. He had her back. It was a nice feeling. Something she could get used to for sure. Phoebe attempted to gather her wits—and her dog. Where had Bisou gone? She clapped her hands and the mini ran into the kitchen, the comical looking pug on her heels.

"Lucius wants to know if it's all right to feed your dog." Bert signed. "It's breakfast time for the pug and poor Franny is giving her owner the business. He has to take the collar off—it's a production."

She smiled. "Yes, thanks. She found a friend."

Bert looked at the small dogs chowing down on kibble and gave Phoebe a sideways look and smiled. "What about you, Under Secretary? Do you think you might have found a friend—or two?"

Was he flirting with her? Or was she just hoping? Her heart stuttered, and she licked her suddenly dry lips.

"Like being in a room full of live wires. Other than my mother, I've never met any other real psychics." *Oops.* Using the *A* sign, she tapped her bottom lip with her thumb. "Secret."

He nodded. "Many secrets."

"I never expected to feel this way. Like old friends. Home."

"It's this place." He smiled. "You won't want to go back to D.C."

"We'll see. Now where am I sleeping?"

Lucius led her and Bert through the lobby. Uniformed officers clustered by a white board with sheets of papers in their hands, while Deputy Otterlegs checked things off the list with a marker. Three new women sat behind the registration desk, headsets on their ears, lips moving. The sheriff leaned over a table in the bar and pointed at a laptop, while a woman made notes. Everyone was doing something—everyone but her. Burned out from all the emotional connections in a high-tension situation, Phoebe had to get to bed soon or she'd collapse.

Bisou in her arms, Phoebe, Bert, and Lucius rode up in the gleaming brass and wood elevator. A quick shower and a nap. Then she'd come downstairs and get to work, do something, anything. She had seen enough TV shows about search and rescue to know they'd need an army of volunteers to find Miriam. The ugly little man who wasn't a man couldn't have just vanished. What would a Little-person want with her? Specifically, why Miriam? Out of all the children in Billings, or even Montana, why would he be attracted to her? Was it for revenge against her parents or a family member? Did he want to raise a child of his own? Or was there some demand yet to come? If this ugly little man was a supernatural being, what could he possibly want from a human?

Bisou licked her face, and her tail smacked Phoebe's arm. At least someone was happy. The pug with her funny face and head tilts was the doxie's new best friend. *Lucky dog.* If only Phoebe could say the same about her relationship with Bert. The man in question's door was next to hers. So close, yet so far. Key in his lap, Bert waved, signed, "Sleep well" and glided into his room.

Lucius opened the door for her, handed her the key, and tipped an imaginary hat. At the sight of the four-poster bed, all thoughts of work flew out of her head. She set Bisou on the bed, kicked off her stilettos, fell back into the huge fluffy pillows, and floated into a dreamless sleep.

Chapter Seven

Hotel LaBelle, Billings, Montana

Alone at last, Bert opened his window, moved to the bed, and tore his clothes off. Time was ticking, and he would need to get out there and back without overstaying his *nap time*. Hal expected him to be part of the team, and he needed to be present in his human form for a good part of the day. Taking a deep breath, he began with his legs. Missing from the knee down, his human legs still gave him phantom pains and itches from time to time. As he stared at the stumps of what had once been a strong runner's legs, they began to shrink and change color. The stabbing pain of his emerging razor-sharp talons was replaced quickly with the joy of knowing he'd be soaring soon. Simultaneously, his torso shrank, his arms dwindled and morphed into light-weight bony appendages. His heartbeat kicked up to over one hundred beats per minute. No real stress—yet. Feathers, long, short, downy, and layered to keep him warm at subzero temperatures stabbed, itched, and tickled their way out of his skin on almost every surface. He lifted one foot, then the other flexing his talons, and preened at his wing feathers with his strong, bright yellow beak. Flapping his wings, he hopped up on the massive antique dresser and examined himself in the mirror, checking for any remnants of human skin. Glorious white head feathers set off his yellow eyes, as large as humans, but far better at seeing. He spread his wings— and sent a lamp crashing to the floor. *Shit*. So much for being subtle. He hoped the hubbub of the lobby covered the noise. Satisfied he was ready to go, he hopped onto the windowsill, grabbed an updraft, and sped toward the other side of the sparkling Yellowstone River and the acres of land to be searched.

An hour and a half later Bert returned to his room empty-handed and frustrated. Despite his extraordinary vision and the ability to see every tiny animal hopping, scurrying, slithering, and flying in the search zone, not a single clue to find Miriam had jumped out at him. Already exhausted from the trip, he needed to restore his depleted calories. He had foregone the desire to catch a fish, not wanting to waste a moment of time away from his search. Shivering from low blood sugar as he morphed back into human form, Bert's first priority was nourishment. If he didn't get something to eat soon, he risked passing out in his birthday suit. Not a good way to be found if someone came looking for him, especially if that someone was his boss. He shook his head, struggled back into his clothes, and headed downstairs to find some food.

As the Yellowstone County Sheriff, Hal was the Incident Commander for the search and rescue effort. Financially strapped and short on manpower, the sheriff's office had recently put out a call for volunteers for the Special Services Division Search and Rescue Program. However, since the program was so new, and the Montana Code was so specific regarding age, specialized skills, the ability to pass a physical test, and a thorough background investigation, the actual number of new recruits was low. Less than a dozen people wore the fluorescent vests identifying them as Special Services Officers. Every deputy, including Otterlegs fiancée, Wanda, had been pulled off whatever they were doing to work the case. By coordinating with the leaders of wilderness search and rescue teams from other counties, including a local K-9 organization, Hal had been able to beef up his resources. A good beginning, but simply not enough man or womanpower to comb the rugged areas of Big Sky Country. With the tall sandstone cliffs running north-east to the city, two major rivers, grassy plains, foothills, and seven mountain ranges, the sheer size of the potential search area would be overwhelming without a well-thought-out plan. Unmanned surveillance drones would be helpful, or a flock of eagle shifters, but neither were readily available.

Shoving glazed donuts into his mouth and quaffing scalding black coffee laden with sugar, Bert surveyed the assembled team leaders and waited for Hal to approach him. He wished he could call in his shapeshifters to augment his team of psychics. Better than hunting dogs, their enhanced senses—smell in particular—would have come in handy for the search. However, a Persian lion would not fit into the local wildlife and werewolves would *not* be safe from hunters. Bronco, Emma, Lucius, and Tallulah—now dressed in blue jeans and a light sweater and looking more alert—sat at a dining room table with Bert, watching the lobby grow thick with uniforms. A large thermos of coffee, condiments, and a box of pastries rested in the center of the table, a trail of confectioner's

77

sugar leading to the white dust on Bronco's shirt.

"Where's the FBI in all this, Bert?" Lucius asked in a low voice.

Thank God for Lucius and his calming influence on Tallulah. Not that he faulted her for falling apart when Miriam went missing. He didn't have any children, but he imagined it would be like having your still-beating heart ripped out of your chest.

"Hal told me the Montana Department of Justice and the Criminal Justice Information Network is on top of this. They managed the AMBER Alert and entered Miriam's information into the Montana Missing Persons Clearinghouse. The FBI jumps in right away. Nowadays, with child abductions, no one waits for ransom notes or calls. The FBI deployed their Western Child Abduction Rapid Deployment—or CARD—team. See those silverbacks in suits over there? They earned those gray hairs the hard way. Years of experience and a proven track record in dealing with non-family child abductions."

"Gotta say, they don't look like they're doin' anything but jaw jacking and hunt and pecking on their laptops. Shouldn't they be out there looking for my baby girl?"

Tallulah clutched Lucius' hand, and a fat tear dropped on her arm.

"They *are* doing something," Bert replied. "They work closely with FBI Behavioral Analysis Unit representatives, National Center for the Analysis of Violent Crime coordinators, and Child Exploitation Task Force members. Right now, analysts are inputting the information the team is providing to them, digging through local, state, federal, and international databases, narrowing down the list of probable suspects."

Bronco put his elbows on the table and leaned forward. "When do we go in, boss?"

"We're like vampires, my friend." Bert gave him a grim smile. "We have to be invited in."

Shaking his head, Bronco stood, wandered to the bar, and helped himself to a soda. "Anyone else want a drink? Water? Soda? I don't know about you guys, but I'm getting a bit over caffeinated."

Emma stretched, strolled over to her husband, slipped her arm around his waist, and placed her head on his shoulder.

A pang of jealousy jolted Bert, spearing him without warning. He'd had *that* once.

Susan Foxtail had been the sun and the moon to Bert. Smart, kind, compassionate, patient with Bert and his eruptions of frustration and self-pity, she had aroused his passions—all of them—including anger. His body had healed from surgery in under a month, but his self-image had not. When he had first looked in the mirror, he had nearly vomited. He had pushed himself away from the reflection—and away from any hope of a future love life. *Until he met Susan.*

A rehabilitation nurse, Susan had taught him to live again—and to hope. Due to the forced intimacy of their relationship, the trust between them had grown over the months of therapy. The only time they had clashed had been over the use of prosthetic legs.

Bert hadn't dared to reveal the real reason he wouldn't use them. Over time, if he left them on and walked, his talons would become damaged. Forced to choose between being able to walk as a human and being able to shapeshift fully intact, he chose his birthright—his bald eagle.

Once he was discharged from the hospital, he still required extensive physical therapy to regain upper body strength. Susan worked with Bert and the VA to ensure he obtained a placement at a Center for Independent Living while he transitioned back to civilian life and learned to be on his own again. The day of his discharge, mouth dry with fear of rejection, he asked her out. She agreed on the condition that he complete all his therapies the week before the date. In the absence of appropriate transportation, she came to his apartment in the center with takeout food, a bottle of wine, and a pair of candles. After dinner she had insisted they work on one more critical activity of daily living—sex.

Susan and he agreed he had completely recovered in that regard—and exceeded all expectations. Simply put, they were great in bed together. Over the next few months, they practiced as often as humanly possible, because as Susan would say in a husky voice as she led him into the bedroom, "Rehabilitation *must* be practiced every single day."

Bronco and Emma returned to the round table, hands intertwined, speaking softly to each other as they sipped their drinks. He shook his head. Too late. He'd lost a once in a lifetime gift from the Supreme Being to a drunk driver. Now at age thirty-eight, he was Uncle Bert, the confirmed bachelor of the family. His opportunities for a love life were over.

Hal approached the table and eyed the team in an appraising manner. "Just want to give you an update. The videos from the cameras mounted on the sides of the hotel were blurry from oh-three-hundred to oh-five-hundred. Before and after that time frame, there are mule deer wandering past, but no ugly little man, no Miriam. The FBI agents in Billings are working on enhancing the images as we speak." Pointing at the FBI CARD team, Hal said, "Those guys sent FBI agents to interview their top picks on the suspect list according to the Behavioral Analysis Unit's profile. If they're innocent and smart, they'll be willing to spill their guts on anything they heard on the grapevine."

He pointed at the whiteboard. "As you know, Miriam's point last seen, or PLS, was her bedroom. Her last known position, or LKP, based on the footprints in the sand was the edge of the Yellowstone. We have dive teams and boats on the river. Using a K-9 team, we searched the hotel, her room, and the outbuildings. A vehicle canvass has been conducted, and we covered roads, trails, and railroad tracks by helicopter. We've looked under tarps, trash receptacles, crawlspaces, downed trees—any place large enough to conceal a child." He took a breath. "At this age, kids can wander as far as two or three miles depending on the terrain. The flatter the area, like trails or railroad tracks, the faster they can go. Children are naturally curious and fearless. They'll follow a butterfly or an animal. They don't even know they're lost—until they get hungry, or something makes them think of mommy."

Tallulah choked back a sob.

"Sorry, I have to give you the rundown. We need you as partners in this search. When it gets dark, little ones will look for a sleeping spot. Under a picnic table, a hollow log, anything that seems like a good bed, even under a pile of leaves. Fortunately, we've had an unseasonably warm spell, so last night wasn't too cold, another thing in our fav—"

"What's the countdown clock? Forty-eight hours?" Bert interrupted.

Hal shook his head. "We follow the three, twenty-four, and seventy-two-hour rules. The greatest danger to Miriam is in the first three hours." He pointed at Tommy who stood chatting with Wanda. "Otterlegs said the tribal medicine people told him she was with an ugly little man after that time frame. It's a good sign—if true. They didn't see him in person, they had visions. No matter how unlikely, we *must* follow every lead." Pointing to a map on a wall, he said, "Based on her point last seen and her last known position, we've predicted a cone of travel and established a containment area. Volunteers with radios have been assigned to stand along the highway, at the river, and in the fields across the river. The dogs and their handlers were dropped at the edges of the containment area to catch anything that gets past our people. If the ugly SOB comes through with Miriam, we will nab him and rescue her."

Tight-lipped and pale, Tallulah listened to Hal without saying a word. A heavy silence fell on the group. Bert needed to cut the tension, give the parents hope.

Before he could open his mouth, Emma spoke up. "What's left for us to do, Hal? Sounds like you've got your bases covered. How can we help?"

"Thank you for asking." He jerked his thumb over his shoulder. "These Special Services Officers are great, but if they do their jobs and really search for clues, they can only cover a mile in three and half hours. Horses can go faster and farther. I was hoping you'd help us out by organizing the horse teams."

"Of course." She smiled. "What about the dogs? You want me to put in good word with them?"

He grinned. "Not sure their handlers would take too kindly to that, so I'm going to say no. We've got a call into an out of state blood hound search and rescue group. Those dogs are sixty times better at tracking than German Shepherds and can track scents on the ground and in the air. As soon as the team gets here, they'll join the search."

"What about me?" Bronco asked. "I'm a former ATFE agent. What can I do?"

"We've already interviewed you and Emma, which is good." Hal scratched his head. "Could you help me with the people who showed up because the story was on the news? They want to help—but they have no expertise and zero experience—plus some of them are just freaking weird."

"Sure."

"You know those damn TV shows always like to film people walking across fields in grids." He shook his head. "I don't want untrained people messing up our containment area, trampling clues. We've got a hundred volunteers camped out front—in trucks, RVs, SUVs— all chomping at the bit to help. If we ignore them, they won't go away. It could turn into a public relations nightmare. I want to give them an out of the way area to comb through, so they're not underfoot—but they can feel like they're being Good Samaritans. Plus, the area will be thoroughly searched, so they actually will be helping. If you can organize this crowd, we can send a couple of people out on horseback to help keep an eye on them. Work for you?"

Bronco nodded. "Just say when."

"We need to keep them out of the hotel and away from the family. I'll have one of the uniforms help you set up an area out front. You're going to be responsible for checking in each and every one of them. Get a logbook from Wanda. You'll need to record their name, address, phone number, employer, organizational affiliation, search location, and time in and out." Hal shook his head. "I would love it if we could video each person who signs in, but we don't have the equipment."

"What about my smartphone?" Bronco suggested. "I could have them tell me their names, address, phone number and place of employment while I video record them. Would that work?"

Hal smiled for the first time since he'd come to the table. "If you don't mind running up your bill and if your cell has the space, it would be great."

"Unlimited data plan," Bronco said. "This is a talkative family—and I have the newest, biggest version."

"This group hasn't had criminal background checks, so keep an eye out for strange behaviors, like overly attentive searchers who ask a lot of questions. You know the drill. Use your training and your gut."

With all the dogs outside waiting to be set to work, Bert was glad he'd advised Bronco to leave his bobcat partner, Gaucho, at home. He wondered how the cat would react to Phoebe's mini dachshund. If she was going to be here awhile, they'd find out soon enough. *Stop it.* He gave himself a mental head smack. This was a weekend trip. Today was Saturday. By tomorrow evening, Phoebe and her adorable smiling dog would be on a plane, heading back to D.C. He glanced up at the sound of the elevator's descent.

There she is now. Omigod. Cotton-mouthed, heart racing, Bert squirmed and looked around the room to see if everyone else was staring too. Like him, quite a few men had taken note of how damn sexy she looked in those skin-tight pants and top. With her long hair pulled back into a tight braid, she looked like a Norse goddess—albeit in the wrong outfit. Resisting the urge to shout at them to put their eyes and tongues back in their heads and get back to work, he moved his wheel chair forward a few inches, firmly placing his lap under the table so no one could see just how happy *he* was to see her.

****

Phoebe's shower had fortunately returned her to the land of the living. A cup of coffee and she'd be ready to go another twelve hours. Bisou wriggled, and she placed her on the floor. Racing toward the kitchen in a blur of red, the little dog was on the hunt for more kibble, Franny, or both.

Stepping smartly in her favorite breeches, riding boots, and round-neck long-sleeved sport top, she carried her sturdy western horse-riding helmet over her arm on its strap, her gloves tucked inside the cap. Proficient at riding from the age of seven, she'd selected everything with an eye toward a rough trail and uneven terrain. The only tiny indulgence she'd permitted herself to bring was the elk tooth necklace from Beautiful Blackfeather. She kept it tucked under her shirt, out of sight. Superstitious, maybe, but for some reason, it made her feel protected.

Heart stuttering in sync with the flock of butterflies attempting to escape from her stomach, Phoebe approached the table where Bert sat surrounded by his team. He was a natural leader, she could see it in the eyes of his team members and their body language. They waited for his responses and deferred to him on everything. She wondered how many other division directors at Homeland had that kind of loyalty from the troops. *Bet I could count them on one hand.*

Bert signed hello and pulled a chair out for her. "Good nap?"

Not only was he a gentleman—but he actually asked her how she *felt*. When was the last time a man treated her with such courtesy? She didn't sense his good nature was forced. It was part of who he was and why his people were so bonded to him. Perhaps she could learn a thing or two from Bert about leadership.

"The best. Softest bed and pillows." She glanced at Hal and the solemn faces around the table. "What did I miss? Did they find Miriam?"

Bert shook his head and brought her up to speed, speaking as he signed. "Hal is telling us what we can do to help."

Phoebe pointed to her helmet. "I'm ready to ride."

"Have you ever been on a search and rescue, or trained for one?"

Her heart sank. Was he saying she couldn't be involved? She shook her head. "But you told me I could help. You promised. And you know about my gifts."

Not repeating the last part of her signing to the group, Bert replied. "Yes. I promised. We need to know so we can put you with the right group. We have dive teams, K-9 teams, EMTs, all kinds of talents." He smiled and winked at her and something warm and soft coiled in her abdomen—and further down. "It's probably best if you go with the group Bronco's going to organize. None of those people have search and rescue experience, either, but there will be two leaders who do. Okay?"

Flustered by her body's response to him, her breath came a little too fast, her legs quivered a little too much, and for an instant, she wished she was there on vacation and had just met this unbelievably hot man and invited him up to her big, soft bed for a very long night of slow lovemaking until dawn.

Get yourself under control, woman.

Biting her lower lip, she nodded. "Fine. I don't want to be underfoot—but I do want to help."

"Excellent. We just need to see if we have someone who can sign to go with you."

Hal spun on his heel, raced away, and returned so fast, the floor shook beneath her feet. He gave a thumb's up sign.

"Boy did we get lucky. One of the volunteers has a brother who attended the Montana School for the Deaf and Blind," Bert signed. "Says he used to go out there for weekends to visit. Signs and finger spells. You'll have to stay close to him. Okay?"

"Yes, yes. Perfect." She glanced around. "I think I should leave Bisou here."

Bert agreed. "I'll keep an eye on her, she likes my lap when she's not chasing Franny." He tapped the helmet which sat on the table. "You won't need this. The horses are very laid-back, used to hunting. Nothing bothers them."

Phoebe put her palm out. "I always wear one. Had a friend in middle school who fell off her horse. Head injury. Partially blind. I can't afford to lose my vision."

"Your call. I just wanted to let you know in case you wanted to avoid lugging it along. You will be wearing a fluorescent vest with pockets for matches, a flash light, folding knife, water bottles, snack bars—and bear spray."

The last item gave Phoebe pause. "Joke?"

"Not a joke. We have grizzly bears—just ask Emma. The spray will keep them at bay, but not for long."

"Why matches if I have a flashlight?"

"Wilderness survival one-oh-one. If you have matches, you can start a fire to keep warm—and to signal for help if you get lost or separated from the group." He paused. "Here's what you do for smoke signals. First you have to find a clearing so your fire doesn't go out of control. Use small dry twigs to start the fire. Then, when the fire is roaring, put green branches like pine on top to—'

Not a fan of any camping, including low budget motels, Phoebe laughed and snapped N-O. "I hope I never need to use that information."

Bert smiled. "Me, too."

A man in faded jeans, dusty cowboy boots, an orange vest, and a Stetson walked up to the table. "I'm Joe Bighorn," he signed and spoke. "Who's riding with me?"

She smiled and waved at the whip-thin man in the black hat. "My name is Phoebe." She left off her last name, not wanting to set off an uncomfortable round of *Any relation to Senator Wagner?* She started to offer her hand, then recalled Bert's warning: *From now on, no handshakes. Okay?* He was right. Better not do it again. She needed to conserve her energy to focus on finding Miriam. She wanted Bert to be happy he brought *the boss* along—despite his protests. She was going out on a calm horse, with a trained searcher, along with other volunteers. What could possibly go wrong?

Chapter Eight

Hotel LaBelle, Billings, Montana

Bert nodded at Bronco, signing at the same time. "Your first customer. You might as well start out with an easy one. Plus, this is a good way for Joe Bighorn to start working with Phoebe as her interpreter."

Bronco stood and waved at Phoebe and Bighorn to come with him. "Let me grab a logbook from Wanda, so we can get started."

Emma jumped up. "I'll go look for the leader of the horse team. See if they need any of my mares to augment the search."

Phoebe stood and signed. "Thank you for looking after Bisou—and for making sure I could participate. It means a lot to me." Then she turned and followed Bronco who was making his way toward the petite deputy.

"What can I do, Hal? Normally, I'd offer to be the guy in the chair on the computer, but it seems you have those bases covered."

Hal smiled and sat in Bronco's empty chair. "While I'm finishing the Incident Action Plan, the equipment has to be inventoried. Every vehicle, GPS, fluorescent vest, radio, flashlight, pad of paper and pencil, whatever, has to be accounted for. Not to mention the team assignment sheet, so we have a record of every team and who's on it. Otterlegs is superb at those kind of nitty-gritty details, so you're off the hook for that job. Besides—" he grinned "—it will keep him out of my hair."

Bert let out a huge sigh of relief. "You had me going. I *hate* clerical work."

"I know." Hal continued with a grin. "The flyers are done, and the local faith-based groups and scout troops are distributing them in person. We've got it up on social media and other Internet outlets. Lucius registered Miriam with the National Center for Missing and Exploited Children, so they'll be posting her photo on their website as well. The ladies at the desk are answering the hotline number on the flyer and attending to the fax machine. You, my friend, are still going to be my guy on the computer, but on the volunteer side. Tallulah and Lucius—" he nodded at the couple, "—need a gatekeeper. The media are already reporting this, which is good. We know we'll get calls from cranks and crazies and people saying they're psychics and had dreams. Every single clue that comes in has to be sorted out and followed, no matter how wild it may seem."

Bert turned to Lucius and Tallulah. "Is this okay with you guys? Do you want me to do this?"

Lucius put his arm around his wife's shoulder. "Okay with you, darlin'?"

She nodded, licked her chapped lips, and said in hoarse voice, "Yes, please."

"From the moment we've met, you've had my back," Lucius sounded as if he wanted to cry also. "You got the Indian Brotherhood to protect me in the hoosegow and bailed my sorry butt out of jail. You proved I didn't set fire to this hotel or try to kill Will

Wellington—not that the thought hadn't crossed my mind at the time. You're my lawyer, my friend, my relative. I can't think of anyone I'd rather have in my corner than you."

"Thanks for the vote of confidence. When do I start, Hal?"

"Now." Hal strode to the registration desk and spoke with the women in the headsets. They passed over a logbook and a stack of papers. He nodded, returned to the table, and set the book and papers down. "A lot of these are requests from the media for interviews. It would be optimal for Lucius and Tallulah to go on camera and speak. If they get overwhelmed or just can't do it, someone needs to be the family spokesperson. You're the best person for the job. The three of you need to work on a press release and selecting photos and videos of Miriam they can use to the best effect on TV. One radio spot can get out to people in the hinterlands with no Internet and no TV, so you want to answer those calls, too."

"I'll grab my laptop out of my room and get to work." He backed his wheel chair up and turned to the stricken couple. "I'm kinda hungry. Is there any food in the kitchen? Maybe the three of us could go in there, get away from this noise?"

Lucius nodded. "Good idea. I'll rustle up some grub for the three of us. Tallulah hasn't eaten anything since Miriam—" Voice breaking, he cleared his throat, and tried again. "I've got plenty of eggs, bacon, and fresh cornbread. Sound good?"

"Sounds great. I'll be there in a bit." Bert wheeled his way to the brass gate and waited for the vintage elevator to arrive at a leisurely pace. Back then it seemed no one was in a hurry. His mind on the other hand couldn't stop racing. He'd been involved in thousands of investigations, but none more poignant or closer to home than this one. The only other case nearly as disturbing as this had been back in Iraq.

Bert closed his eyes and could smell the dust of the camp and the sweat of the latest batch of detainees. It had been another horrible day in the midst of an endless war.

Summoned by his CO, Bert's job was to help deal with the large influx of prisoners taken from the most recent skirmish. A motley crew of about fifty raggedy men wearing clothing ranging from dark khaki uniforms with a traditional headdress to desert camouflage paced back and forth in the prison yard. Armed American soldiers stood guard, never taking their eyes off the prisoners. The only man not pacing the small area leaned on a wall picking at his nails, looking bored. The other prisoners glared at him with open hatred.

"What's his story?" Bert asked the officer in charge. "The one who looks like he's waiting for a train?"

"Ha." Lieutenant Johnson snorted. "Just another day in paradise. He's a special kind of creep, one even the criminals hate. Abducted boys from villages and sold them to tribal forces and other hostiles for child soldiers. Kids as young as six. You know, too young and scared to think for themselves or talk back."

"Good God."

The younger officer looked at the logbook. "Says he's a Russian, trying to pull some kind of diplomatic immunity crap."

"Hmm. We'll see."

Bert interviewed the Russian who continued to appear uninterested throughout the conversation. A massive man covered in tattoos of Russian mob origin, Sergei Kuznetsov, the Blacksmith, as he called himself in lightly accented English, insisted he had ties with the Kremlin and this was all a big mistake. He rambled on and on about the dust in the air, the stinking prison, the inedible Iraqi food, the lack of clean toilets, and the abundance of goats, many of whom were more attractive than the local women. Not once would the arrogant, condescending thug answer any direct questions. Bert nodded and took notes, saying they'd follow up. Then he told the guard to return the Russian to the general population.

Eyes wild the Blacksmith turned and shouted, "You cannot keep me with these people. I need a separate cell. Someone told them lies about what I do with the boys. They will attack me."

"The luxury suites are filled up. Let me see if we have any queen size beds left." The lieutenant flipped through the log book as if searching for an available room. "Nope, sorry. You're gonna have to bunk with your new friends. Sleep tight. Don't let the bedbugs bite."

As the soldiers forced the cuffed man back into the prison, Kuznetsov screamed, "This is your fault, Lieutenant Johnson and Captain Blackfeather. I will hunt you both down and make you beg to be killed. I know your names, I know your names!"

By the end of the day, Bert had processed all of the new detainees and determined about half of the poor souls had been in the wrong place at the wrong time—

caught up in the chaos surrounding an attack on an American unit. He recommended to his CO they be released. The Russian, on the other hand, had not been innocent. As night fell Bert had left the building, the Blacksmith's words still ringing in his ears.

The elevator dinged and brought Bert back to the present. Almost a decade ago, and he still shuddered at the memory. The Blacksmith was either dead or still in prison in a Middle Eastern country. Either way, justice had been served, and he would never have to deal with Kuznetsov again.

****

After registering with Bronco, getting her vest, which was filled as Bert had predicted, Phoebe grabbed water and snacks and stuffed them in the ample pockets. Cowboy, as she mentally called him, told her his horse trailer was up on the side of the road leading to Hotel LaBelle. As they walked up the incline, they passed a line of news vans with satellite dishes and earnest looking reporters speaking into microphones and pointing at the hotel in the distance. One of the news crew ran up to her and jammed a recorder under her face. Just like Washington, D.C., only she was being forced to face the press instead of her mother dealing with them. Phoebe waved the sandy-haired man away. The Cowboy, signed as well as said, "No."

Cowboy swung open the back gate of the double trailer and led out a gray mare and nodded at Phoebe, finger spelling *Dobbin*. Well, she thought, it's sort of old fashioned, but cute. She took the reins, and rubbed the horse's forehead while she waited for him to saddle her up. The animal shuddered at her touch, and a ripple of fear ran through Phoebe. Hoping to calm her down,

95

she reached into the vest and pulled out a granola bar, which the mare sniffed with interest. Wrapping the reins around her wrist, she extracted the snack from the package and held half a bar out in her open palm. The horse's warm breath and soft lips tickled her hand. Reaching up to pet her again, Phoebe noted the stiffness initially present was gone. She pressed her brow to the animal's forehead, and the tension melted away.

Dobbin and she were going to get along fine.

Cowboy held a radio up to his mouth and his lips moved. He nodded and hooked the device to his denim jacket. "Bronco said we should ride ahead to the designated GPS coordinates for our search area and wait for the volunteers to show up," he signed. "It will take us a bit to get there by horse, and they'll be coming over by ATVs in groups of four."

Cowboy opened the driver's side door of his huge pick-up truck, and a brown and white beagle with a circle around one eye like a bull's eye leaped down, tail wagging with joy. He finger spelled *Daisy* and held the circle of the letter *d* up to his eye for her name sign.

Dobbin and Daisy? Easy to remember.

At least the dog seemed happy to be there. She ran in circles and jumped up on Cowboy's legs. He rubbed her large ears, and she sat down to wait for him as he saddled up his ride, a large red with a white splash between her eyes.

"This is Star," Cowboy signed.

After snapping her helmet into place and pulling her leather gloves on, Phoebe placed her foot into the stirrup, threw her leg over the horse's back, and settled in. If nothing else, it was a beautiful day for a ride. They followed the road down to the hotel and went around back, skirting the yellow tape around the child's window. The sun glinted off the river, nearly blinding her. Grateful she'd remembered them, Phoebe slid on her shades. Birds startled by their approach took flight. The breeze stirred the long grasses, and a small herd of mule deer waded into the river for a drink. As a grim reminder of the reason for the outing, divers suited up on the deck of a boat anchored downstream. She shuddered and prayed they found the little girl soon, alive and well.

Forty minutes later, they arrived at an area where a deputy stood waiting. As soon as he spotted them, he waved them over. An ATV with a pile of red flags on metal posts sat nearby, its trailer stocked with water, snacks, first aid kit, and other emergency supplies. When the on-foot volunteers arrived, they would be lined up in a tight grid with lanes the width of their extended arms. Their job was to walk slowly and do a visual sweep of the area.

Each volunteer would be given red flags to mark any clues they came upon. If they found clues—a shoe or sock, for instance—they were to stop, flag the item, and call it in. Nothing was to be disturbed. Phoebe and Cowboy were to ride along the borders of the search area and keep an eye on the volunteers. If Phoebe spotted an issue, she was to wave a second red flag to catch Cowboy's attention, as they would be in visual range at all times. Cowboy would then communicate with the deputy standing by the ATV.

Via Cowboy, the deputy reminded her to keep a sharp eye out—look up, look down, look left, look right, and look back—for clues. Sometimes things blend in, until you look at an area from a different angle and then it jumps out at you. She nodded. One advantage to being deaf was that unlike others, she was not distracted by sounds. Her sense of smell and touch were acute, but her world was dominated by sight. Tiny shifts in people's expressions telegraphed information others missed. She spotted patterns before others did— whether in data or people's behavior. Her mother said she was *eagle eyed*. When Mom misplaced things, Phoebe was always able to find them. She spotted irregularities when items didn't belong in a particular place or background. Which was why, as she told Bert, she *never* lost her keys.

While she didn't know this specific environment, she was completely at home in this type of terrain. Growing up in Virginia, her equestrian training hadn't been confined to the show ring. Her mother also rode horses, so the weekends when she wasn't being Senator Wagner, she spent time with Phoebe on the trails in the Shenandoah National Park. While some of the trails were relatively even, the woods, hills, and narrow rocky mountain paths challenged the best. Not to mention the fact there was always the excitement of coming upon deer, bobcats, snakes—and one time, a black bear foraging in the bushes. Startled by the large horses, the furry berry picker had bolted.

Straining at the end of her lead, Daisy seemed more interested in chasing rabbits than in looking for clues. Cowboy yanked at the leash, and Phoebe winced for the poor dog. He should have left her home, like she had Bisou. This was a job for trained tracker dogs, not your average household pet. Shaking her head, she used the reins and her legs to urge Dobbin to her side of the field, under a small stand of aspens. It was going to be a long day, she might as well take advantage of the shade while she could. The horse's nostrils flared, and she headed right for a small stream running through the trees. How long had the mare been in the trailer? Like cars, even with the windows open, the enclosed metal boxes became ovens in the sun. Had Cowboy fed and watered the horses recently? Dobbin took a long drink, which only made Phoebe feel more concerned. She didn't like the pattern she was beginning to see.

Volunteers began to arrive and cluster around the deputy. After a while, the ATVs stopped delivering passengers. Hands waving like a flight attendant describing emergency exits, the uniformed officer indicated where people should stand. Starting on Cowboy's side of the field, he set up a line of about fifty people. By noon, the slow march across the field began. Heads down, looking to the left, right, and behind, each person kept in lockstep with the next. Combing the field for any sign of trampled grass, shreds of clothing, and even gum wrappers was a painfully tedious job. Seated on Dobbin, Phoebe wondered if she would have been better off joining the walkers. At least she would have gotten some exercise. She stretched and turned her head to loosen up the crick in her neck from watching the searchers creep along—and something in the shadows caught her eye.

A short, dark figure clutched the trunk of an aspen and stared at Phoebe.

Dobbin jerked her head up, snorted, danced, and turned in a circle. Phoebe pulled on the reins to make her stop. By the time she had the animal under control and pointing in the direction of the irregularity, the man—or whatever it was—had disappeared. Or had he?

Not a moment to lose. No time to wave a red flag. His presence was not normal. She had to find him and drag him back by any means she could. She squeezed Dobbin with her legs, and the mare raced as if her life depended on it. Marveling at the horse's sudden speed, Phoebe leaned in, gave the horse her head, and kept her gaze glued to the horizon. One hundred feet ahead, scrabbling on his hands and knees for a hold on the slope covered with small loose stones, was the ugly little man.

Chapter Nine

Hotel LaBelle, Billings, Montana

Bert wiped his mouth with a napkin and pushed his plate aside. Bisou and the lampshade-hatted Franny placed their paws on him and looked up with beseeching eyes. As he leaned over to sneak the beggars some leftovers, Lucius cleared his throat.

"Just so you know, both those little con artists were fed and walked while we were meeting in the dining room." His large moustache twitched. "The woman who made the cornbread comes in everyday to help us with food prep and clean the rooms. Toni's in love with our bug-eyed creature—and now the little badger hound, too."

Tallulah finished her coffee, and added, "She's our pet sitter, too, so you know Phoebe's baby is in good hands. Toni's the one who spotted the problem with Franny's face last week—she got a scratch on her buggy little eye. It's closer to the ground than her nose. Which is why she wears the cone of shame." More alert by the hour, she'd become more attentive as the sedative wore off. "Where do we start? With the media packet or the calls?"

"How about if you and Lucius work on the press release while I sort through the phone log and the faxes?"

She nodded and stood. "I'll get my laptop from the office. Faster than writing longhand."

After she left the room, Lucius leaned over to Bert. "She collapsed yesterday, completely hysterical. She's doing better because you're here. I can't thank you enough for coming."

"That's what family's for." He smiled. "We're Crow. This is war and *we're* the war party."

"I like the way you think," Lucius replied. "So, what's up with your boss lady?"

"What do you mean?"

"She likes you, you like her. How come you're in separate rooms?"

Bert stared at his relative who, despite being a quick study, occasionally came out with completely inappropriate comments. Then again, he was a hundred and thirty-something years old, so he should probably cut the old guy some slack.

"In this century, we do not refer to our female supervisors as *boss lady*. Nor are we permitted to be romantically involved. Furthermore, I don't know what you're talking about."

Lucius roared with laughter, just as Tallulah walked back into the kitchen. "That's a sound we haven't heard for a while. Gonna tell me the joke?"

Wiping his eyes, Lucius' moustache twitched, and he said, "Bert says he ain't interested in Phoebe, and she ain't interested in him."

Tallulah set the laptop on the kitchen table. "For such a smart investigator, you are *so* clueless, Mr. Blackfeather. Even *I* saw how you looked at her when she got off the elevator. It was a wonder you didn't burst into flames."

Lucius patted Bert's hand. "Wake up and smell the coffee, my friend. You've got it bad for her, and if I'm not mistaken, she's got it bad for you."

"Sparks are flying," Tallulah agreed. "I can't believe the smoke alarm didn't go off."

Embarrassed by the conversation, but understanding their need for a distraction of any kind, even one this ludicrous, Bert cleared his throat and tried to get them back on task. There were more important things to deal with here than his non-existent love life.

"I'm going to go through the phone log and the faxes and sort them by caller, type of clue, and priority for follow up."

A few minutes passed in silence, interrupted only by Lucius' soft comments to his wife as they searched on the computer. Heads nearly touching, Tallulah said, "The website has an example of what to include in a press release. It says we might want to consider offering a reward. What do you think, Bert?"

"It's up to you, but if you offer a reward for something it's a contract. So whatever you do, you need to word it with care." He set his pencil down. Using money always sounded like a good plan, but there were people who would take advantage of a frantic family's vulnerability and prey on their need for hope—of any sort. "If you do it, don't use your own money. You could get sucked dry pretty quickly, depending on what you specify in the language of the reward. You'd need to set up a bank account for donations. Right now, we're not even at the forty-eight-hour mark. How about tabling that decision and work on the information for the media?"

Lucius nodded and exchanged a glance with

103

Tallulah. "You're right. We want her back quick like and it seemed like money would do the trick. Never considered what it would take."

"When you had your grand re-opening of the hotel, you had quite a few journalists at the party. Do you recall who they were?"

"I've got their cards in my office." Tallulah said. "But those were lifestyle reporters. Isn't it out of their lane?"

Bert shrugged. "Maybe one of them wants to move up, become an investigative reporter."

"Hold on a red-hot minute." Lucius shook his finger. "You're onto somethin'. One of those gals did tell me she moved here from the east, used to be a crime reporter for the Baltimore Times. She came out here on vacation, fell in love with the area, and never went home." He stroked his mustache. "What was her name? Jessica? Janie? Josephine—"

"Jackie Gay!" Tallulah shouted. "I loved her. Yes, let's give her a call." Tallulah strode out of the kitchen with more pep in her step than she'd had at the start of the day.

The men looked at each other.

"Momma Bear's back." Lucius blew out a sigh. "Thank God. I felt so alone when she lost it and had to be sedated. I can't do this by myself."

"You're surrounded by friends, family, and neighbors. We are here for you. We want her back, too."

Waving a business card in one hand and holding her cell in the other, Tallulah smiled. "She's on her way. Said she's honored to be trusted with the story. Will do whatever she can to help us. Told me to gather photos of Miriam from different angles so she can include them in her story."

"You guys get them, and I'll work on these calls."

Two hundred calls and counting. People asking if they could help were put in one pile. Those claiming to be psychics were put in another. He ran his finger down the list of callers and recognized a name. "Marjorie Longjaw. Reported a strange man in town. Big guy, wore a long-sleeved hoodie pulled up in warm weather. Didn't fit in with the locals or the tourists." *Hmm. Jimmy Two Toes mother was a talker, but not a teller of tall tales.* After he was done sorting the calls, she'd be at the top of the list for one of Hal's deputies to interview.

An out of state caller said her daughter had been abducted last year—about the same age, also a redhead—and found a week later, alive and well. She wanted to give the parents hope, let them know she was there if they wanted to talk to her. Plus she could connect them with support groups. He was sure just making the call must have brought up old dreadful feelings for the woman. Instead of burying herself and her wounds, here she was offering to help Lucius and Tallulah. She proved there were good people in the world.

A woman walking her dog in the evening said a windowless, black panel truck drove by her slowly. Frightened, she pulled her flashlight out and shone it at the driver's side window. She thought the man was Middle Eastern, he sped up when she put the light on his face. She gave a partial license plate number saying the rest had been obscured with dirt or mud. One for Hal's team to work on. He could run the plate and the style of the van.

A man said there were lights in the sky over the fields the night Miriam went missing. The gray aliens were back, and they were looking for him to do more experiments on him. He ran and hid in his cellar, so they must have taken the child instead. *Oh-ho!* Bottom of the pile.

A woman called in to say if the parents paid her a thousand dollars, she'd take the missing child's belongings off their hands, since they wouldn't be needing them. Disgusted, he put the bottom-feeder's message in the *should-be-trash* pile. Nothing would be discarded—not yet.

A psychic gave an address of a property he went to in a dream. Okay, that one goes straight to Hal, right *now*. Anyone with specifics could be the perpetrator, looking for attention and the thrill of the spotlight. He backed his wheel chair up and nearly bumped into Bronco.

"Hey, Bert," Bronco said, scooting around in front of him. "I don't want to alarm you, but that cowboy, Joe Bighorn?"

"What about him?"

"I've told Hal, since he's the Incident Commander, but I figured you'd want to know, too. Supposedly the guy was vetted by a Wyoming search and rescue organization, but when he introduced himself on the video, he kept turning his face so the light from the sun interfered with the images. I called the employer the cowboy gave me, and they'd never heard of him. Then I called the search and rescue group, thinking they'd vouch for him, too. They did—in a way. The real Joe Bighorn answered the phone and talked to me. The guy who could sign? The one who took your boss out? He's an imposter."

****

Hot on the man's trail, Phoebe pushed Dobbin as hard as she dared on the uneven ground. When she was within a yard of her target, she dismounted, praying the mare wouldn't wander off. Feet sliding on the rolling gravel, like him, she fell to her hands and knees, grateful she'd worn her riding gloves. Sprinting as fast as she dared on the unpredictable surface, at last she caught up to the ugly little man and grabbed his ankle. Foot shod in an unadorned deerskin moccasin, he kicked and wriggled. When he rolled over on his back to kick at her, Phoebe had had enough. Blocking his leg, she leaped on his chest and pinned him to the ground. Hair in her eyes, Phoebe thought for an instant she was seeing things.

Squirming beneath her was a little person with dark brown skin. Eyes scrunched up, he turned his head as if anticipating a blow. With his pointed ears, long chin, and sharp teeth, he reminded her of a leprechaun. His shirt and breeches were made from animal skin—she guessed deer—and on his hip he carried a drawstring bag and a switch. She pulled the rod out of its binding, and his mouth fell open in an *o* of astonishment.

Using her teeth to pull off a riding glove, she gripped his wrist with her right hand, and tumbled into a well of images, as if she were dreaming in broad daylight.

Miriam, happily skipping after this creature.

The little man banging sticks and rocks on pine trees, delighting in the child's smiles.

Three old men stand before a cave and present

Miriam with three items—a knife and two bags. The girl chooses the third bag, and the ugly little man jumps up and down. The old men clap their hands and smile.

The ugly little man crosses a field with Miriam at his side, and the hotel comes into sight across the river.

A large man steps out of the shadows and snatches the child out of the little man's grasp.

Phoebe released his tiny arm, lost the connection, and stared at her captive in a state of shock and confusion. He wasn't human—nor was he a god. He was something in between—a forest dweller of some sort. Who were the old men? Why had they been so happy with Miriam's choice? Who was the large man? Did he work with the ugly little one?

She glanced around, searching for Dobbin—but the horse was nowhere to be seen. How would she get back to the hotel with this little person in tow without a ride? From between the stand of trees, Cowboy appeared and her heart gave a little skip of relief. She waved frantically and snagged his attention. He galloped up to her and glared down from his mount.

"What the hell are you doing?" He signed furiously. "You were supposed to stay put."

Her butt firmly planted on the elf, leprechaun, whatever, she signed. "Look." She pointed at the creature's face. "I found the ugly little man. This is him. We have to take him to the sheriff." And to Bert, she thought, he'd understand.

Jumping off his chestnut, Cowboy strode next to her, and yanked her to her feet. Stunned, unable to understand why he would do this, she ripped her arm out of his grip. "Get your hands off me. Who do you think you are?"

"You're crazy, I should have never agreed to come out with you." His gaze snagged on the switch on the ground. "If you struck my horse, you'll pay for it."

Staring at the stick as if seeing it anew, she signed. "It's not mine—it's his." She turned to point at her captive—he was running up the hill, getting away.

Cowboy swung his hand at her face, and she blocked the blow with her forearm. As she had learned in martial arts, Phoebe turned his momentum against him. He fell onto the rocky ground, his hands and arms extended to break his fall. He rolled over onto his back, rage twisting his face, spittle flying out of his mouth. He reached into his jacket and pulled out a hunting knife. She hadn't a moment to spare, she *had* to get away from this madman. Tears welled in her eyes, and she prayed for God to send help.

As she turned to run up the foothill, Dobbin galloped out of the stand of trees. Halting next to Phoebe, the mare pranced and tossed her mane as if urging her to climb on. No second invitation required. Throwing herself onto the horse's back, she wheeled and went up the slope after the little man and away from the large one. She now suspected the Cowboy was responsible for Miriam's abduction—and possible murder. She had to find a way to grab the little man and drag his scrawny little ass back to the hotel.

****

Anxiety crushing his lungs, Bert hung on every word as Hal radioed all the deputies to be on the lookout for a tall, rangy man in a denim jacket and cowboy hat claiming to be Joe Bighorn. Hal shook his head. "We just described about half the searchers. The only thing we've got going for us is that he was on horseback."

Bert rolled out onto the front porch and scanned the horizon. He was still tired from his morning flight, but if he didn't shift again soon, he'd lose the sunlight. At the top of the hill, where the driveway began, a man on a red horse appeared with a brown and white beagle. *It's him!* Popping a wheelie, Bert sped back into the lobby.

"Hal—call your guys! It's him, at the top of the hill. You need to grab him before he can get his horse in the trailer and get away."

Two deputies jogged up the driveway, calling, "Bighorn, hold up, we need to talk to you."

The cowboy let go of the horse's reins and jumped into his truck, wheels squealing, the empty trailer fishtailing as he sped away. The beagle howled as the horse nodded its head, as if to say, "You got that right."

"Now he's pissed me off," Hal said. He keyed his radio. "All mobile units, we need you to pursue a black four by four pick-up truck—pulling an empty horse trailer, heading east on I-90. He's a person of interest in the Stewart abduction. Use all needed resources to stop him and bring him in for questioning. We need him ALIVE."

Bert shook his head. "Great, but what about Phoebe? Any sightings?"

Hal changed the channel and keyed his radio again. "Deputy Carlson, have you seen a tall, blonde woman in fancy riding gear out by you?"

Static buzzed and a man's voice wavered, "Last time I saw her was about noon. Sheriff, it's gonna be dark soon. You want me to send the volunteers back to the hotel to log out?"

"Affirmative." Hal set the radio on the counter. "She's your boss. You know her better than I do. What do you want me to do?"

A groan escaped his lips. "I'm so screwed. If I don't get her back to D.C. in one piece, her mother is going to rip my skin off. Let me think about it." He couldn't ask Tallulah to do a remote viewing to find her, but he could ask Bronco.

Just then Lucius walked into the lobby, a young African American woman trailing in his wake. "Oh, hey Bert, this here's Jackie Gay. She's going to work on the story like you suggested."

He nodded at the woman. "Thanks for doing this. A good story will be a big help. Lucius, have you seen Bronco?"

"Yup. They ran out the back door about twenty minutes ago. He and Emma had to take off, said they got a call from Stephanie. The twins are running a high fever."

In the blur of activity, Bert had missed his sister and brother-in-law's hasty exit.

One of the women behind the registration desk called out, "Hal, Sheridan County Sheriff's on the line. Wants to know if you've seen a stolen pick-up truck, a horse-trailer, two horses, and a beagle. Says some deaf guy's brother who just got out of the county jail took off with the stuff and the animals. Says the owner's concerned about the animals. His brother was locked up for domestic violence."

Hal stepped up to the counter and grabbed the phone. "We've got one horse and the dog. Truck, trailer, and second horse are missing—along with one of our female volunteers. Un-hunh. He beat his wife—

111

put her *and* her little boy in the hospital? Jeez."

A wife and child beater? The cowboy wasn't just an imposter—he was a monster. Bert's heart plunged into the watery abyss of his stomach.

"We've got a BOLO out for him now. Soon as we grab him, we'll let you know. Tell his brother to hang tight. We'll take good care of his animals." He handed the phone back. "What a slime ball. Can you imagine stealing someone's truck, trailer, horses, money, *and* their service animal?"

"Maybe he thought he'd cash in on a reward if he found the girl?"

Hal shook his head. "No accounting for the weirdoes crawling out of the woodwork when a kid goes missing."

Given the circumstances Bert had no choice but to change into his eagle—and do it fast. Time and sunlight were running out.

Chapter Ten

The Pryor Mountains, Crow Reservation

Phoebe needed to find a stream for the horse and a place to hole up for the night. If her foot would reach her butt, she'd be kicking herself. Once she escaped the madman, she should have turned back, looked for the deputies, volunteers, somebody. Instead, she'd pursued the ugly little man like a bloodhound chasing a scent. Now she was lost, it was getting dark, and her water was running low. She'd let her pride and ego take charge instead of her brain. She'd been so *positive* she could grab the leprechaun—or whatever he was—she'd hadn't considered what she'd do with him once she caught him. How would she get back? She pulled out her smart phone, hoping for a signal so she could text someone, but there were no bars. In fact, if possible, there would have been negative bars. What had she been thinking?

Climbing off Dobbin, she stretched her back and sides, and patted the horse's neck. She rummaged in her pockets and found another granola bar. Placing it on the palm of her hand, she petted the mare as she nibbled. Phoebe flicked her torch on and shone the light on the tumble of boulders a few yards away. A dark hole on the right side of the rocks might be a spot to check out for shelter. The temperature had dropped when the sun went down, and a breeze had sprung up. If she didn't find a protected spot soon, she'd be hungry, thirsty, and cold. She hoped the space wasn't already occupied by something with claws. Despite carrying bear spray, she'd been warned its effectiveness was limited. The best way to deal with those creatures was to avoid them.

As she led the horse toward the cairn, movement in the black void caught her attention. It was about the right size. She quickened her pace. If it was who she thought it was, this time he was not getting away. Just as she was two steps away from the mouth of the cave, the ugly little man shot out. Stepping into his path, she put her foot out and tripped him. Then for the second time she sat on him. Having lost her glove in the melee, nothing impeded her touch. She latched onto his upper arm and allowed his thoughts to pour into her. This time the images were more chaotic, as if his fear and panic caused them to jump and leap in her mind. Oddly, although impossible to follow, unlike the others' powerful emotions, his did not drain her. The only way to make sense of this jumble was to get him to trust her. Hoping to get through to him, she took a deep breath.

Calm down, she thought. *Relax. I won't hurt you.*

The creature stilled. The images stopped tumbling and settled into an orderly flow.

His home—a forest—appeared in her mind. His name was Bohpoli Kowi Anukasha, the Thrower who Stays in the forest. He had traveled a long way from home to find Miriam, who was like him, part of the Choctaw tribe. Only prophets and doctors could see him—and Miriam had seen him just fine. As with her ancestors, his job was to take the child to the forest and

114

help her learn about her gifts. The forest closest to her home was here at the foot of the Pryor Mountains in the land of the Little People. The old men Phoebe had seen in Bohpoli's memories were conducting spiritual tests, which Miriam had passed. Rejecting the knife and a life of violence, she had ignored a sack of poisonous plants, and chosen the bag of healing herbs. The child was going to be a powerful Medicine woman, just like her great-grandmother. When she was older, he would come to her to teach her how to make medicines. After spending a little time playing with her in the forest, Bohpoli's plan had been to return her to her home. Instead a very bad man had snatched Miriam as they walked down the hillside.

Phoebe permitted him to stand, but did not release her grip on his arm.

Tears began to roll down his face to his pointed chin, his thoughts clearer in Phoebe's mind. "She's in danger. It is all my fault. I was supposed to teach and protect her. Instead I led him to her."

Perplexed, Phoebe thought, "How did he miss you?"

"He couldn't see me," Bohpoli answered. "Only medicine men and women can see me."

"I can see you. I'm not a medicine woman."

A smile crossed his face, and he pointed to her chest. "You wear the elk tooth necklace with the beads in a special pattern. Only medicine women and men have them."

"Me? A medicine woman?" So Beautiful had gifted her with this, not just as a piece of jewelry—but to mark her as a spiritual conduit. How had Bert's ancestor known?

"I'm the healer of healers, the teacher of medicine men and women. I did not recognize you before. Please forgive me." He bowed his head. "I'm your servant. The man who took the child is no medicine man. He's evil. A trickster. Pretends to be one thing and is another. He grabbed the child roughly, had a gun, and rode off on a machine. I thought you were him—so I hid."

"Can you show me which way he went?"

"I can lead you to his cabin. Let me ride on your horse, please?" He pointed down. "My legs are short, and the day has been long."

Climbing up on Dobbin, half expecting Bohpoli to bolt despite his conciliatory words, she was surprised when he allowed her to reach down and lift him up to ride in front of her. He smelled of pine, and his legs bounced with the horse's galloping steps. After a fifteen-minute ride, he pointed to pin-pricks of light in darkness. As they drew closer, the outline of a cabin and an ATV emerged. Bohpoli placed his cool hand on hers indicating she should stop. This was as close as they could get without alerting him to their presence. She pulled at the reins and gnawed at her lower lip.

If she waited there was a good chance Bert had people looking for her. Despite being prickly about her mother, and insisting this was her personal time, Phoebe was well aware a missing senator's daughter would trigger national alerts. On the other hand, what if the man packed up and left in the middle of the night? How would they ever find Miriam? She had to see the child, know she was safe, then she could wait for the search team to find her—and the child. *Just stay put.* Isn't that what they always said in the survival exercises she'd practiced for her leadership classes? Those had been academic exercises and none of them had included *this* scenario. No matter how well rehearsed, no classroom training could have prepared her for this. Raw emotion took over and rational thought vanished when a life was at risk. Especially a child. How could she leave her to that man's devices? What was he doing to her? No. She couldn't just wait it out. No way was she about to walk away. Reckless or not, she had to get closer to the cabin, get a look inside.

Time is of the essence. A child is in danger.

Climbing down from the mare, Phoebe tiptoed closer to the building, pausing every few steps to see if more lights went on, or if the door flew open. Sore from hours of riding, her legs and thighs trembling, she edged even closer. Nothing. Just a few more steps and she'd be able to see inside. Flattening herself on the side of the building, she inched along the rough surface. Mouth dry, fearful of what she would find, she told herself the baby was okay. She *had* to be okay. An open window beckoned to her. Peeking around the casing, Phoebe spotted a lantern. No sign of Miriam. Where was she? Knees wobbling, she crept to the next window. This time she could see more of the one room cabin—a shack, really. A small stove. A bed with brown blankets and a pillow. A table with a lantern in the center. A crib and a huge box of disposable diapers? *What the hell?* This wasn't a random snatch and grab— this place had been prepared for a child—but not just any child. Miriam. Someone with a grudge against the parents must have set this all up, waiting, planning, for God only knew how long. The parents seemed like the salt of the earth—kind, gentle, well-liked by the community. No matter what business conflict or land dispute someone could have with them, nothing on earth warranted kidnapping their child. What kind of monster would do such a thing? Bohpoli was right. This was *evil*.

The door flew open, a gun muzzle flashed, and a boom resonated in her chest. He'd aimed past her. She glanced over her shoulder. The pale gray horse reared into the air, and Bohpoli disappeared. When she turned back, something hard struck her temple and the world went dark.

****

Bert flew back through his hotel room window and perched on the seat of his wheelchair—frustrated and angry at himself. He should have never allowed her to go out with that cowboy. He should have insisted she stay at the hotel with him, no matter how great her gifts were. She'd never survive a night in the wilderness. If they found her, if she got back alive, he'd apologize to her and tell her it was all his fault. And how sorry he was for judging her based on her looks. Not that her looks were bad. *Quite the opposite*. From her pale blonde hair, her perfectly shaped face, her full red lips, down to her lithe, muscular legs, she personified grace, beauty—and brains. They'd spent little face-to-face time together, but her emails—annoying at first—had proven her to be thoughtful, and spot on in her analyses. Out of stubbornness, he'd bucked attending the Blue Ribbon Committee meetings in person. Knowing she had been in attendance at all of them, he now regretted that decision and the lost opportunity to get to know her better. Much as he hated to admit it, he'd been an arrogant ass. She was one of the smartest women he'd ever met—and their instant connection made him think of flowers, wine, and moonlight. Not since Susan had he dared to hope he'd find another woman—and romance. A year after Susan died, his sister told him, "Remember, bald eagles mate for life, but when one dies, the survivor takes a new mate. Don't let your eagle die of loneliness." He'd pushed her advice away at the time. But now, just as he was on his way to admitting he wanted to spend more time with Phoebe it might be too late. Life wasn't fair. Just like the song, he hadn't known what he had until it was gone. If he could have another chance, a do over, he'd start the relationship out right and be the kind of man she would want to be with.

If only.

Morphing back into his human form, he shed his feathers, expanded into his larger mass, shimmied back into his skin, shook his arms, wiggled his fingers, twisted his neck, and lifted his thighs. All in working order. Now for some clothes. Unlike flying comic book superheroes, he couldn't do a quick change into his secret identity. *Where the hell is she?* The horse could have only gotten so far. And she needed food and water. As he feared, the sun had set while he was in flight. He'd been able to pick out a few lights in the Pryor Mountains, but when he dove down to inspect, they'd been nothing more suspicious than campers roasting marshmallows over small fires. As soon as he finished dressing, he'd go downstairs and see what happened while he was *on a long phone call with Washington*, the lie he'd told Hal to explain his absence. But first, a quick wash to remove the distinctive raptor scent.

Feeling refreshed, but starving, a short while later, Bert found a haggard looking Hal with a stack of computer print-outs in front of him.

Bert inhaled muffins from the tray sitting next to his friend's elbow. Speaking around an apple crumb topping, he asked, "Any news?"

"We got him—the imposter." Hal rubbed his eyes. "His brother—who refuses to press charges per the Sheridan County Sheriff—is on his way from Wyoming to pick up his truck, trailer, and animals—all but one. The horse Phoebe was riding."

"No accounting for families, is there?" Bert shook his head. It was tough when a family member was a criminal. Some cut the person off, others took up their battle, and still others wavered, not knowing what was right. Family love and loyalty were touchstones of his life. But to a wife beater and child abuser? That's where he drew the line. "You're not releasing him, are you? At the least, he must have violated some law— impersonation? Refusing to stop for an officer of the law? Speeding?"

"No way are we letting him go. He's the last person to see Phoebe. We've got him in a holding cell. Of course, he's all lawyered up, even demanded medical attention. Claims she beat him up and he's the victim."

"She hurt him? He's lying." The idea boggled the mind. He could imagine she might give him an ASL dressing down. But a physical attack? "If she did, it had to have been in self-defense."

Hal nodded. "I agree. With his rap sheet, I wouldn't trust him if his tongue came notarized."

If she gave that creep a beat down, then he must

have deserved it. *Damn.* He liked her, he *really* liked her. Bert made a mental note to add another adjective to his growing list for Phoebe: ass-kicker. His kind of gal—and still missing.

As pleased as he was to know she could take care of herself, her continued absence worried him—and ratcheted up his fight-flight response. The wilderness, beautiful and inspiring as it was, could be harsh and unforgiving. Not to mention populated with wild animals that might consider her and the horse a good meal. Bert pressed his palms into his eyeballs to reduce his heart rate and keep his eagle under wraps. He *had* to find her.

"Are you going to send a helicopter out tomorrow to search for Phoebe? Maybe someone will spot the horse?"

"First thing in the morning," Hal said. "By the way, while you were on the phone with Washington, did you happen to speak with her mother?"

"Good God, no. Why?" Bert winced at the idea of telling Senator Wagner her daughter was missing. She might be psychic, but he doubted the woman would be forgiving. He wouldn't survive the verbal lashing—or the backlash to his career. He could kiss the agency and the division good-bye.

"Someone recognized Phoebe as the senator's daughter." Hal shrugged. "Now the reporters want to know what she's doing here, and if Homeland's involved in the search for the missing child."

"Shit. Shit. Shit." He pounded his thigh with his fist, punctuating each word. "Shit."

"Yup, my sentiment exactly." Hal nodded. "It's only a matter of time before someone reaches her mother and asks for a comment."

"SHIT." Bert's mind raced. As soon as the senator found out her daughter was missing, the state would be swarming with more agents, more media, and even more crazies. A veritable circus would come to town, complete with political clowns pretending to be concerned, but actually capitalizing on the sensational event. He could see the humongous headlines on newspapers and websites in all caps: SENATOR'S DAUGHTER MISSING! UNDER SECRETARY TOOK PERSONAL TIME TO SEARCH FOR MISSING CHILD—NOW SHE'S MISSING, TOO!

"We have to contain this, get some damage control in place now." Bert drummed his fingers on the table. "Tell the deputies to put a lockdown on any stories. Say they can't confirm or deny any rumors of her participation in the search. If pressed, they can say all the volunteers have gone home and are exhausted. We're sure they went to bed early. Searching for the missing child was hard work. The Good Samaritans have earned their rest, yada, yada."

"That will give us twelve hours, tops." Hal yawned. "I just hope no one shows up from Helena tomorrow. The governor loves to get his face on camera, always acts like it's an election year. He also likes to meddle with investigations, I've heard. Pissing on the paper is what I think, trying to take credit for everyone else's hard work."

"I know." Bert shook his head. "I see it every day in D.C. Some are genuine—like Phoebe's mother— she's a good one. Others? I could do without. I'm waiting to hear back about getting some satellite time. If they let me use it, we might be able to find Phoebe and Miriam with our eyes in the sky."

"I hope so, too." Hal checked his watch. "We're coming up on seventy-two hours for Miriam and twelve for Phoebe. The temperature is dropping and the wind is picking up. This isn't good."

For the love of God, could things get any worse?

Otterlegs crashed through the front door, red-faced and out of breath. "Boss. Get. Out. Here." He sucked in air. "The horse. Phoebe's horse. It's back. Bleeding. Looks like it got shot."

Chapter Eleven

The Pryor Mountains, Crow Reservation

Brightness slid under Phoebe's shuttered lids, and she winced with pain. Grateful she'd worn the *unnecessary* riding helmet, she automatically sought the strap to remove it—but it was gone. Her head pounded like the Gallaudet football team's big bass drum—but it wasn't to call her onto the field to play. This drum was calling her to arms. She opened her eyes with caution, afraid of what she'd see. Overhead, the roughhewn ceiling of the cabin, darkened with age and smoke wavered in the lantern's light. When she turned her head, the room spun and rocked. She thought she might be sick, and tried to swallow down the bile. Probably a good thing she hadn't had much to eat today.

A large shadow extracted itself from a chair and came to stand over her. Not a shadow. A huge man, the back of his hands covered in ink, crouched next to her, his open red plaid flannel shirt revealing thick gold chains, a naked chest, and a veritable tapestry of eight pointed stars, staring eyes, skulls, and saints all surrounding a tiger. Her mother had chaired hearings on Russian transnational criminal organizations' involvement in crimes on U.S. soil. She'd poured over research reports and shared what she could with Phoebe. Her most vivid memories of the investigation was the piles of photographs of tattoos. This wasn't any normal criminal. This man was a Russian mobster. Known for ruthlessness in all aspects of their crime syndicate, these men used women and children as commodities to be bought, sold, and traded. For the Russian mafia, the easiest way to deal with a problem person was to kill him—often with extreme prejudice.

Heart racing, her gaze riveted to his chest, she dared not look up. He reached under her chin, lifted her face, and made eye contact. She shuddered. His left eye was normal, dark brown if her vision could be trusted. The right eye was pale blue and didn't move in concert with the other in a leathery face crisscrossed with scars. A buzz cut revealed a missing ear. Terrible things had happened to this man, and she didn't know where to look. Blinking back tears and failing, she stared straight ahead, too terrified to move.

He grinned and several gold capped teeth winked at her. His lips moved. He frowned. Repeated himself. And grew angry.

She held up a palm, signed deaf, and pointed to her ears.

He dropped her chin, strode to the table, and returned with a pad and pen. He wrote, "Who are you?" showed her the note, and handed her the pen, motioning for her to respond.

"Phoebe." She paused. Telling him her last name could be dangerous. For a man like him, blackmail, extortion, and ransom demands were second nature. Her mother would never allow Phoebe to be kept by a Russian thug. But what price would they want to extract from a senior U.S. senator? Her sterling reputation as a pillar of integrity would be more desirable than a priceless Fabergé egg. Her mother and her political influence were not for sale. Grasping at the first name that popped into her head other than her own, she wrote, "Blackfeather."

His grin terrified her. It was neither friendly nor humorous—the only way to describe it would be malicious.

"Mrs. Bert Blackfeather?" he wrote.

How did he know Bert's first name? Sickened and trapped in her lie, Phoebe wished she had said Smith instead. She nodded.

He yanked her to her feet and pushed her against the wall. Hands roaming across her breasts, he shoved his face against her neck, and began to grind his groin against hers. His fetid breath combined with the violent images pouring out of him, and the chorus of bass drums in her head. If she didn't get him off her soon, she would burn out, just as Bert had warned her. This toxic sludge of evil would suck out every ounce of strength and leave her an empty husk. She turned her head in a desperate attempt to remove the skin to skin contact—to no avail. Phoebe closed her eyes to keep the room from spinning—until a gut-wrenching spasm overtook her. Horrified, she watched as a geyser of green bile hit the man in his face and eyes. His features twisted in disgust. He backhanded her, and she fell to the floor sobbing.

Coming here was the worst mistake in her life.

She should be back at the hotel, flirting with a handsome employee, one who personified the opposite of this vicious brute. Bert, a man filled with kindness and compassion, was the one she'd been waiting for all her life. No one had ever gotten under her skin like he had. With his mischievous smile, easy humor, and warmth, he had beguiled her and extracted her deepest secrets. Tonight, she should be in the bar with him, trying to figure out if he was as interested in her as she was in him. Instead she ran straight into harm's way—and for what? That sneaky little forest dweller had lied to her. The child wasn't here. But the crib and diapers? Why were they in this remote cabin? Had Miriam been here at one time? And if she had, was she—Phoebe dared not even think the word.

Wiping her eyes with her sleeve, she stopped to catch her breath and take stock. She wasn't helpless. Hadn't she defended herself against the cowboy? The elk tooth necklace shifted on her neck and grew warm as if to let her know it was there, waiting for the real medicine woman to emerge. What would Beautiful do? Unlike her, Phoebe couldn't disappear. She had to fight him here and now. There had to be *something* in the cabin she could use against this thug, even a bottle or a lantern could be a blunt weapon. Her gaze fell on the crib in the corner. A little redhead, eyes as blue and large as robin's eggs, sucked her thumb and stared at something Phoebe couldn't see at the moment.

Miriam's alive!

Nearly weeping with relief, she vowed to protect the child at all costs. She smiled at Miriam, but the tiny girl was too engaged to notice Phoebe. She followed the toddler's gaze. There in the shadows was the ugly little man, dancing and twirling, keeping the baby entertained. Somehow, Bohpoli had managed to get into the cabin. Nearly laughing with relief, she sat up and straightened her back against the wall. If he came at her now, she would be fighting not just for herself, but for Miriam.

The big man's shadow fell across her legs. Towel in one hand, he threw the notepad down. Scrawled across it were the words, "Your husband did this to me. Now he will pay." Phoebe glanced up and the man removed the blue eye from its socket and turned it around, inspecting it with his good eye and nodding. He popped the glass orb back into the socket and pointed to the side of his head missing an ear. Then, he pointed to the scars on his face.

How could Bert have been responsible for this man's disfigurement? *Bullshit*. Nothing in Bert's memories had revealed any sort of abusive nature. The man was a liar.

She wrote on the pad. "May I get up?"

He nodded and she slid up the wall, not removing her eyes from his face. This man could not be bothered taking care of a child. But for some reason, based on the diapers, crib, and toys, he had taken pains to prepare for her.

As bad as he reeked, she hazarded a guess that somewhere along the way he'd lost his sense of smell, too. Pointing at the baby, she wrote. "She needs her diaper changed."

His head jerked back, and he glanced between the child and Phoebe.

She pinched her nose with her thumb and index finger, the sign for "stink."

He shrugged and waved her toward the child.

Walking as fast as she dared with her still throbbing head, Phoebe reached into the crib, lifted the girl, placed her little noggin in the crook of her neck and pulled her into a gentle hug. All of the toddler's memories and emotions exploded into Phoebe's mind and heart. Taking a deep breath to still her churning reaction, she rocked the now sobbing child and kissed her brow.

As God is my witness, you will go home to your daddy and mommy and be happy again.

****

After all the frenzy with the volunteers and uniforms off duty and the initial buzz of the phone lines having died down to only a few calls an hour, the hotel had become eerily quiet—too quiet. The calm belied the work going on behind the scenes and in the field, especially since they were still within the seventy-two-hour window. However, he worried Tallulah and Lucius would interpret the dwindling law enforcement presence as a decline in urgency and interest. And there could be nothing farther from the truth. The reality was people needed rest, even people with special powers. Speaking of whom, he had to make a call to Bronco in the off chance the twins were better.

Wild-eyed, the bloodied mare had side-stepped and danced away from the veterinarian, requiring a small army of deputies to assist with the exam. If Emma had been here, she would have been able to communicate with the poor animal, let her know they wanted to help her. The tip of the mare's ear had been clipped and bled like crazy. She'd have a permanent notch out of it, but fortunately nothing more. He drummed his fingers on the table top. Maybe Emma would be willing and able to come by and connect with the mare. Then they could find out where the horse left Phoebe—and with any luck, cut out half of their search time. He reached for his cell phone.

"The twins are burning up," Bronco said, worry etched in every word as they came through the spotty service. "We're at St. Vic's ED now, waiting to be seen by a pediatrician. Seems like every little kid in Billings has this bug." He lowered his voice. "You know it's scary when Beautiful shows up and says we need to change the kids' Crow names to change their luck." A child wailed in the background and another joined in. "There's the twins. They do everything together, even crying. I gotta go."

Bert pressed the end button. Maybe Tallulah could do a remote viewing? No. Too much to ask. She'd exhausted herself when Miriam had first disappeared, practically going off the deep end. She was back and functioning now. He dared not upset the delicate balance she'd achieved by dint of sheer courage.

Pulling his laptop close, he went online to see if his satellite request had been approved. The email stung like a slap in the face. "Due to the personal nature of this request and the current demands on satellite time, we are unable to approve this application for federal resources."

He slammed his hand on the table, startling the ladies at the registration desk out of their conversation. Frowning, they turned and stared at him. Bert put his palm out. "Sorry. Didn't mean to scare you."

What the hell could be so pressing that Homeland couldn't spare him ten minutes of time when the satellite passed over Montana? Were they being invaded by terrorists? He clicked through his other emails and surfed over to the home page. His heart stuck in his throat. Phoebe. Her smile stabbed him in the heart. He had let her down—no worse—he had betrayed her trust in him, agreeing to go with a convicted felon because he had said she could go out with him on the search. If only he had done a better job of checking him out. Instead, he had trusted someone else's vetting procedure, one that clearly had holes the size of Montana in it. If not for Bronco and his gut instinct, that bastard would be on the loose, free to con and abuse other unwitting victims. As he started to close the lid, a red alert on the bottom of the screen grabbed his attention. Flipping it back up, he double clicked on the notice.

"Human trafficking alert: Sergei Kuznetsov, aka, "The Blacksmith" a violent offender who traffics in women and children was traveling under an alias of Boris Kasparov and wearing a disguise of a wig and mustache. Officials did not identify him until after he left Canadian immigration. Presumed to be in Canada, he may have crossed into the U.S. in a wilderness area..."

The Blacksmith. His stomach knotted. *Heavenly Creator, please don't let him be the one who took Miriam.*

The man held a grudge against him. Sure. But that all went down a decade and a war zone ago. If he could see me now, Bert thought, Sergei would realize he wasn't the only one who paid a steep price. While locked up with the general population, Sergei had been brutalized by the other prisoners. Even among criminals, child traffickers were the lowest of low. Afterward Bert had made sure Sergei was placed under medical care in solitary, under guard. It hadn't made any difference to the Blacksmith. Sergei had blamed Bert for his injuries, including the loss of his eye and an external ear, and had sworn his revenge. Was this the man responsible for Miriam's abduction? How had he found Bert's family? Had he been planning this for a decade? Russians played a long game, but this was longer than most revenge seekers would wait. It didn't seem possible, but then again—

"Hey, Bert." Tallulah and Lucius stood beside him. He snapped the laptop closed.

"Oh, hey, how are you guys holding up? How was the interview?" They looked tired, but otherwise were still standing. Damn they were strong.

"Interviews," Tallulah corrected. "We started with Jackie and then moved onto AM radio and Internet radio shows. We're pretty beat."

Lucius squeezed her hand. "She was a trooper, only cried a couple of times. I could barely keep it together to talk. She was the star."

"My talk show experience promoting my haunted hotels book helped, but you my dear, were my rock. I couldn't have made it through them without you. Someone is going to hear us, I just know it, and lead us to our girl." She scanned the lobby. "Where is everyone? I thought this was an *active* investigation?"

"It is," Bert said. "Law enforcement is using every resource at its disposal to find Miriam. Everyone is either in the field following up leads or working with data analysts to generate more leads." He dared not mention Phoebe being missing. They had enough of a burden already.

Tallulah's mouth turned down. "I hope they're not giving up."

"No." Bert shook his head. "Listen, when Hal set the Command Post up, he told me he debated on whether he should do it here. In cases like this, they usually don't set up in the child's home, but nearby. In your case, the choices were limited. You're an hour away from Billings or any other area with the appropriate resources. You will see an ebb and flow of uniforms, but I swear, no one is giving up. No one."

A tear streaked down Tallulah's cheek. "Thanks, Bert. It's so hard to read the tea leaves, and know what's going on with the sheriff's office."

"Just ask. They're your partners in this. You have the right to ask them any question you want. Okay?"

"Okay."

"Where's your girlfriend?" Lucius asked in an obvious attempt to change the subject. "Do we need to move you two to the honeymoon suite?"

Bert thought his face would burst into flames. "You are a joker, my friend."

Unfortunately or fortunately depending on who you spoke to, Lucius was able to sniff out a budding romance from a thousand yards. He put Cupid to shame.

"You're such a matchmaker, you should have been an old lady," Tallulah said. "What's that song?"

"I think they make a great couple," Lucius countered, his moustache twitching. "I told you Bronco and Emma would get together, didn't I? The wedding can be here. Summer would be nice, you know, with the gazebo and garlands for the outside seating. Maybe the quartet from Montana State University could play. They'd have everyone up on the dance floor. On the other hand, if you want winter, that's a beautiful time, too. A roaring fire, everybody in their winter finest. Hot toddies and Moscow mules. Can't you see the invitations now?" He put his hand in front as if writing. "The Honorable Ruth Wagner invites you to the wedding of her daughter, Phoebe and Mr. Bert Blackfeather—"

Two suitcases thudded onto the floor and the voice of a woman who was not to be crossed shouted, "I'm inviting people to the wedding of my daughter and *who?*"

Shit. Shit. Shit. Shit.

There in the lobby, dressed in a black pantsuit, white blouse, and black coat, wearing an equally dark expression stood the last person Bert wanted to see at this moment. The chairman of the U.S. Senate Select Committee on Intelligence. Phoebe's mother, the extremely honorable, and dreadfully angry Senator Ruth Wagner.

Chapter Twelve

The Pryor Mountains, Crow Reservation

The connection seared through Phoebe as if she'd grabbed a downed power line. Raw, jagged, unchecked emotions flooded into her from the child. Images and feelings, inseparable from each other in Miriam's memories, swirled in a vortex in Phoebe's mind, immobilizing her. Love for her mommy and daddy. Joy of a new playmate in Bohpoli. Curiosity at seeing new things in the woods. Pleasure at being praised by three old men. Panic and terror at being grabbed by a scary giant. A torrent of all these sensations and more rushed from Miriam. Ripped out of Bohpoli's friendly grasp, the little girl had been petrified of the Monster—a man whose smile made the child think of nightmares where pumpkins came to life and sharp teeth gnawed at her fingers and toes. Sobbing, Miriam wilted in her arms and went back to sucking her thumb.

Depleted by the child's gamut of feelings, Phoebe wanted nothing more than to eat and rest, but she dared not show any sign of weakness, lest the Monster pounce. After changing Miriam as quickly as possible, wiping her hands clean with a baby wipe, and taping the diaper to itself, she held the soiled bundle out to the man. Disgust twisting his scarred face, he recoiled and pointed to the door. Child on hip, she went outside, looked for a garbage pail and found a metal one with a lid four feet away from the cabin, next to an outhouse. She didn't know much about the wilderness, but she *did* know bears were drawn to human odors. Did the monster standing in the entry watching her every move know? If she left the top of the can a little ajar, what would happen? Making a big show of lifting the lid one-handed, placing it on the ground, and dropping the soiled diaper into the can, she pretended to snap it closed—but left it up a smidge. If there were any bears in the area, she was certain they'd show up during the night—and maybe provide enough of a distraction for her to try to escape on the ATV. Crazy, wild thinking, yes, but grasping at any straw—even bears—was the best she could do for now.

When she returned to the warmth of the building, the Monster leered at her and made an obscene gesture. Instead of reacting, she used her last ounce of reserves and made the sign for eating—fingers pinched together in an *o* tapping at her chin. The vile man shrugged, nodded, and pointed at a cooler and a box on the floor next to the table, clearly annoyed at her lack of response. He had no idea how many obscenities had been directed toward her throughout her life because she was a woman. Every despicable word used toward women had been hurled at her while going about her life, walking down the street, whether in Washington or Mexico City. Being a woman meant she was a target for verbal harassment from ogling men, some of whom appeared to be in junior high. Just because she couldn't hear them didn't mean she wasn't aware of the nature of their catcalls and gesticulations. She'd learned to make no eye contact and to stride with confidence—the walk many friends said was her *model-on-a-cat-walk* strut. If a creep had the balls to get in her path, she stepped aside—and on a couple of memorable occasions had been forced to use her self-defense skills, a combination of Eastern, Israeli, and Western martial arts. Cockroach squashing.

And being deaf? Icing on the cake for some men. Growing up in Washington, powerful, ignorant men had talked down to her, belittled her education and experience, and even shouted at her when they discovered she couldn't hear. The fools mistook her well-bred demeanor for deference and vulnerability. Mentally rolling her eyes at them without changing her ever polite expression, she had used their ignorance as her secret weapon. In law school and in advocacy cases, these jerks had underestimated her and had been stunned when she bested them. Phoebe called it mental jiu-jitsu—yielding to the force of an opponent to use it against them. Today she needed both her physical and mental skills to best the Monster—and keep Miriam safe.

With the child's legs wrapped around her waist and one soft sweaty arm clinging to Phoebe's neck, it was a challenge to undo the lid of the cooler. Inside she found juice boxes and single serve portions of milk with attached straws and pulled out two chocolate milks. She set the milk down on the table, then rummaged in the box and pulled out individual cups of cereal, plus nutrition bars. Again, she was struck by how much preparation time, effort, and resources, he had clearly invested in this operation. This was no spur of the moment snatch and grab. How long had he thought about doing this? Miriam was barely two years old.

How long had he been waiting for the perfect moment to extract revenge on Bert?

The child still clinging to her, Phoebe sat at the table and began to open the containers. Miriam, listless and wan, watched with glassy eyes. She had to get her to eat. Milk first, then cereal. Putting the straw to the child's lips, she urged her with motions to drink. At last the child roused enough to sip. It was a start. The sugar would revive her—she hoped. She opened a cardboard bowl of pastel colored cereal and shuddered at the thought of eating all that food dye. *Well, better than nothing.* As she brought a few pieces to Miriam's lips, she jumped when a hand grabbed her left leg. She looked under the table, as if she had dropped something and spotted Bohpoli. *Shit. Shit. Shit.* He didn't realize she needed skin-to-skin contact to communicate with him.

Seating the child on her lap facing the table, Phoebe toed at her riding boot, praying for traction in the absence of a boot jack. To her surprise, the little man pulled as she pushed, ultimately getting it off. He placed his cold hand under her sock and connected.

"What can I do?"

"I need a distraction so I can search the cabin for tools or weapons. Can you do something?"

Laughter bubbled up in her mind. "I'm the Thrower." Memories of tossing rocks at unsuspecting forest visitors and banging on trees to wake sleeping campers danced through her mind. "Keep him busy."

Nearly faint from fatigue and fear, the image of the Monster running around from one place to another in the foothills lifted her spirits. This was what she needed. The child's head fell back on her shoulder.

Poor baby, Miriam likely passed out from exhaustion. Carefully placing the little girl in her crib, Phoebe turned to find the creep standing right behind her.

He pointed at her unbooted foot.

Using both index fingers, she made an inward motion toward her stomach, the sign for "hurt."

He handed her the pad of paper and the pen.

She wrote, "Foot hurts."

A lecherous expression on his face, he wrote, "Something else is going to hurt you now," and pointed at his groin.

If only I could vomit on demand. She thought of something else, perhaps equally revolting to him. She held her abdomen, and wrote, "Pads?"

He looked confused.

She wrote, "Menstrual pads?"

Now he looked like *he* might vomit. *Good.*

The Monster pushed her away and pointed at the diapers. She wasn't an expert lip reader, but it sure looked like he called her the *B* word. She bit her bottom lip to keep from grinning. *Focus, Phoebe.* She picked up the diaper and nodded. She pointed at the closed door and raised her eyebrows.

Lips twisted in a sneer of disgust, he nodded.

Nailed it.

She turned the knob and Bohpoli scampered out. Hobbling behind him, she entered the outhouse, found the opening, and set about attending to her genuine need—and her fake one.

****

Stunned silence filled the lobby of the hotel, followed by chaos. Bert, Lucius, and Tallulah all spoke at once, talking over one another.

Senator Wagner put her fingers between her teeth and whistled.

Talking ceased.

"Thank you. Now. One at a time. Where is my daughter? And what's going on here?"

Bert raised his hand. "Senator Wagner, I'm Bert Blackfeather—I work for your daughter—and indirectly, you. I'm the Director of the Anomaly Defense Division."

The older woman's blue eyes—so much like Phoebe's—narrowed. Was she scanning him, looking for lies? If she was able to probe his mind, he had nothing to hide.

A breathless young man in a black suit, white shirt, and black tie, skidded to a stop beside her. "I parked the rental, Senator. The reporters are trying to get past the deputies—they want a statement from you about the missing girl and your daughter's work here."

The mask of suspicion dropped, concern wreathed her face, and her tone of voice changed. "Of course. A child is missing." She peeled off her gloves and coat and handed them to her aide. She crossed the lobby in long, quick strides, going straight to Tallulah. She took one of the younger woman's hands in both of hers and tilted her head. "What is your name, my dear, and how old is your child?"

"Tallulah." Tears rolled down her cheeks. "Miriam will be eighteen-months old next week."

"I'm so sorry." Releasing Tallulah's hands, she grasped Lucius' big paw next.

"And you are the father?"

"Lucius Stewart." His face softened, he nodded, and choked out. "Yes, Miriam's my little girl."

Awestruck, the enormity of what he was witnessing hit Bert like a kick in the chest. Phoebe had understated her mother's powers. Senator Ruth Wagner, wasn't just an elected official and hard-working servant leader—she was an empath. *Just like her daughter.*

He waited for her to come to him, half-expecting the magnetic clasp he'd had with Phoebe. However, when Senator Wagner gripped his hand, the pain was so excruciating, he may as well have been in a bear trap. He winced and tried to extract his aching fingers, but she was relentless.

She stared at him with those ice blue eyes and said in a low, cold voice. "You and I need to speak in private. Now."

"Yes, ma'am," he said. "Tallulah, may we use your office?"

"Of course."

At last Senator Wagner dropped his hand. Without missing a beat, she turned to her aide, and said, "Kyle, I need you to work with the hotel owners to get us rooms. When you're done, put my bags away, and *you* get some rest. You've had a long day."

Lucius waved the young man over to the registration desk, and pulled out the old-fashioned, hand-written hotel register. "This is on us."

Otterlegs appeared in the doorway as if materializing out of thin air. "Senator Wagner? The Mayor said he wants to meet with you?"

She turned. "Please tell him thank you, but it's not possible right now. We have other, more pressing matters to deal with." She gave Tommy an appraising look. "Fix your uniform. Your tie is crooked. If the press sees you like that, they'll think your investigative work is sloppy too. Appearances matter, Deputy…?"

"Otterlegs." Flustered, he began to fix his tie. "Yes, ma'am. Thank you, ma'am."

"Now," she said, staring at Bert. "Who can find me a good cup of coffee?"

"You guys head into the office," Tallulah said. "I'll have Toni bring you a tray."

Rolling past Lucius, Kyle, and the telecommunications specialists—both of whom stared at the senator with wide eyes—Bert led the imposing and imperious woman to the large office behind the mahogany desk. He waved her to a small couch Lucius had added to the room in the last year and closed the door behind him.

"This is a beautiful hotel," she said as she folded herself into the love seat. "I just wish I could be here under different circumstances—" Someone tapped on the door, and she stopped to call out, "Come in."

Before Toni could get completely through the door with a pot of coffee and freshly made pastries, the mini dachshund burst into the office with the yipping lampshade pug behind her.

"Bisou," Senator Wagner signed the wagging letter *B* and called her name at the same time.

Placing the tray on the table in front of the love seat, Toni backed out of the office saying, "Holler if you need refills. Come on, Franny. I have treats for you in the kitchen."

Phoebe's little dog lunged at the senator's legs, dancing to be picked up. Leaning over to lift the dog to her lap, the ice queen melted, rubbed the happy creature's floppy ears, and cooed, "What have you been up to, widdle girl? Who's your new fwend?" Showering her with doggy kisses, Bisou's tail wagged so fast it became a blur. "Where's your mommy?" The little dog sat at attention under her hands and stared deep into Senator Wagner's eyes.

Bert barely had time to wonder what the dog had told her.

"You're lucky Bisou likes you, because right now, I'm not sure I do." Senator Wagner glared at him. "When was someone going to tell me my daughter was missing?"

Direct and to the point, the Honorable Ruth Wagner was coming in for the kill.

Bert winced. "How did you know?"

"Phoebe always texts me about what she's doing and where she's going." She poured herself a mug of black coffee and sipped. "After my husband died under unusual circumstances, I kept close watch on my daughter. I never let her out of my sight, except when she was in school. I gave her a cell phone—a *big* deal at the time—with the condition she text me when she went to a friend's house, the mall, wherever she went. Since then, she has texted me at least once a day throughout college, law school, and even when she went to Mexico." Her lips thinned. "We video chatted the day she decided to join this search. I was in Denver for a human trafficking conference. We planned for me to join her here in Billings when I was done. I expected to hear from her yesterday and today. Nothing. The only reason that would occur is if something happened to her."

Leaning over the now sleeping dachshund, she placed the mug on the tray, and stared at him.

"I can explain," Bert said, regretting the lame

Sharon Buchbinder

words the instant they left his lips.

She poured herself another mug, took a pastry, and leaned back in her seat. "By all means, please *do* tell me how you thought it was a good idea to bring my daughter here."

"When you last communicated with her, I take it she left out the part where I told her I *didn't* want her to come. She insisted." Bert briefed the senator on his meeting with his new boss, the phone call from Lucius, and her unyielding insistence on coming on her personal time—for a weekend. He brought the senator up to date on events since they arrived and left no detail out, from the imposter cowboy to the return of the bloodied horse she'd been riding. "I was emphatic she not join me on this trip. Your daughter is very persistent. She does not take no for an answer."

Her mother smiled. "She comes by it naturally."

"I see. If one thing doesn't work, she goes after another." Bert shook his head. "She even used the National Security card, suggesting my niece's disappearance might be related to a foreign national attempting to use leverage against me to reveal secrets."

Senator Wagner stiffened. "She said *what*?"

He shrugged, "I think it's a stretch, but she was very persuasive, pointing out the nature of my division—and the people who work for me."

"I'm not so sure it's so far-fetched. I'm still not convinced my husband's death was an accident." She paused. "When he died, I was chairing hearings on Russian involvement in American crime—transnational criminal organizations. I was never able to prove he was murdered, but my gut tells me the Russians were involved. They left clues, not so subtle threats via

144

voicemail messages to my office, to back off. Their attempts at intimidation had the opposite effect on me. I doubled my security, bumped up my daughter's protection, and was one of the early supporters of the Magnitsky Act."

"Sounds like you took a lot of personal risks to fight corruption—in a different country."

"Not just corruption—those criminals tortured and murdered a man because he wouldn't lie. Justice needed to be served." She looked him straight in the eye. "At the end of the day, all we have is our integrity and our desire to make the world a just place, one where people can live without fear of being killed for telling the truth. And, if I'm not mistaken, you feel the same way. You do the right thing—and you've paid a high price, too."

Glancing away, Bert slid his hands down his thighs and silence fell between them. He didn't like to think of it that way. She made it seem like he was some kind of hero. When the IED went off, he was doing his job—like a million other soldiers who had done their jobs in Iraq and Afghanistan—and come back injured, many worse off than him. Yes, he had suffered and, at times, thrown a pity party for himself. But it was in the past. Here and now, in the present, he had the privilege of being director of a division in one of the most important agencies in his country, a job he loved, one which made him proud every day.

The senator cleared her throat. "Of course, I would never suggest using federal employees' salaried time on a personal matter—that would be *completely* inappropriate. But why haven't you asked your agents to volunteer to search for the missing child—Miriam,

145

right?"

Nodding, he steepled his fingers and measured his words with care. "Because they're otherwise occupied with equally pressing matters."

"Such as?" she demanded.

Fingers curled into the letter *a*, he tapped his chin twice with his thumb. "Secret," he signed without speaking. "The parents work for me."

Her eyes widened, and the color drained out of her face. She signed back. "Any other agents nearby?"

He nodded and signed, "Sick babies in hospital."

The senator expelled a long breath.

"Yes, ma'am. My feelings exactly." He rubbed his thighs. "To top matters off, when I tried to get satellite time to use our eyes in the sky, my request was denied because it was personal."

"Oh, *really*? We'll see about that." She placed the snoozing dachshund on the floor and strode to the door and yanked it open. "Kyle!"

Her aide—the one she had told to get some rest—flew into the office. "Yes, ma'am?"

"Get me MILSATCOM on the phone. Now." She nodded at Bert. "Our friends at the Military Satellite Systems Communications Directorate will be very sorry they turned down your request. Trust me."

He shuddered at the thought of being on the receiving end of the call.

And then Bert smiled.

Chapter Thirteen

The Pryor Mountains, Crow Reservation

Phoebe returned to the cabin after taking great pains to ensure the bulky outline of the diaper was clearly visible beneath her tight riding breeches. As she hoped, the Monster glared at her with undisguised disgust. He grabbed the notepad and wrote, "Get in the crib."

Astonished he would even think it was possible, she stared at him, at the sleeping girl, and then back again at him. The child was tall for her age and nearly filled the small portable bed. She grabbed the pad out of his hand and wrote, "I'm too heavy. It will break. I will sit next to crib. Promise not to move."

He glared at her, and at last nodded.

Without taking her gaze off him, she backed up, slid to the floor, and placed her head against the wall. The monkeys in her brain wouldn't stop racing around, alternating between panic, fear, and resignation. Where was Bohpoli? What was he doing? Where were the searchers? Why hadn't anyone come out here? What was taking them so long? She took a deep cleansing breath and thought about her mother's iron-will and resilience. If only she could be more like her. *Mom.* Her heart hurt just thinking about her. They were so close. Not a day went by that she and her mother didn't connect. She missed her mother, her home, and her little dog, too. Her mom would be worried—no terrified—and propelled into action by now.

She'd video chatted with her mother before she left D.C. and told her she was heading to Billings on her personal time to join a search for a missing child. Her mother, while sympathetic to the parents' anguish and Phoebe's burning need to prove herself, had tried to dissuade her. She had not been enamored with the idea and urged her to consider the potential emotional impact if the search was unsuccessful. *Oh shit.* In the frenzy to get into the search and rescue, to save the child, Phoebe had forgotten to reserve a room for her mother—or even to mention to Bert she'd be coming.

Oh dear. Poor Bert.

Feigning sleep, she put her arm over her face to hide her expression from the Monster. Talk about protective. Her mother put momma bears to shame when it came to Phoebe—from birth. As an *elderly* first-time mother at the age of thirty-five, per the obstetrician, Senator Ruth Wagner was not a naïve, easily intimidated young woman. Mom had told her how a pediatrician had insisted Phoebe *needed* a cochlear implant, or she would never have a *normal childhood* and would suffer from learning disabilities. The doctor hadn't known what hit him. When she moved Phoebe to a new practice, her mother had requested her child's medical files. On them the pediatrician had noted, "Mother is aggressive." In his mind, a mother standing up for her child and providing extensive literature and lived experience to refute his claims, was not an advocate or even assertive. No, she was *aggressive*. Phoebe wished all children could have a mother as aggressive as hers when it came to their child's health and well-being.

Now, her laser beam of protectiveness would be pointed at Bert, whom she actually liked—a *lot*. Aside from the fact she was his boss, she now wondered if she would ever see him again, much less have the opportunity to test the boundaries of a workplace romance. As her mother would say, "That ship has sailed."

Maybe not. She had a few bumps, a thumper of a headache, possibly a concussion, but she was alive— thanks to her riding helmet. And she had found the missing child. If anyone ever needed an aggressive protector, Miriam did. Phoebe decided she could either sit here and feel sorry for herself, or kick herself in the butt and do what she did best. Be an advocate for kids. It mattered not that Miriam wasn't deaf, or that this wasn't a court of law or a children's rights agency. The only real advantage the Monster had over her, aside from his size, was his weapon. If she could get it away from him, she'd level out the playing field. Plus, she had the element of surprise. He probably thought she was a helpless little flower, vulnerable and weak. Well, she was more like kudzu, the vine from hell that over ran and choked out other plants. If only he didn't have the damn gun.

She lowered her arm and studied the creep. Head bent over a phone, his fingers moved quickly across the tiny keyboard. Fingers poised to strike, his head jerked up, and he stared at the window. He continued to stare for a few heartbeats, shrugged, and went back to his work. Again, his head jerked up. Again, he returned to his phone. The third time, face twisted with rage, he threw the phone down, jumped up, withdrew his weapon, and yanked the door open. Returning only to snatch up the lantern, he strode outside, leaving Phoebe alone with the child—and a glimmer of hope.

The phone sat unguarded—and glowing, the text still in progress. This was her chance. She prayed Bohpoli could keep him busy chasing ghosts in the forest. Watching the door and moving as quickly as she dared, she grabbed the phone, scrolled through the texts. Some numbers. GPS coordinates?

What time you come tomorrow? Someone named Gregor responded with noon. She continued to scroll— and her stomach roiled.

Little girl fine, tell couple we want more $$$$$.
Got a NEW woman. Blue eyes. Big tits. Nice ass.
DEAF, scared, easy to control.
Can use @ whorehouse & 4 high rollers.

Phoebe looked up. A pinprick of light in the woods came closer. Heart thudding in her throat, she returned the phone to its last message, and raced back to her spot against the wall. She leaned her head back, let her mouth fall open, and feigned sleep. Her mind raced. The time on the phone had been twelve-fifteen in the morning. She had less than twelve hours to do something to save Miriam from being sold and to keep herself from being imprisoned in a brothel.

The floor shook with the Monster's boots, and his steps came closer. He kicked her foot and she looked up.

Face twisted in rage, he held the lantern in one hand—and lifted the light over his gun hand—or what was left of it. Blood pouring onto the floor, the Monster still stood—albeit wavering on his feet.

Shaking, she slid up the wall and grabbed a nearby diaper. Wrapping it as tightly as she could around the mangled mess, she directed him to sit at the table where he set the lamp down. Moving around the room, busying herself as if looking for something to use for bandages, she wondered what had happened out there. Had her ploy with the dirty diapers worked? Had he been attacked by a bear? Or had Bohpoli led the Monster into a bear's den? Either way, she didn't care, she was beyond grateful to the ugly little man and would have kissed him if she could.

With his injury and apparently having lost his weapon, he'd also lost his advantage over her. She had no reservations about using his suffering to her benefit. Seize the moment. She must strike a debilitating—if not lethal blow. She recalled her martial arts instructor's admonition: *In battle, you must choose wisely. For every blow you strike, your enemy will have a counterstrike.*

If she used her fist on his bloodied stump, he could strike her in the head with the lantern. If she struck in the groin with the hard heel of her riding boot, he might fall over in pain—or flip back on the chair. It might give her enough time to grab a piece of fire wood, step on his injured hand and beat his head in. Taking a deep breath, she tensed her leg muscles to raise her knee— just as he withdrew his weapon from his pocket and pointed it at her chest.

****

Bert's secure phone vibrated with texts and emails. MILSATCOM informed him that the next time the satellite would be in position to scan this part of Montana specifically would be at eight in the morning, one hour after sunrise. Assuming there was little to no cloud cover, he'd have some visuals in six hours. Enough time to grab some sleep—if he could.

As he debated going up to his room, his phone rang and Bronco's number appeared.

"Hey, Bert, any word on Miriam?"

"Sad to say, no." He paused. Should he tell him about Phoebe? Only if the babies were better. "How are the twins?"

"They have RSV—respiratory syncytial virus— and they're being admitted to the pediatric ICU for IVs and oxygen therapy." His voice cracked. "I gotta tell you, Bert, this is scarier than when Emma and I took on the neo-Nazis. Back then, it was just our lives at stake. This is different. I feel so helpless. All I can do is stare at them and pray. Thank God Stephanie insisted on coming with us. She was acquainted with the admitting clerk, so she got us checked in and upstairs ASAP." He lowered his voice. "Beautiful has been with us the whole time. Won't leave their side, keeps telling us to change their names. Emma agrees."

"It's the custom among our people to change a child's Crow name if they become sickly in hopes of making a change for the better." He stroked his chin. "You need one, two, or four people—four is a sacred number. You can do it yourself, but usually clan uncles and an aunt help by suggesting names. The parents make the final decision. If Beautiful wants four people, you're going to need some back-up. Everyone on the rez is out looking for Miriam. Let me think. You've got Stephanie, Lucius, and me." He paused. "And Tommy."

"Otterlegs?" Bronco's voice was filled with disbelief. "You're kidding, right?"

"No, not joking. He's a distant relative, and he'll do in a pinch."

"Oh, come *on*. He still has a thing for Emma."

"Nope. All gone. Ms. Wanda has him wrapped around her little finger."

Bronco blew out a long breath. "Let me talk to Emma—and Beautiful."

"How's Emma holding up?" Bert had been so entrenched with events of late, he hadn't spoken to his sister since the twins had fallen ill. He didn't need to talk with her to know how she felt. The connection between them was as tight as ever, and she was anxious, depressed, and angry. "Why do I get the feeling she's mad. What's up?"

Bronco sighed. "She's pissed at herself for letting some neighbors come over to see the babies. They brought some little kids with them. Even though they never touched Adam or Emily, she's convinced the kids got them sick."

"What's she going to do? Keep them in a bubble?" Her fears were understandable. Bronco had been in a coma for weeks after they brought down the neo-Nazis. Emma had sat at his bedside daily, trying to reach him and bring him back. If it hadn't been for Beautiful, Lucius, and Emma working together, Bronco would have never made it out of the world between worlds, limbo. If she had to do it again, it would take an army— and Lucius was out of commission.

"I tried telling her she couldn't have predicted this, but she's not having what I'm selling. They may never be allowed out of the house after this."

"New mother jitters. Give the doctors some time to work their medicine—and we'll get started on coming up with some names for you to choose from."

"Okay. Let me know if you hear any good news."

"You got it." Bert pressed the end button. So much for asking Bronco for a remote viewing. Good thing Senator Wagner had used her position—and the fact her daughter was missing also as bargaining tools with MILSATCOMM.

Speaking of the devil, there she was now—heading straight for him, the little dachshund at her heels. Still in her black pants suit and a crisp white blouse, he had to marvel at her stamina. Nearly three in the morning and she looked as if she was ready to tackle an army of miscreants—or a committee of politicians, whichever came first.

"Mr. Blackfeather," she called. "May I have a word with you?"

"Of course. The office is wide open." Back to the woodshed, he thought. He wondered what she'd say to him this time. Was he afraid of her? No, not at all. His feelings were more along the lines of terrified admiration. "Should I get more coffee?"

She waved her hand. "If I have any more caffeine, I'm going to jump out of my skin." She sat on the loveseat with Bisou on her lap. *How does she keep the dog hairs off her pants?* Franny required one pet-roller per person when she trotted into a room, much less sat on a lap.

"Since my husband died, I've had to assume the role of mother and father for Phoebe."

"A burden, I'm sure." *Where's she going with this line of conversation?*

"Not a burden at all. I may be a U.S. senator, but my daughter is my world."

"That's clear. I know you've moved every military and intelligence connection you have to get satellite time."

"It's not as big a deal as you think it is. You'd be surprised what the Speaker of the House uses satellite time for."

"I don't think I want to know." These days, if he had five cents for every politician's perverse pleasures, he'd have a very large pile of nickels.

"Sure you do." She laughed, looked up, and shook her hands at the ceiling. "Weather reports. He's obsessed with meteorology. If I hear one more lecture from him about clouds and what those spaghetti maps mean when a hurricane is coming, I'll throw up."

"When he leaves office, he can go to work as a weather forecaster."

"You're right. The next time I see him, I'll suggest just that." She shifted gears. "Look, Mr. Blackfeather—may I call you Bert?"

He nodded. "Sure." This was getting cozy. And odd.

"I know my daughter very well, better than most mothers. We are very close. She tells me *everything*. Now do you get my drift?" She stopped talking and switched to signing, "I suspect you know our secrets. True?"

Well, that was unexpected.

Worried about potential eavesdropping, he said aloud, "Ma'am, I have no idea what you're talking about." Then, he signed. "Yes. Phoebe is an empath and has psychometric abilities. You, too?"

She nodded and said, "Oh, I think you know where this conversation is leading."

He shrugged. "I do?"

She signed, "You know my secrets, now you tell me yours."

Holy crap, this woman made the KGB look like boy scouts. "What do you mean?"

Sparks flew out of those ice blue eyes, and her signs became faster, more agitated. "You have something over me, something that could get my daughter killed—or worse. What is your biggest secret?"

Wow, she was not taking any prisoners. He held his palms up and shook his head.

She stood and grabbed his hand. *Shit. That hurts.*

Senator Wagner pinned him with a stare. Unable to resist her mental probe, his fingers began to morph into feathers, and his nose began to grow larger and more yellow. She dropped his hand and returned to her seat on the sofa. He shook his hand and head and shifted back to his human form.

Looking satisfied, she leaned back on the love seat, crossed her arms over her chest, and gave him an appraising look. "Mr. Blackfeather, what are your intentions toward my daughter?"

Exhausted, punchy, and surprised beyond belief, he burst out laughing.

"Oh-ho, you really had me going, Senator Wagner. You are certainly a great practical joker." Nervous and uncomfortable, he shifted in his seat. It wasn't just the fact her mother was asking. No. He wasn't sure about his own feelings. Was he in love—or lust—with Phoebe? "Whoo hoo. Good one." When he looked up, she wasn't smiling.

"If you ever do anything to hurt my daughter, you

will live to regret it for the rest of your life. Phoebe told me she has *never* connected with a man like she did with you. Now, I need to know. Is the feeling mutual?"

Chapter Fourteen

The Pryor Mountains, Crow Reservation

To her chagrin, Phoebe found the Monster's hand still intact, albeit bitten by an animal smaller than a bear. After a while, she stopped counting the puncture wounds. If she had to hazard a guess, she'd say he'd had a run in with a raccoon. Finding no emergency first aid kit, she was forced to rely on cleaning his hand with hand sanitizer and bottled water—which was running low. In the cooler, she found a bottle of whiskey. In the absence of any other painkillers, this seemed to be a reasonable, albeit poor, substitute. Taking the cap off, she offered the booze to the man, and he accepted—using his gun to point to the table for her to set the bottle down. After she placed a clean diaper under his injured hand, Phoebe gently washed off as much blood as she could, then began to apply the antiseptic. On occasion, the man grimaced and took a swig out of the bottle. Each time he did the monster picked up the gun and pointed it at her chest. Only once did the weapon waver, but he regained control in a flash, frowning at her as if it was her fault. The close encounter of the uncomfortable kind over at last, she stood and shrugged her shoulders, putting her palms up.

He grunted, inspected her work, and nodded.

Seizing the notepad and pen, she wrote, "You need

doctor. Bite & rabies."

Grinning, he shook his head, pointed at his crotch and Phoebe—then opened his mouth and waggled his tongue at her.

Skin crawling, she backed up so fast, she slammed into the wall next to the crib. Disgusting and superhuman in an evil villain way, the man appeared to have a pain threshold so high, he could withstand his arm getting chewed on as if he'd only sustained a papercut. The thought of what he wanted her to do to him made her gag. Of course, if he had his way, she'd be performing that and many other things on hundreds of men—weekly. Her mother had been waging war against human trafficking for years. Phoebe wasn't a babe in the woods when it came to the topic. The fate of women sold into the sex trade was horrid—and deadly. Those who thought prostitution was a victimless crime made excuses to turn their heads and pretend the women wanted to be sex workers. Most prostitutes started as minor children, forced into the life by parents, pimps, or organized crime. If they lived past the seven years of slavery at which time most victims died from drugs or violence, robbed of their childhood and education, they had no other vocational skills. They stayed on the streets and became part of the hierarchy, bringing in new, younger victims—once prey, now predators.

Her mother's passionate work aside, in her own efforts as a child advocate Phoebe had brushed up against some of the scum of the earth who would do anything for a buck, even sell an infant. A baby was worth a lot of money on the black market. If the Monster had an anxious couple on the hook already, he could ratchet up the demands for cash on a daily basis, threatening not to deliver. Who would they go to? The police? Not likely. Anyone with half a brain was well aware baby trafficking was illegal—not to mention immoral. People with money had *connections*, people who worked on finding babies for them. Phony adoption agencies, sniffing out vulnerable couples, would pretend adoptive parents had walked away, leaving a cash-strapped mother holding the bag. Voila! Enter the marks—a childless couple unable to conceive, or worse, one who'd lost a child in some tragedy and wanted to fill the void. And the traffickers would pounce.

She had to do *something* or Miriam might never see her real parents again.

The Monster had slammed the door behind him when he came in—leaving Bohpoli out in the cold, literally. While working on the thug, she had been too intent on her task to take notice of the room temperature, but now she shook with chills. Tucking the baby more firmly under her blankets, Phoebe rubbed her arms while the Monster dozed on and off at the table, his head snapping up at unexpected intervals like an evil Jack-in-the-Box. She decided to take inventory, see if there was anything she could put to good use, either as a weapon or a tool.

A large fireplace, a neatly stacked pile of wood, a kindling box. A two-burner propane cook top minus the fuel tanks. A narrow cot with a sleeping bag—covered in the Monster's putrid odor no doubt. The cooler, the box of snack food, and the diapers. One adult-sized heavy camouflage jumpsuit, suitable for cross-country riding on snow mobiles or ATVs, and a matching child-sized version, were draped on hooks on the wall. One suit—but two criminals—one named Gregor. Was his accomplice joining him here before heading to that GPS point? She was strong, but she couldn't fight two men. Her gaze returned to the unused fireplace. A flicker of hope sparked in her heart. She was cold—a good enough excuse to start a fire. And maybe, just maybe, send a smoke signal. Too bad the Monster had stripped her searcher's vest of anything useful when she was unconscious.

Taking care to skirt the snoozing thug, she crept over to the fireplace and cast about for matches, looking over her shoulder every few seconds. Feeling along the high mantel, her fingers fell on a small box with a striker patch on its side. Ten matches. Placing tinder on the bottom, then arranging firewood in a teepee configuration around the smaller pieces, she glanced back once more and struck a match. It sputtered and went out. *Shit.* How old were these things? Crouching next to the open fireplace, Phoebe moved a piece of wood, and struck a second, third, fourth, and fifth match next to the kindling. Each one fizzled in her fingers. *Shit. Shit. Shit.* Five left.

She rocked back on her feet and absently rubbed the elk tooth on her necklace, wishing she really was a medicine woman. *I should at least be able to start a damn fire, shouldn't I?*

Closing her eyes, she prayed, "Dear God, please help me help Miriam. She's just an innocent child. Please, please, please. We need your help." A tear trickled down her cheek, and she brushed it away with the back of her hand. Five more matches. Five more chances. *Please, Lord, if you're there, help us.* Leaning into the mouth of fireplace, hands next to the tinder, she struck number five—and the whole box burst into flames.

Thank you, God!

Phoebe rocked back on her heels and clapped her hands in gratitude and triumph.

The floor shook—the Monster was up and coming at her, his face twisted with anger.

Heart leaping in her chest, she put her hands out to the fire, and rubbed her arms. With both hands in the letter *S*, palms facing each other and in front of her body, she shook her arms in and out at the same time. *Cold.*

He stopped a foot away from her. Instead of kicking or hitting her, he pointed at the crib. Miriam stood wide-eyed with tears running down her bright red cheeks.

Phoebe ran to the crib and placed her palm on the child's forehead. The baby was burning up. She grabbed a bottle of water and attempted to get Miriam to drink. She pushed it away, crying harder. Phoebe poured the water on a diaper and placed it on the back of the baby's neck. The poor little thing leaned in, grasped the elk tooth necklace in one petite hand, and sucked her thumb.

Baby on her hip, anger bubbling up like acid in her chest, Phoebe grabbed the pen and wrote, "Baby has fever. Needs doctor." Shoving the pad at him, she stomped her booted foot.

Lips turned down, he read the note, and waved her away.

Furious, Phoebe wrote, "NOT LYING. SICK. NEEDS HOSPITAL." This horrible man understood money. Even he would understand a sick or dead child would be of no value to him, wouldn't he?

Quirking an eyebrow, he put his gun in his waistband, reached out, and placed his good hand on Miriam's forehead.

Time slowed down to a crawl. The accumulated emotional charge of every torment since Miriam had been snatched by the Monster raced from the child's mind into Phoebe's. Immobilized and awestruck, Phoebe's arm lit up with a luminous corkscrew. The coil crackled from Miriam to Phoebe and back to Miriam, like an electromagnetic battery building up power. On what seemed to be the one-hundredth rotation—she had lost count—lightning arced from the center of the spiral and struck the Monster in the chest. A bewildered expression on his face, he staggered back, slammed his head into the stone mantel, and fell to the floor.

The baby dropped the elk tooth, and her head fell onto Phoebe's chest. She was hot, breathing heavily—and asleep. Placing the overheated girl in the crib, she approached the Monster with caution.

Head bleeding and dangerously close to the fire, the thug appeared to be dead—or at least unconscious. Phoebe snatched his gun off the floor, put it in her waistband, and dragged his limp, heavy body away from the fire. She withdrew the gun, before she placed her fingers on his neck to check for a pulse. Weak and thready, but the Monster was still alive. She needed to tie him up. But with what? She dared not leave the cabin to search the ATV for tie downs. Rolling him over onto his belly, she pulled his flannel shirt down and used the sleeves to tie his wrists together. It was the best she could manage for now. He'd have a whopper of a headache when he woke.

Sucks to be you, whatever your name is.

Now if Gregor showed up, she had a gun—and the will to use it. Breath burning in her throat, every muscle in her body screaming for rest, Phoebe fell in the chair, picked up the satellite phone, and glanced at the time. Twenty minutes after seven. In less than five hours, the Monster's partner in crime could be here. Worried he'd wake up any moment, she decided to forgo texting 9-1-1 and the ensuing lengthy explanations. No. There was only one person in the world who would understand her situation in a flash. She punched in her mother's cell and texted three numbers.

****

Glued to his computer in the dining room at seven-thirty in the morning, Bert rubbed his gritty eyes and waited for the email from MILSATCOM to tell him when the satellite was in position. His mind wandered back to the off the record meeting with Senator Wagner and her death-grip handshake. Wincing at the memory, he looked down at his hand and flexed his fingers. If he ever needed to interrogate a suspect without leaving marks, she'd be the first person he'd call.

Sounds of the hotel waking up flowed over him. Toni called Franny for breakfast. Lucius and Tallulah, showered and dressed, descended the stairs, and greeted the deputies. Kyle, dressed in a suit and tie, bounded down the stairs, and bounced out the front door.

Hal walked into the lobby and called out, "Summer's over. Nippy out there." He rubbed his hands together and welcomed a steaming mug of coffee. "Thanks, Wanda. What's the word, Bert?"

"Twenty-four minutes to our target." Tallulah and Lucius stood behind Bert, watching the computer screen and praying softly. Tallulah gripped Bert's shoulder and he patted her hand. "Keep saying those prayers. We need all the help we can get." He glanced at his watch. "Twenty-three minutes."

A door on the second floor slammed open. "Mr. Blackfeather," the senator shouted. "I have a message from my daughter!" Still in her dressing gown, her salt-and-pepper hair down from her usual school marm bun, Senator Wagner raced down the stairs. Hands shaking, she extended the phone to Bert and showed him the text message: six-six-six. "It's our emergency code. We use it when she needs to be rescued from a date from hell."

"Hal," Bert called. "Where'd those bureau guys go? We need their technical expertise."

"I'll get them on the horn right now."

The senator sank into a chair next to Bert, her face stoic. "I want to be optimistic—but some stories don't have happy endings."

Tallulah's soft sob caused both Bert and Senator Wagner to turn around. He hated that in his anxiety for Phoebe, he'd forgotten they were listening. "Lucius, why don't you take Tallulah upstairs, and you both try to get a bit more rest. It's still early, and the day could be a long one."

Lucius nodded, his eyes bright with tears, and steered the now crying as if her heart and soul were shattered Tallulah to the elevator. "Bert, I'm begging you to find both Phoebe and our little girl," he called over his shoulder.

Bert nodded at his ancestor and then turned back to Phoebe's mother.

"This is good news, Senator Wagner. Very good news." He pointed at the computer screen. "The satellite is almost over our search parameters. We should hear something soon." A message flashed in his secure inbox with a link. "Here we go." He clicked on the address and was taken to an aerial view of the surrounding wilderness. "We're in luck. No cloud cover today."

Patches of light and dark green at lower altitudes rose upward into deeper shades of emerald, forests of pines following the mountain ridges. At lower levels, roads snaked between folds leading across the high plains. As the view slid over the foothills, Bert tapped the screen. "There." He noted the latitude and longitude. "Smoke coming out a small stand of trees in the middle of the clearing. Probably an illegal hunter's cabin. The Pryors are so large, you can hide things away from the roads and hiking paths. May be the owners, but it might be a squatter—the one we're looking for."

Hal raced back into the hotel. "Took a bit, but the bureau techies got the coordinates of the satellite phone." He read off the numbers.

Bert and Senator Wagner exchanged glances. "We have a match," Bert shouted. "She's in Pryor Mountains—Crow Sacred Lands."

"Get me Jacob Graywolf, Tribal Chief of Police and the National Guard or Bighorn Air, whoever's available. We'll need a Medivac from St. Vic's, too," Hal barked into his phone. "This is going to be a coordinated rescue. Tell all units we have a kidnapping in progress and to be prepared for a hostage situation. Our missing child, Miriam Stewart may be with Phoebe

Wagner. Yes, the senator's daughter. Have the rescue chopper pick me up on the highway at the turn off from I-90 to Hotel LaBelle." He turned to the deputies who stood stock still. "This is not a drill, ladies and gentlemen. Otterlegs—grab your vest, three teams of two, and head for these coordinates."

As the whirlwind of activity and barked orders swirled around him, Bert drummed his fingers on the table. An iron hand grasped his, and he flinched.

In a low voice, Senator Wagner said, "Mr. Blackfeather, I know you want to be out there."

"I don't feel comfortable leaving you here alone," he said. "The waiting is the worst part."

"You don't need to babysit me." She released his hand, gave a rueful laugh, and rolled her eyes. "That's why I have Kyle."

On cue, the earnest young man appeared at her side with the morning paper, a steaming cup of coffee, and a toasted bagel with cream cheese and smoked salmon.

"You found lox?"

He grimaced. "After I went to three delis."

"You are the best aide, Kyle. I think I'll keep you." She set the bagel aside, sighed and frowned at Bert. "Don't you have someplace to go?"

"Yes, ma'am, you're absolutely right." He spun his wheelchair around and headed for the elevator. With a tailwind, he might just beat the air rescue team to the cabin—which he would see just fine. Racing down the hall, he sideswiped an antique spittoon and sent it spinning down the hall. *Whoops!* Good thing it wasn't porcelain.

Someone called out, "Everything okay?"

"Just me in a rush, Lucius—nothing broken." He

couldn't get to some privacy fast enough. "Come *on*." He swore at the key under his breath and the door creaked open. Why had he bothered locking the room? *Oh, yeah, national security.* Ripping off his shirt and sliding out of his trousers took less time than getting into the room. Unimpeded by clothing just as he was about to start the shift, he stopped. *Who closed the damn window?* The windowsill covering him from the waist down, he flung the sash open and looked across the hill leading up to the highway. Binoculars at her face, a female deputy stood with her mouth open in an *o* of surprise. He waved, and she pivoted on her heel so fast, she wobbled and nearly toppled over on the uneven surface. He laughed. "So much for trying to spy on celebrity guests."

He closed his eyes and said a prayer in Crow to the Supreme Being, asking for safe travels and for the strength to help Miriam and Phoebe. Heading into the Sacred Land, where Little People used to welcome his tribe and where his ancestors were buried on rocky ledges and in deep ravines, meant he had to ask for permission to enter. Bert asked the Little People, the animals on the land, the birds and the sky, and the fish in the streams to be allowed into their home. He hoped his prayers would be accepted, despite not being able to place a rock on the pile to acknowledge the covenant with the Little People. When he finished praying, he was ready to shift.

****

Phoebe checked on Miriam and wet the diaper on her brow with cold water again. The child was out like a light. Not surprising given she had discharged enough energy to shock a grown man—something on par with a police stun gun. She rubbed the elk tooth and stopped. Beautiful had given her the necklace—not just to honor her as a medicine woman, but to protect her. Had Bert's ancestor known what would happen when Miriam connected with the necklace and Phoebe? It was all so new to her, she had no idea what to think. If—no—when she got back, she had a lot of questions for Bert.

Right after she'd sent the text to her mother, she'd opened the door to the cabin and let Bohpoli in. Bug-eyed with amazement at the Monster trussed up on the floor, he'd grasped her hand and asked if the little medicine woman was okay.

"Sick," Phoebe responded. "Bad fever. Not waking up."

Releasing her hand, he climbed into the crib, and placed the girl's head on his lap. As he stroked her brow, his lips moved in what Phoebe assumed was a prayer. If only she had some of those healing herbs Bohpoli had told her about. She'd find a way to get them into Miriam and get her fever down.

The Monster stirred.

Heart struggling to escape her chest, she held her breath, hoping he'd go back to sleep. Instead, he began to thrash like Gulliver entangled in snares by the Lilliputians. As she debated what to do, Bohpoli took the matter in his own little hands. Springing across the room, he wrenched a hefty stick of firewood out of the neat stack and brought it down on the big man's shoulders, back, and legs. The Monster writhed and rolled over, blood smearing beneath his head. Mouth moving, teeth gnashing, the giant bucked like a wild horse and fought his restraint—and one hand came loose.

Roused from her state of frozen immobility, Phoebe leaped to her feet, gun in hand. As she strode toward the Monster, Bohpoli raised the stick one more time and brought it down on his face. The Monster stilled—but she doubted it was for good. He was like something out of a horror movie where the villain did not die, but just kept coming back, time and again, plucking off helpless victims with each return. The ugly little man examined the giant, nodded with satisfaction at his work, threw the stick into the blazing fire and returned to the crib. Phoebe made a mental note never to get on his bad side.

All she could do now was wait—and feed the fire.

****

Catching a thermal convection, Bert climbed to ten-thousand feet in the air and arrowed toward the Pryor Mountains and the cabin now imprinted on his brain. Between the updraft and his flying speed, he arrived at the cabin in a little over an hour. Swooping down, exhilarated with the rush of the air in his feathers, he almost missed the ATV coming across the hills from the north. Wheeling, he launched himself in the direction of the vehicle to get a better look.

A burly man in a one-piece suit and goggles bounced over the rocks and kicked up dirt on a direct path to the cabin. Tires spewing up dust and gravel, he gunned the engine, downshifted, and spun a one-eighty, ripping long trenches, violating the land and the law. The man pushed his hood back, removed his eye protection, and stripped down to a sleeveless T-shirt and jeans. Baldheaded and covered with Russian mobster tattoos, the man flexed his brawny arms and stretched. In English, he bellowed, "Honey, I'm home!"

and bounded toward the cabin.

If Phoebe was inside as he suspected, she wouldn't know the man was coming.

He had to do something. *Now.* Without hesitating for a moment, Bert dropped onto the man's bald head and dug his razor-sharp talons into his scalp. Shrieking in pain and screaming in Russian, he batted wildly at the air. Blood poured into the man's eyes, and he twisted in an effort to dislodge the eagle. Tearing at the man's ears with his beak, Bert did not stop his attack until the *thwup-thwup-thwup* of a helicopter approach. Only then did he release the whimpering mobster who curled into a fetal position.

Phoebe strode out of the cabin into the morning light, one boot off, Miriam on her hip, and a gun in her hand. She was a kick-ass sight for sore eyes. Bert flew over Phoebe's head, circling closer and closer until she looked up. Amazement filling her face, she grinned. Satisfied, Bert perched on a nearby pine tree and kept watch until the thugs were arrested.

Chapter Fifteen

St. Vic's Hospital, Billings, Montana

Phoebe sat in a hospital bed, awaiting the verdict on her head injury, and continued to worry about Miriam. A flashback of the child's feverish face in the cabin rose in her mind, along with a shard of panic. She grabbed a nurse by the sleeve and motioned for pen and paper.

"Where is baby girl?"

"Pediatric ER. In good hands."

Everything had happened so fast, it had all been a blur. The helicopters. The air ambulance ride. The eagle tracing figure eights in the sky, coming down to her, as if connected to her in some way. Had it all been a terrible dream? Did the police get the kidnapper? Just as she had feared, the Monster's accomplice had shown up. But by that time the vibrations from the two helicopters shook the floorboards and she ran outside, and found him curled in a ball, his hands covering his bleeding head. Who—or what attacked him? Her head thumped, and she asked the nurse in the green scrubs for aspirin.

She shook her head and wrote, "Sorry. Not before CT scan."

Phoebe nodded and wondered how long it would be before someone came to take her to imaging. The curtains swirled and she looked up, expecting an orderly with a wheelchair. Instead her mother materialized at her side.

The nurse raced out of the room leaving them alone.

The very honorable, very tough, very aggressive Ruth Wagner clutched a wad of tissues and sobbed. Not just a weepy, sniffling, I-just-saw-a-tearjerker-of-a-romance-movie cry. No, her mother was in a full-blown, red-eyed, big gulps, someone-died cry. She'd never seen her mother so distraught. It wasn't like her. She never, ever, cried in public. Even in the terrible days following 9-11, her mother had been stoic, holding it together for a week—until she was in the privacy of her Washington home, holding her daughter close, thanking God she was safe.

"I'm fine, please don't be sad," she signed. She held her arms out and turned them. "See? All one piece."

"I know," her mother signed back, still crying. "Not sad. Happy, so happy you are back. Worried sick. Thought I'd lose you like I lost your father. You are all I have. Since you were born, you've made me happy. You're so smart, beautiful, caring—when you went to Mexico and that child died, I was devastated for you. Your joys are my joys, and I'm only as happy as my happiest child. *You.*"

Phoebe's protested, snapping her fingers repeatedly. "No, no, no. You have important work—you're a senator."

Her mother shook her head. "My job means nothing without you. I try to make our country a better place for everyone, but *especially* for you. Because I

173

love you." Hands trembling, she signed, "I want you to be safe and happy, no matter what happens to me."

Tears welling in her eyes, Phoebe opened her arms to her mother, and the two women cried tears of joy and exhaustion together.

****

Bert found a weary looking Bronco in the twins' room, the TV playing silently overhead. "Looks like you could use a good night's sleep."

"Oh, hey, Bert." Bronco jumped out of the orange folding chair-bed and shook his hand. "It's the so-called bed." He pointed at the offending piece of furniture. "When someone makes a more uncomfortable slippery fake vinyl material for these things, let me know so I can buy them all and burn them in a bonfire."

"That good?"

He nodded. "Worse on my back than riding cross-country on my bike."

"How are the kids?"

"Doc says the twins should be going home sometime today or tomorrow. They're doing much better. Beautiful says we still need to change their names." He shrugged and pointed at a rattle floating over a crib without any strings attached. "Adam's feeling well enough to play with his toys." The ceiling lights on the other side of the room flicked on and off. "And Emily's up to her old tricks, so she's definitely on the mend."

"Where's my sister?"

"Stephanie told her Lucius and Tallulah were in the pediatric ER with Miriam, said she was sick. You know anything about this?"

"I know enough to tell you Phoebe probably saved

her life—not to mention the fact she rescued Miriam from being sold to another family."

Bronco's mouth fell open. "That's some nasty business."

"Yes, it is. There's more, involving some foul play, but you don't need to hear about it now."

Bronco waved his hands around the room. "Not like I have a lot to do here. Nothing but time on my hands—and five hundred channels of nothing to watch."

Bert nodded. "Fair enough." He filled Bronco in on everything from the moment they left the LaBelle to rush home to the twins, the frantic rescue in the mountains, and the discovery of the identity of the human traffickers. "Those bastards not only endangered Phoebe and Miriam's lives, but also violated Crow Sacred Lands. The Pryor Mountains are like the Absaalooke people's church and cemetery. My tribe goes there to pray, fast, and have vision quests. They violated our sanctuary." He shook his head. "Not surprising, considering who those thugs are."

"Wow. He really held a grudge, didn't he?"

"Yes. And took it out on my family." Bert flexed his fists, recalling his talons ripping into the thug's scalp. "They will pay for it."

"Where are they now?"

"Under armed guard here at St. Vic's." He grinned ferociously. "The one called Gregor seemed to have had a run in with a wild animal. His face and scalp were pretty torn up. Phoebe opened up a can of whoop ass on the Blacksmith."

Emma walked in the door with two sweaty cans. "I'd like to open some whoop ass on them, myself. Poor baby's been through a harrowing experience. I hope Miriam is young enough to forget it ever happened."

Bronco kissed her and took a soda. "How is she?"

"She has RSV, just like the twins." Emma rolled her eyes at her husband. "You were right. It's in the community."

"Let the record show," Bronco intoned, "that on this date, my wife told me I was right." Emma gave him a light punch on the arm. "Okay, Mr. McSmarty Pants. Miriam's on IV bronchodilators and humidified oxygen, too. Her temperature is down from one-oh-four to one-hundred, so very good news."

"Wait." Bronco held his index finger up. "Let's back up a bit. I'm still trying to piece this all together. Did we ever determine who the ugly little man is?"

Emma raised her hand. "Pick me, I know the answer."

Bert shook his head. "You always were the teacher's pet."

She took a swig of her soda. "Long story. Tallulah's grandmother was a Choctaw medicine woman—which is why she can see Beautiful. Because of her heritage, she is allowed to see the ugly little man, whose name is Bohpoli, by the way. His main purpose in life is to find children who will become medicine men and women. He's like a supernatural talent scout, looking for gifted kids. When he finds a potential candidate, he takes the child into the forest. The kid meets three wise men and are given three choices—two evil and one good. If the candidate chooses poorly, he returns him or her to their home and never sees them again. If they choose wisely, he sticks around to teach them how to become healers and doctors."

"Let me guess," Bert said. "He's staying?"

"Oh, yes." Emma laughed. "He's already made friends with the Chief of the Little People."

"Hope he gets along with Beautiful."

Emma nodded. "Apparently they've become buddies sort of. Not sure how it works, since he's Choctaw and Beautiful is Crow, but whatever works, right?"

Bert's phone vibrated with a text from a number he didn't recognize.

This is Senator Wagner
Can you come see me please?
Emergency Room 15

"Duty calls. I have to roll."

"Before you go," Emma's words stopped his exit. "Check your dance card, please. See if you're available to come over for dinner later this week, say Thursday? For a baby naming ceremony?" She fixed him with her gaze. "You are working on names, right?"

"Yes, yes, Otterlegs is too. But are you sure you want to make dinner, what with the babies and everything?"

"Absolutely." Emma nodded. "I'm bringing the babies and the bear root incense. Stephanie's cooking the main course, and Wanda and Tommy are bringing the side dishes."

"You got it. At least they don't throw hot bread at me," Bert said.

Hand on hip, Emma snorted. "I could arrange to make it happen again. One more thing."

He was halfway out the door. "What?"

"You and your girlfriend can bring dessert."

Face blazing, he retorted, "I *don't* have a

girlfriend."

"Stop lying to yourself. Bring Phoebe and some berry pudding."

He protested, "I don't know how to make *baalappia*."

"Aww. Think of it as an opportunity to get to know your blonde goddess better. You could whip up a batch in Tallulah's big old kitchen in no time—and feed it to each other. That's what lovers do."

"You've lost your mind, little sister." Ears and face burning, he popped a wheelie and flew out of the room with Emma's laughter following him down the hall.

****

Phoebe thought her heart would leap out of her chest when Bert entered her room. His mischievous smile and sly wink set a flock of butterflies into a frenzy in her stomach—and a coil of heat lower down. *Hold your horses.* He's probably praying you'll be on the next plane out of town. She couldn't blame him, really. The last thing he probably wanted was publicity about his division and his role in it. She had *promised* to keep everything off the clock and low-key. Instead, as soon as the media found out her mother was here and Phoebe was missing, the town turned into a circus. Like sharks in a feeding frenzy, reporters descended upon Billings from all over the country—even a few stringers from international outlets had popped up in the mix, throwing probing questions at her mother on her way into the hospital.

Face blazing, feeling like she had with her first huge crush in high school, her fingers flew ahead of her brain. "So happy to see you!" *Sheesh.* She must look like an idiot.

He responded, "I'm happy you are safe. Are you okay? You have a big bruise on the side of your head. Does it hurt?"

Hand to the side of her face, she touched the tender lump with care. "A little. Supposed to have a CT scan."

"Good thing you wore the riding helmet. It could've been much worse."

Her mother tapped Phoebe's shoulder, interrupting their one-on-one.

"We need to debrief." Senator Wagner interjected. "Phoebe and I have been discussing the men who kidnapped Miriam and imprisoned my daughter. Do you have any idea who they are?"

"The first one is Sergei Kuznetsov—the Blacksmith. I encountered him in Iraq when I was with the JAG Corps." Bert provided details about the human trafficker and how the Russian had blamed him for the other prisoners attacking and disfiguring him. "It was so long ago, he wasn't even on my radar as a threat."

Senator Wagner, her hair back in its signature coif, her make-up perfect, signed, "For some, *revenge is a dish best served cold.* My years in the Senate have taught me many lessons, including *know thy enemies.*"

"The second guy, his partner in crime, is a guy named Gregor Petrov. They spent time in prison together. They're little fish. Right now, Immigration and Customs Enforcement is trying to make them talk about their bosses, the big fish. Not sure they'll get very far. I think they're more afraid of what the Russian mob will do to them than they are of ICE."

"Trust me, they're right." Senator Wagner shook her head. "I've seen what those mobsters can do."

"So Phoebe." Bert pointed at her. "What happened

in the cabin? How did you overcome the thug?"

She raised her eyebrows. "This will sound crazy."

He waited.

"I was holding Miriam, she was sucking her thumb and holding the elk tooth necklace I was wearing. I was angry. Told him she was sick and needed a doctor. He didn't trust me, but he knew if she died, she wasn't worth anything to him. He put his hand on her forehead—" she shook her head "I still don't believe it myself. Electricity spooled around Miriam and me, faster and faster. Then a bolt of lightning arced out and struck him in the chest. He flew backward and went down as if he'd been shot with a taser.

"After I grabbed his gun and checked to see if he was really out, I tied him up with his shirt. When he started to come around, the ugly little man, Bohpoli, beat him with a piece of firewood and knocked him out." She smiled. "He was very pleased with himself."

"As well he should have been," Bert signed. "I could be mistaken, but if I remember the stories correctly, it sounds like you and Miriam harnessed the power of the Thunderbirds. If Miriam is a baby Thunderbird medicine woman, I can only imagine what she'll be like with the right training. The forces of thunder and lightning in you two must have been a sight to behold. Kuznetsov wouldn't know what hit him. I wish I could have been a fly on the wall. I would have paid to see it."

The baby. What about the baby? Phoebe signed, "How is Miriam? Is she okay?"

"She has RSV, will be on IVs for a few days. She's pretty dehydrated. But you know that. She's where she needs to be, here at St. Vic's with her mother and father."

Swallowing down tears over a lump in her throat the size of a baseball, Phoebe signed, "Glad she is safe."

Bert looked at Phoebe's mother, then back at Phoebe. "I guess you can't wait to get out of here."

Senator Wagner laughed and signed, "You're not getting rid of me, Mr. Blackfeather. Before everything went sideways, I was coming to spend some girl time with my daughter." She pinned him with a gaze. "Unless you have other ideas."

Face heated as if she stood next to a roaring fire, Phoebe threw her mother a pleading look.

Bert shrugged. "If you and Phoebe are going to be here for a while, I'd like you to come to dinner and a baby naming with me."

"You mean you want *Phoebe* to come with you."

He shook his head. "Senator, if you're in town and don't come, my family will pester me and your daughter with questions about you. It will be easier on both of us if you're there to answer them yourself."

"Well, since you put it that way, how can I refuse?"

"Good, it's a deal." He nodded and slapped his thigh. "I'll give you the details when I have them. I'll be going now."

"Hold on a minute." Phoebe shook her finger at him. "You need to do something for me."

He grinned. "You name it."

Gathering her courage, she glanced at her mother briefly. *It was now or never.* Phoebe signed, "Would you like to go for coffee with me? My treat?"

"An offer I can't refuse."

A nurse pushed a wheelchair into the room and handed her a note. "Ready for your CT scan."

"Time for me to go," he signed. "Text me when you get out."

As soon as he rolled out the door, Phoebe fell back on the pillow and laughed. *I did it! I asked him out for coffee!* Now maybe, just maybe, they could have a little romance, one step at a time, like two regular people.

Chapter Sixteen

Hotel LaBelle, Billings, Montana

Two days later, Bert sipped a cup of steaming hot coffee and while Wanda directed the deputies to collect the equipment and papers from the lobby. *Her nickname should be Ms. Organized.* If Hal didn't watch out, the little redhead might just be the next sheriff of Yellowstone County. *Speak of the devil there he is now.* His friend looked younger and more rested than he had in the previous four days. He could've sworn his buddy had even squeezed in a haircut since he'd seen him last. *Good for him.* He'd run a great operation and he deserved to take care of himself and get some rest. Not every missing child case ended on a positive note.

"Hal," Bert called out. "You must be a happy man."

"You can say that again," Hal said. "Anytime we get to reunite a missing child with their family is a terrific day. Thanks to your feisty friend, we got Miriam back." He shook his head. "She was a rock star in the debriefing with her mother. Her story was almost unbelievable. To survive, she had to be one very tough cookie."

"Do you mean Phoebe or her mother?"

"They're both tough cookies, but I meant Phoebe."

"I have to say, I was *not* thrilled about my boss

insisting on coming along on this trip. But I'll be the first to admit, she really kicked ass and saved the day."

"Yeah, about that." Hal nodded and held up an index finger. "Don't go anywhere. I want to continue this conversation, but I need to speak with my deputies for a minute, make sure Otterlegs got all the paperwork done before we pack everything up. I *hate* loose ends."

If Hal hated loose ends, then he would despise all the dangling threads on Phoebe's story—and he guessed that's what he wanted to talk to Bert about. Senator Wagner, Phoebe, and Bert had spoken before her first interview with the sheriff. Together they had decided Hal didn't need to know about Bohpoli *or* the Thunderbird effect. The senator was most insistent on keeping the true events a secret, and Bert agreed. Hal might accept the use of psychics for leads in cases like this, but Bert doubted he'd be able to wrap his head around Phoebe's very different abilities.

Beautiful, smart, talented, and gifted, she and Miriam had awakened the power of the Thunderbird. Could Phoebe's powers be synergized and enhanced with other psychics? Or did it only work with Miriam? What if she were to try to pair with Bronco or Emma— or their babies? He rubbed his hands. How exciting it would be to experiment. *Come on. You know you're not just thinking about work.* He'd also like to try other things with his blonde goddess to warm her up. Say a nice big bed and an entire night alone to enjoy each other. He shook his head. It was only coffee nothing more. *Don't get your hopes up too high. She's your boss. Never forget it.* Soon she'd go back to Washington and her socialite existence and forget all about his team—and him.

His chair vibrated with a hard tap and a cool hand fell on his—then pulled away abruptly.

"I was going to say a penny for your thoughts," Phoebe signed. A rosy hue crept into her cheeks, and a smile grew on her face. "But you seem to be—"

She got more than she expected. Did she feel the same way? Was it possible?

"Thinking about coffee." His grin grew. "With something on the side."

She made the "R" sign with both hands and circled them in the air. "Donut?"

"Something sweeter—"

"Hey, Bert, could you ask Phoebe a couple of questions for me?" Hal interrupted. "I'm still trying to piece together the scene in the cabin."

Talk about bad timing.

"Phoebe," Bert signed and spoke, "Hal would like to ask you a few questions. Okay?"

She cut a quick glance at the sheriff, then shifted her gaze back to Bert and nodded. She glided into a seat next to him.

"Could you please walk me through what happened?"

"When I was in the shade by a stand of trees in the search area, the horse must've smelled water and headed toward a little stream." Phoebe glanced at Bert. "I saw what I thought was a dark little man. I followed him, got lost. Never saw him again. The mare took me a long ways into the woods. When I got off the horse to go ask for help, a big man came out of the cabin, shot a gun, and then hit me in the head."

Bert smiled, signed, and said, "You're doing great."

"When I came to, he was standing over me, his lips moving. The thing that stood out to me the most were his Russian mobster tattoos. I was terrified. I told him I needed a pen and paper. He asked me who I was—I told him my first name—but could not tell him my real last name."

Turning to Bert, she signed, "I'm sorry."

Puzzled, he signed without speaking. "For what?"

"What I'm about to tell you—and the sheriff." She pointed at Hal. "Please tell him I gave the monster the first name that popped into my head. I told the man my last name was Blackfeather."

As he spoke the words out loud, Bert stumbled over the last one—his own name. Stunned, he took a deep breath to regain his composure. *The first name that popped into her head was his?* Heart galloping like one of his sister's prize broncos, he reached over and grabbed her hand. A rush of feelings racing through him at that moment—amazement, pride, and the overwhelming urge to crush her in his arms and pull her lush, full lips to his.

Phoebe ducked her head and blushed.

Hal cleared his throat, interrupting a moment—again. "What happened after you told him your last name was Blackfeather?"

Wishing he had more hands, Bert pulled away to sign the question for Phoebe.

Her face turned crimson. "He asked me if I was Mrs. Blackfeather, and I said yes. I thought he would leave me alone but instead he laughed, dragged me to my feet, threw me against the wall, and started groping me and grinding his hips against my groin."

A deep-seated rage coursed through Bert, and his

eagle threatened to explode. Barely controlling his anger, he gritted his teeth, signed, and growled, "The bastard. It's a good thing I didn't know this before. I would have killed him."

Tears shimmered in Phoebe's eyes. "I had no idea he wanted to hurt you. I'm so sorry I made it up."

"You did the right thing. The senator—your mother—needed to be protected at all costs. It's not your fault this guy tracked me down to extract revenge. I'm sorry you got in the middle of this—but I'm not sorry you were there to rescue Miriam. Without you she wouldn't be with her parents now."

Tears slipped down her cheeks. Bert handed her a handkerchief.

Like a hound after a rabbit, Hal kept going. "Okay, let's put it aside. Take me to how you overpowered him. He's twice your size. Survived Russian prisons— and an Iraqi detention center—and had a gun. What did you do?"

Senator Wagner, Phoebe, and Bert had agreed no one else needed to know about Phoebe or Miriam's gifts. It would only muddy the waters and create more questions.

Phoebe looked the sheriff straight in the eye, and responded via Bert. "Like I told you last time, he came in after going outside and was badly injured. I was hoping he had lost his gun. However, he made sure to let me know he still had it. While I bandaged his hand—I assumed he was attacked by a raccoon—"

Hal nodded and said, "Yes, the hospital gave him the post-exposure prophylaxis and he's on IV antibiotics. I don't give a crap if he died from an infection, mind you, but he's a little fish and we want to catch the big fish. We need to keep him alive so we can interview him and his partner."

Worried about conflicting stories, Bert interjected, "Is he talking?"

"Nah. He lawyered up. Has a Russian attorney, Natalie something, flying in from New York."

Bert laughed a little too loudly. "Good luck getting anything out of him. He'll tell you everything about anything—the jail, the food, the sky, the clouds—and nothing about what you want to know."

"You were saying." Hal pointed at Phoebe.

"So I bandaged him up as best I could. He fell asleep. I decided to start a fire." She glanced at Bert and smiled. "I hoped for smoke signals, too. I had my back to the Monster and the baby. He tapped me on the shoulder and pointed to Miriam. She was crying." Phoebe shook her head. "The child was burning up with fever. I wrote a note to the Monster telling him she needed a doctor. He didn't believe she was sick. When he put his hand on her forehead, I lost it."

Hal said, "Show me."

Bert protested. "Hal, don't you think it's time to stop this before someone gets hurt?"

"This'll be the last time, I promise." He motioned to Phoebe to stand.

She rose and held her arms as if embracing a child. The sheriff reached out. With the speed of lightning, Phoebe kneed him in the groin and kicked him in the chest, throwing him backward.

Lying on the floor, coughing and clutching at his crotch, Hal groaned, "We're done here."

Bert looked down at him and snickered. "Don't say I didn't warn you."

From the gallery on the second floor, Senator Wagner's voice rang out. "Never mess with my daughter, Sheriff. If she doesn't kick your ass, I will."

"Sorry." Hal rolled over onto his side and struggled to get to his feet. "I just needed to know for certain. When this goes to trial, you know how these thugs are, they will try every trick in the book to discredit Phoebe. When I'm on the witness stand, I'll be able to speak from personal experience. She throws a mean kick."

Smiling, Phoebe gave Bert the thumbs up. He grinned back and signed, "You are a bad ass."

He hoped that in the not-too-distant future, she might allow him to discover if she was equally athletic in bed. He shook his head and gave himself a mental slap on the forehead. *She's your boss. Not happening.*

****

Phoebe tried to keep her excitement tamped down, but given what had just happened it was impossible not to feel *something* was going to happen. When she told Bert she used his name instead of her mother's, she'd been worried he would be angry. Instead it was clear he was quite the opposite—he was happy, proud, and wanted to kiss her. She'd almost followed up on his wish, but Hal had been there, not to mention all the other people. No, when they kissed, she wanted it to be a private moment, a moment that might lead to something else.

The butterflies in her stomach circled and swooped, and her rubbery knees threatened to betray her. She grabbed the closest seat and dropped into it, her heart racing. *It's the adrenaline rush of knocking the persistent sheriff on his ass, nothing more.* Phoebe dared not touch Bert for fear of setting off flashes of desire and not-so-subtle signals that she wanted to behave inappropriately with her subordinate. Then again romance in the workplace wasn't uncommon. There were reams of paper in HR to address such situations, weren't there? There had to be a loophole somewhere in all those regulations. If she didn't find one, she'd make one.

Or quit the damn job.

What a liberating thought. She hadn't wanted the job in the first place. She'd only taken it to please her mother. And here her mother was, embroiled in the middle of a mess *she* created. Maybe it wasn't such a good idea for a senator to have a daughter working in such a high-profile government position. She'd get a job on her own, something she loved, *not* in government service. Wasn't being kidnapped by a Russian human trafficker a good enough reason to step down from this position? Others might be emboldened to try to do the same. And since she wasn't the President's daughter, she wasn't entitled to Secret Service protection. No, the best thing for her mother and for herself was to find a different job, one that utilized all of her talents. Something like the Anomaly Defense Division—but non-governmental. If there was such a thing. If not, she could start her own. Staff it with people like her, gifted people who would fly under the radar because of what the world perceived as their *disabilities. Ha!* Nearly clapping her hands with delight, she turned to find her mother standing next to the table with a steaming cup of coffee and a plate of pastries.

The very formidable, very smug looking Senator Wagner nodded at Phoebe and Bert, and pulled up a chair. "Good work," she signed. "You two make a great team."

Heat crept into Phoebe's face and Bert smiled. "Careful," he signed, "some people do know ASL here."

The senator replied. "So, where you going on your first date?"

Phoebe signed, "MOTHER!" and Bert burst out laughing.

"We haven't even had a chance to talk about it," Bert signed. "I think we've had enough coffee to open our own cafe. There's a place in town called the Garrett. It's a club with great shows and interesting performers."

Just then a strikingly beautiful titan with long black hair in a flowing purple sundress swept into the foyer. A man dressed like Elvis strolled behind her nodding and waving. The deputies and others all smiled and waved back.

Phoebe signed to Bert, "You know these people?"

"Not only do I know them, they're my relatives. Well, the woman in purple is my cousin. Elvis is her boyfriend."

"Is his name really Elvis?"

"No." Bert laughed. "It's Rod. He's an Elvis impersonator at the place I'd like to take you."

Billings was becoming more interesting by the minute. "What time is the show?"

"Let's ask my cousin," Bert replied. He motioned for Stephanie and Rod to come over and made the introductions. Their expressions telegraphed their awe at having a U.S. senator in their midst.

Her mother shook her head, pointed to Phoebe, and

signed, "This is your heroine. She saved Miriam." Senator Wagner excused herself, pointing to Kyle, and indicating they had work to do.

Stephanie's mouth moved faster than a whip-poor-will's tail, and Bert raced to keep up.

"Omigod! Thank you, thank you, thank you, you are so wonderful. We are all so grateful to you. I don't know how you did it, but we are all so happy to have Miriam back."

Bert signed, "Too bad you didn't get here sooner. You could've seen Phoebe demonstrate on Hal." Bert waggled his eyebrows. "He's walking a little funny now."

Stephanie and Rod winced almost in unison. "You know," his cousin said, "Hal lost his wife last winter to breast cancer. Now the poor man's whole life is wrapped around his job. Wish I could fix him up with someone. He really is a good guy—even if he does wear a badge." Stephanie glanced in Senator Wagner's direction in the corner of the dining room and said, "Is Phoebe's mom available? She's a looker."

Nearly doubled over with laughter, Bert interpreted in double speed for Phoebe.

She clapped her hands and laughed until tears rolled down her face. "My mother is married to the Senate. I doubt anyone could pry her away from her work, even if the sheriff used handcuffs."

"Honey, that is just a crying shame." Stephanie shook her head. "Every pot has a top. A girl needs to take some time out from her work and enjoy being a woman. She won't know unless she tries. Just look at me and Rod. I gave up finding a good man—and look—I got two in one."

Phoebe blinked and gave Bert a quizzical look. Was Stephanie talking about her mother and the sheriff? Or about her and Bert?

"Look at you." Waving her hand, Stephanie plowed on. "You are gorgeous. Stand up so I can take a good look at you."

Phoebe complied, coming up a few inches shorter than Stephanie.

"Girl, you belong on the catwalk. Why are you here with my cousin? You should be doing something glamorous." She jerked her thumb at Bert. "He's so boring with his desk job."

Bert signed, and growled out loud, "I'm in the room."

"I can see why he's so taken with you."

Bert glared at his cousin. "You know I have to interpret everything you say, right?"

Stephanie grinned. "Yes, I do. Now, where was I? Oh, right. Emma told me she told Bert to bring berry pudding to the baby naming on Saturday." She reached into her large purse. "Here's the recipe. It's very easy. I recommend you taste it while you make it, make sure it's sweet enough. The berries can be tart."

Toni entered the dining room with a huge tray of sandwiches and chips, the chubby pug in her plastic lampshade close on her heels, the dachshund prancing behind Franny.

Ecstatic to see her owner, Bisou raced over to Phoebe and begged to be picked up. Between face licks, she communicated joy and a sense of belonging. Phoebe agreed. The place and the people had grown on her, just as they had grown on Bisou. She hadn't realized how much she had become attached to this special place until she'd been trapped in the cabin, longing to be back with the people who welcomed her with open arms. She thanked God for the happy ending for Miriam—and dared to hope for one for herself.

Stephanie reached out and Bert signed, "She wants to hold Bisou. Is it okay?"

Phoebe smiled, handed the doxie over. "Lots of dog people here."

"Want to see the show tonight?" Bert asked. "My cousin can get us in for free."

"Yes, that would be fun." She paused. "What should I wear?"

"Something that looks good with stilettos," Bert smirked. "I bet you have a suitcase full."

"Show's at eight o'clock. Come hungry—we've got a new small plates menu, so many tasty treats. Delicious." Stephanie handed Bisou back to Phoebe and kissed her on both cheeks. "Don't let his gruffness scare you off. He's a teddy bear underneath."

Shaking his head the whole time, Bert translated for Phoebe, adding, "I'm really more of a grizzly bear than a teddy bear."

She flipped her hair over her shoulder and rolled up imaginary sleeves. "Maybe I'm just the woman who can trim your claws."

Chapter Seventeen

The Garrett, Billings, Montana

As he rolled into the club with Phoebe at his side, Bert's chest puffed out involuntarily at the stares from both men and women. *Yes, she is stunning, isn't she? And she's with me. Me!* Even given the degree of unlikely events and people he dealt with in the course of his job, he could never have foreseen Phoebe would waltz into his life—and steal his heart. Following his spell at Walter Reed and rehab, he'd returned to Billings and the grandmothers in the Crow community pushed women his way—all of them bearing gifts of food. When the refrigerator and freezer were filled to the brim with casseroles and bison chili, he had given the food to his sister and anyone else who would take it. A parade of women—tall, short, skinny, athletic, plump, single, and divorced, with and without kids—marched through his life and not one ever sparked his interest. He'd been polite, kind, compassionate—but in the end, he'd been relieved to escape the machinations of the marriage makers when he took the job in Washington.

The Supreme Being was the ultimate matchmaker. If Bert hadn't taken the job with Homeland, he would have never met Phoebe. He hoped he didn't screw this up, because when he was around her, he felt like Chief Plenty Coups. In Iraq, the JAG Corps were always first and foremost soldiers—and he counted three of the four coups to become a chief. He'd been in charge of a war party, touched his enemy without killing him, and grabbed a gun out of an enemy's hand. He hadn't stolen any horses and goats didn't count. Plus, in modern times, education had become more important to his Crow Nation than leading a war party. Perhaps stealing a beautiful woman's heart would count? He'd confer with his cousin Stephanie, the Two-Spirit guru of all things Crow.

As *the* place to go in town for the LGBTQ community, especially on drag queen revue nights, the Garrett was hopping. But tonight, it was even wilder than usual—and the reason was right by his side. American Sign Language—ASL—was flying across the room and a crowd had enveloped them, all eyes focused on Phoebe. She was, to put it mildly, a celebrity. People took out phones, snapped photos and videos, incidentally including Bert as well. One after another, people asked to take selfies with her. Almost to a person, each one asked the same question with a different name. "Do you know so and so?" Just as the Crow had the Indian telegraph, Phoebe told him the Deaf Community had its own forms of instant communication. In this crowd, six degrees of separation was the norm, not the exception. Phoebe, as engaging and gracious as she was beautiful, smiled, laughed, and thanked people for their kind words.

At last, she turned to Bert and signed, "Should we find our table?"

He nodded and replied, "I didn't want to interrupt you with your fan club. You seemed to be having fun."

She grinned, "We could gab all night long. I'm

here with *you*."

Warmth suffused his face, and he thought he might explode with happiness. *She likes me. She really likes me!*

Spotting his six-foot-two-inch cousin in the crowd, he waved and pointed at his boss. *No*. Not his boss. Tonight, she was his date, and they had both taken off their government employee hats—Phoebe even more than him. On the way to the club, after admiring his tricked out SUV that Tallulah and Lucius allowed him to keep at Hotel LaBelle, she had shared her intention to resign as Under Secretary of Homeland Security and asked him to keep it confidential. She needed to follow protocols—but she also had to tell her mother, which would be much more difficult than telling the Secretary.

When he asked her why she had taken the job in the first place, a shadow crossed her face and it wasn't from the setting sun. Well, maybe someday she'd confide in him, but not tonight. The good news was he was going on a date with an intriguing, smart, kick ass woman, and he could do so with a clear conscience.

Stephanie flew to his side, her fuchsia gloved hand at her neck clutching her opera length pearls. "Oh my darlings, I'm so glad you're here. You will have *such* a good time. And the food is divine." Shooing a buff male server in a barely there tuxedo—bowtie, cuffs, and pants—out of the way, she led Bert and Phoebe to a reserved table near the stage and in a perfect position to see a large screen overhead with closed captions detailing the time of the show and the number of contestants.

Phoebe turned to Bert and signed, "You don't usually see closed captions in a club. And I'm surprised to see so many deaf people here. What's the occasion?"

Bert interpreted Stephanie's explanation for Phoebe.

"For one thing, it is pretty darn noisy in here when the show gets going. The crowd can get quite rowdy. This is a drag show and a big one, so everyone comes out for this show, gay, straight, bi, transgender. Not to mention, there are talent scouts in the audience. All the girls are on edge. Queen bitches, really, but I digress. For another thing, we have a few more surprises in store for you, darling," Stephanie replied. "Just hold onto your cowgirl hat. I have to go corral my performers, make sure they're all lined up." Stephanie kissed Phoebe on both cheeks and then left her guests at their table.

"Is this your first time at a drag show?" Bert asked Phoebe.

"Heavens, no!" She smiled. "One of my best friends from Gallaudet is a drag queen. Sam loves playing all different celebrities, however his favorite persona is Selene the Queen. If you met him on the street, you would think he *was* Selene."

"Somehow it never occurred to me that deaf people would be drag queens."

Phoebe arched an eyebrow at him. "Deaf people are just like anyone else. Washington has its fair share of drag shows and drag queens. My friend competes in a lot of contests—he's hoping to make it onto a TV reality show for drag queens. I need to look Sam up. We lost touch with each other when I went to Mexico."

"Wow," Bert responded. "Learn something new every day."

"School's open." Phoebe winked. "Happy to be

your teacher."

Another hunk in a mini-penguin suit took their drink and food orders. It was hard to choose between bison bites, parmesan risotto with peas, chicken satay, pad Thai, pot stickers, lamb lollipops, or trout almandine. After choosing three plates each to share, they sent the hunk off to the kitchen to round up their food.

Phoebe's eyes followed the server, and Bert tapped the table. "You seem interested in our waiter."

Blushing, she shook her head. "I was wondering what the chef wore in the kitchen. Oil splatters can be dangerous to tender parts."

Bert roared with laughter and shook his finger at her. "I had you pegged as an Ice Queen. I'm rethinking your nick name."

She mock pouted and those beautiful full lips made him want to kiss her right then and there. Instead, he touched the side of his nose, and pretended to ponder a weighty question—then exclaimed, "I have your new name. It shall be—"

Lights flashed, music blared, and closed captions ticked across the screen. Elvis stood at the microphone. "Ladies, gentlemen, non-binary people, homosexual, heterosexual, bisexual, and Queer—welcome to the Garrett and the Big Sky Drag Queen Contest. Now enjoy the dulcet tones of contestant number one Polly Darton." The audience applauded and Elvis waved. "Unh, unh, thank yew, thank yew, very much."

A petite blonde strutted onto the stage in Western costume. She began to sing about a job, the hours, and a bad boss, then segued into a song about summer loving, followed by one about yellow roses. The applause shook the room and three judges with cotton candy colored hairdos—blue, pink, and rainbow—stood and held up signs with scores of seven, eight, and nine.

Bert signed to Phoebe, "These are some tough judges. I thought she was great."

"Hair and make-up were not perfect. Her costume was off by a country mile. I don't know about her voice, but she did not look like Polly Darton to me."

"If they need another judge, I'll tell Stephanie to send you in."

"I've seen the best," she signed, and flipped her hair over her shoulder. "They're going to have to try harder to impress me."

The dishes arrived, and were as delicious as advertised. And the price was right. Bert was surprised more people didn't come here just for the food. As he twirled noodles onto his fork, Elvis introduced the next contestant.

A breathless Marilyn Monroe in a sparkling silver dress sang happy birthday, faux diamonds dripping down her neck and arms. After a few more numbers, she blew kisses to the audience and waited for her scores. Two cards said eight and one said seven. He wondered what it would take to get all tens from these judges.

Phoebe agreed with the judges, saying her mole was a little too large and her eye makeup was a tad off. Also she was stiff as a board when she sang. "Deaf people," she explained, "use their entire body to communicate, just as performers should. It's a package deal."

A parade of celebrity look-alikes, each introduced by Elvis, each beautiful in her own way, made their way on and off the stage. Roan Mivers, Mette Widler, LaDonna, Starbra Briesand, Paty Kerry, and Miza Linelli each took the crowd by storm, only to be shot down by the judges.

The ninth contestant, Teenie Turner, came out in a body skimming sheath covered in rhinestones and belted out a song about rolling on a river. Hair spiked in a million directions, Teenie grabbed the air, shimmied, and strutted with astonishing legs and high energy. She asked what love had to do with it, offered to be your private dancer, and ended crying about the rain on her window. She was a show stopper. She scored ten, nine and nine.

"Close, but not perfect." Phoebe noted. "Her lips weren't right."

Bert slapped his forehead. "Picky, picky, picky. No one can please you."

"Yes, I am," she signed. "And *you* please me."

He thought his heart would stop right then and there. Had she meant it? Or was she teasing him? The wind knocked out of him, Bert rocked back in his chair and tried to come up with a witty reply.

Elvis's voice broke through his fog. "Ladies and gentlemen, please welcome Selene."

Phoebe jumped up, pointed, and signed. "That's my friend from Gallaudet. Oh my God, I can't believe Sam's here." She threw her arms around Bert and gave him a passionate kiss knocking what little sense he had left right out of his head. He pulled her closer and returned her fervor with his own, her soft lips opening for his probing tongue, the heat of her body threatening to burst him into flames. It was almost as good as flying.

****

Feeling like a movie star, her head already swimming with excitement and happiness, Phoebe thought she would explode when he returned her kiss. Better than she could've possibly imagined, his lips set off a ripple of thrills from her toes to her nose, and all points in between. As she opened herself to him, she soared above the crowd, outside into the night, under the stars. Intoxicated with the flight, she gasped when he released his embrace.

"More," she signed. "I want more."

Bert smiled and signed, "Me too, but not here." He grabbed her hand and pointed at the stage.

The crowd went wild, hands waving in the air, as Selene strutted in skin tight white pants and top and a gold blazer, her long strawberry blonde hair streaming down her back. As the captions rolled overhead, Selene signed a song about being all alone, all by herself. Then she signed about being loved back to life, followed by one telling how love makes you feel alive. Swept away by her friend's passionate performance, tears ran down Phoebe's face. Before Bert, she had been alone all by herself. Just like the song, he loved her back to life, and now for the first time in a long time, she felt alive—and open to a lifetime of new experiences with this amazing man.

Whew. Slow down.

This isn't a marriage proposal. It's only a date—and the first one, at that. She fanned her face, took a long drink of ice water, and focused on her friend and the scores.

The rainbow haired judges stood and one by one flipped over their cards. Ten, ten, and ten! Selene was the winner of the Big Sky Drag Queen Competition—and she was going to be a contestant on the biggest TV reality show for drag queens. Tears streaming down her cheeks, Phoebe jumped to her feet and waved her hands in the air as the floor shook with the thunder of feet stomping. Who said dreams couldn't come true? She leaned down, hugged Bert, and kissed him until she ran out of breath.

Laughing, he signed, "Keep this up and we're going to need to get a room."

"I know just the place," she replied. She laughed so hard, her knees buckled, and she had to sit down. "As soon as my mother leaves town."

Bert smiled. "She'd have her shotgun out and primed for me, for sure."

Stephanie pushed her way through the crowd of people, many of whom were up on the dance floor moving with the beat of the music. Flushed, breathless, and grinning, she arrived at their table. Bert interpreted. "Well, were you surprised?"

"Oh my God! Surprised? I was blown away. How did you know Selene and I were friends?"

"I didn't. Sam told me just today. Saw the news and asked if I could get you here." Stephanie patted Bert's shoulder with a fuchsia colored hand. "Girl, I said, not only can I get Phoebe here, I can get her a chauffeur." She winked. "It was our little secret."

Bert gave her a Cheshire cat grin, and her heart stuttered.

"I can't believe no one in that welcoming committee told me. They must have assumed I knew Selene was performing." Her eyes narrowed. "Or did you swear them to secrecy?"

Smirking, Stephanie arched her eyebrows and rolled her eyes when Bert interpreted. "Maybe."

"When can I see her?" Phoebe asked.

"The girls are backstage getting ready to come out and mingle with the crowd. There are a lot of fans here, ones who travel all over the country following their favorite star. Selene will be out shortly. I'm sure you have a lot of catching up to do but remember to pay attention to your date." Stephanie winked. "Bert has a jealous streak."

Bert shook his head, signed, and said, "I'm right here interpreting your drivel, my *darling* cousin."

"I know, *darling*. That's why I said it." Smiling, Stephanie strutted off to go visit with other guests.

"She's wrong you know," Bert signed. "I'm happy for you. You take all the time you need with Selene. Unless you don't want me here?"

"Don't be ridiculous. I wouldn't be here without you and your crazy cousin. She's a trip." Phoebe shook her head. "Has she always been this wild?"

"I don't know about wild, but she's always been dramatic. She's a Two-Spirit, so she sees things the rest of us don't always see. Stephanie is loyal to the death. Don't stand in her way when she's on the warpath. She will roll right over you, me, and anyone else in her way."

"Like a Thunderbird?"

Bert grinned, "Lots of thunder and her own kind of lightning."

Stephanie returned to the table leading Selene by the elbow. "See, I *told* you she was here."

Bert signed and winked. "There is no resisting Stephanie, she is a force of nature."

Laughter and pride filling her chest, Phoebe leapt to her feet, hugged her friend, and kissed her on both cheeks. "Congratulations! I'm so happy for you." She turned and pointed at Bert. "I'd like you to meet Bert Blackfeather. We met at work."

The ebullient crowd bubbled around Selene, encircling the star, pushing Phoebe back. Fans signed to each other and Selene and asked for selfies. Smiling, Phoebe scanned the crowd curious to see how many other people were using ASL. Her gaze snagged on a giant in a hoodie, his face covered in shadows. Her heart leapt to her throat, and her mouth went dry. *The Monster's back!* As she was about to tap Bert on the shoulder and point to the man, he flipped his hood back revealing a very big, very blonde Marilyn Monroe look-alike who had not been in the show. A fan perhaps? Exhaling a shaky sigh of relief, she shook her head and thought she would probably see that bogeyman wherever she went for the rest of her life. Under the watchful eyes of armed guards at the hospital, soon the Monster would be transported to the prison and put behind bars. The only time she'd need to see him again was when she testified against him in a court of law to put him away forever. An iron clad case of kidnapping and human trafficking against him, there was *no* way the Monster would escape the law.

Chapter Eighteen

Crow Reservation, Billings, Montana

Bert had warned Phoebe about the dogs and the
bobcat, Gaucho, but she insisted on bringing her little
red doxie with her. His sister's fenced in backyard was
part raised bed planters, part dog park, and completely
Emma's making. One side of the yard was lined with
railroad ties and rebar boxes filled with loam. Protected
from grazing deer, sage, basil, bee balm, parsley,
rosemary, dill, and other plants grew in profusion.
Franny pin-balled between Bisou and the other dogs,
careened into the planters, yipped and twirled in circles,
attempting to instigate the other dogs to play with her.
Emma's three patient dogs sat and eyeballed the ankle-
biters bouncing between them. Gaucho, the bobcat,
lounged in the middle and allowed the pug and the
doxie to run at him, occasionally taking a languid swat
at whichever one was closer.

Phoebe, her blue eyes crinkled with mirth, sat in a
folding chair on the sidelines, laughing. She'd taken to
Gaucho and, per Bronco, the bobcat had approved of
her, too. Senator Wagner chatted quietly with Lucius
and Tallulah. Miriam toddled up to Emma's dogs,
patted each one on the head, said, "Good doggo" then
moved on to Gaucho to repeat the blessing. When
Bisou and Franny ran too fast for her to catch them, she

protested by stamping her little foot.

Bert called out and signed, "I see she's living up to her redhead genes. The girl has a bit of a temper."

Lucius rolled his eyes and said, "Can't imagine where she gets it from." He earned a punch in the arm for that remark.

"We're just glad to have her back, safe, sound, and recovered from RSV. Doctors couldn't believe how fast she bounced back. She's clingy, but the therapist says it's normal for a child who's been abducted. She feels safe here." Tallulah flicked a tear off her cheek. "Might have something to do with Beautiful and Bohpoli taking turns looking after her in the hospital and still watching out for her."

"Beautiful is right by Miriam." Phoebe signed and pointed to the corner of the herb garden, "Bohpoli likes this space. He's smelling all the flowers."

Bronco and Emma came out, each holding a twin. A chorus of oos and ahhs went up in the little crowd. "Who wants to hold a baby?"

Arms opened. "Me, me, me!"

Bronco deposited Emily in Phoebe's arms and her smile was so bright, so happy, Bert thought his heart would snap in two. Children were her passion. He wondered how many she would want when the time came. He wanted at least two, maybe more. *Get a grip on yourself. This isn't even a second date and you're having those kind of thoughts?*

She looked up, caught him staring at her, and blushed. Warmth spread through him and he grinned. *Damn, she made him feel good.*

Stephanie swept into the gathering wearing a traditional elk-tooth dress in burgundy and beaded moccasins. Rod, who was out of costume, looked like a perfectly normal, middle-aged man in a large white Stetson, denim jacket and pants, and black leather boots. He placed a large cooler on the picnic table and shook hands with Bronco while Stephanie greeted each person with a kiss on both cheeks.

"Darlings," Stephanie announced. "I'm so sorry I'm late. I had to make sure I had three bags of bear root incense for all three children."

"We're not burning the incense all night, Steph," Emma said. "One packet would have been enough."

Stephanie retorted, "Who's the Two-Spirit here— me or you?"

Emma threw her hands up, "Sorry, my bad, I stand corrected. I'm surrounded by powerful Medicine Women—but you, my darling cousin, are the only prophetess in the group."

"Yes, I am." Stephanie blew her a kiss. "So, what Crow names have you chosen for your little ones? And where's Tommy Otterlegs?"

"He's on his way with Wanda." Emma replied. "They both had to work today."

"We had a lot of good suggestions, thanks to the uncles and aunts," Tallulah said. "We decided *Kalihchiia Balakbia* was the one we liked best."

"Lightning Daughter," Emma said. "Perfect. She has the skill and she did something praiseworthy— knocking that creep out."

"Shh. Let's keep it amongst ourselves." Tallulah cocked her head. "Maybe Phoebe's Crow name should be Thunder Heart. They made a good team."

Emma nodded, "I like that idea. What do you think, Stephanie and Bert, should we give Phoebe a new name?"

Bert signed, "Would you like a Crow name?"

Handing the infant to Senator Wagner's outreached hands, Phoebe signed, "You asking me to marry you?"

Bert's hands froze, and his heart stuttered.

Phoebe laughed and pointed at him, "Joke!"

Smiling, he responded, "You got me." *She posed as my wife once and look what happened.* The Blacksmith was going away for a long time. He'd never get to her again, not if Bert had anything to do with it.

"But, seriously, why would I get a Crow name? I'm not Native American." Phoebe asked.

"We change names when a person has done something praiseworthy, or if a baby is sickly. You did something brave and saved a member of our family. We would like to honor you."

Senator Wagner replied, using the crook of her arm to hold the baby and her right hand to sign. "This is a great honor, Phoebe."

Phoebe blushed. "Thank you."

Bert nodded, signed, and said, "Phoebe's gifts come from her heart. She's passionate. Single minded. Maybe a little stubborn."

Senator Wagner barked out a laugh. "A little?"

"Thunder Heart." He rolled it around in his mind. "It's been done—but I like it. *Suua Daase.*"

Tommy Otterlegs and Wanda strolled through the kitchen door and handed Emma and Bronco two covered dishes.

"Sorry we're late," Tommy announced. "I needed to get home and get cleaned up before we came, a truck carrying manure flipped on I-90—and guess who had to help clear the road."

Wanda pointed at him and held her nose. "Trust me, you *wanted* him to get a shower."

Everyone laughed and Lucius shouted, "We can always take him out to the ranch and dunk him in the horse trough to be sure."

Senator Wagner signed for her daughter, and Phoebe laughed. Bert's chest filled with warmth and contentment—something he had missed since he lost Susan. This beautiful, intelligent, talented woman was here with him and his family, and she looked right at home. The Ice Queen of his imagination had melted, replaced by this warm, funny woman who had stolen his heart. Did she feel the same way?

Stephanie clapped her hands and everyone looked at her. "Since everyone is here now, let's focus on the reason for this event. This occasion is joyous and solemn. Joyous because we can celebrate the return of Miriam to our family." She placed her hand on her breast. "Solemn because we're here to change the names of these children because they were ill. Thanks to the Supreme Being, Emily, Adam, and Miriam have recovered from illness. Who would like to go first?"

Tallulah and Lucius brought their daughter forward and placed her in front of Stephanie. Miriam smiled, hugged Stephanie's knees, and said, "Good auntie."

"Have you chosen a new Crow name for your daughter?"

"Yes, we have," Tallulah said. "Her name will be *Kalihchiia Balakbia,* Lightning Daughter."

"Lovely," said Stephanie. She motioned for Rod to hand her a bowl. She dipped her fingers into the dish. "I'm painting Miriam's forehead with red clay so the Supreme Being will be able to recognize her." She handed the bowl back to Rod in exchange for a smoking saucer made of pink quartz.

A heady aroma drifted toward Bert. He inhaled the intoxicating scent and thought of all the important rituals and ceremonies he'd been involved in with this sacred herb, a pervasive ingredient of Crow spiritual life.

"Now I will pass the incense over Miriam four times. On the fourth time, I will pronounce her new Crow name which she will be known as from this point on. Per Crow tradition, your daughter must never speak her Indian name."

One, two, three passes, and on the fourth, Stephanie said, "*Kalihchiia Balakbia*."

Miriam squealed and clapped her hands in delight. "I'm a good girl."

"Yes," Lucius said, and hoisted his daughter to his hip and moved back to make room for the twins and their parents. "You are Mommy and Daddy's best girl."

A ripple of happy laughter rolled through the group. The dogs perked up and the little ones leapt to their feet, but Emma sent the pack a stern look. Franny sat on Bisou's tail and tilted her head.

A baby on each hip, Emma and Bronco drew closer to Stephanie. After painting both children with red clay, she asked, "What is Adam's new Crow name?"

"*Iishbiia*," Bronco said. "Mountain Lion."

Stephanie nodded. "And Emily will be?"

"*Iishbiixisshe*," Emma said. "Bobcat."

Rod handed Stephanie an obsidian dish. She passed the smoking incense over the boy three times and on the fourth time, pronounced his new name. As she held the dish on the palm of her hand to give it to Rod, it floated two inches up into the air.

"Not now," Emma hissed.

The dish fell into Rod's outstretched palm, and he placed it on the table without any change in his expression, as if this sort of thing happened every day.

A red stone dish held smoking incense for Emily. She cooed and waved her hands. The smoke swirled and danced around her fingers. The infant sneezed, and the smoke scattered.

Bert laughed to himself. These two would be a handful. It was going to be hard to keep their talents under wraps. Emma might need to consider home schooling until they could control their powers—and keep them a secret, like their Crow names.

On the fourth pass of the incense over Emily, Stephanie said her new name.

"This concludes the naming of the babies—"

Bert called out. "This woman—" he pointed to Phoebe—"has done something praiseworthy. We formally declare she has earned a new name."

Stephanie tilted her head. "What reason do you give for this name change?"

"Phoebe Wagner showed great courage and saved Miriam. In doing so, she saved our family. We decided Phoebe has earned a place in our tribe. Her Indian name will be *Suua Daase*."

"She's not a child, but she is new to our family." Stephanie motioned for Phoebe to come to her. "Emma, could you please give me your bear root incense? We'll be needing it, after all."

After painting Phoebe's forehead with red clay, Stephanie passed a fourth smoking dish over Phoebe and on the fourth pass said, "From this time on, she

shall be known as *Suua Daase*—Thunder Heart."
Stephanie waved to Phoebe's mother. "Senator Wagner,
please tell your daughter to go sit with her man. They
can't take their eyes off each other."

Lucius piped up from the back of the group. "I told
you they were sweet on each other!"

Shaking his head, Bert wagged his finger at his
relatives, and laughed. Family. The only group they
couldn't throw you out of—and the only group you
couldn't *shut up*.

****

Phoebe sat next to Bert in a folding chair and
signed, "Your face is red."

"I'm an Indian. My face is always red," he replied
with a grin. "Besides, yours is, too."

She waved her hand. "Mine will wash off. You're
blushing." She smiled. "My mother isn't the only one
good at embarrassing family members."

He swept his hand around the group. "With the
Crow teasing cousins are the norm, not the exception.
We play practical jokes on each other, sometimes
waiting years for payback. You would not believe some
of the elaborate jokes we play on each other."

"Good to know." She winked. "I'll fit right in."

"You already do." He reached over, grabbed her
hand, and squeezed.

Her heart sped up, and her mouth grew dry. That
zing of connection when he touched her hadn't
diminished. It had morphed into something even more
powerful, as if she climbed above the clouds, the wind
rushing through her face. She wondered what would
happen when they had sex. *Whoa.* Not *if* but *when*. She
turned the thought over in her mind—and gasped when

he let go of her hand.

"Something wrong?"

"No, it's just time to eat. Why?"

"I was enjoying your touch—" she paused. "—you make me feel like I'm flying."

He grinned and winked. "There's more where that came from. Would you like to soar with the big birds?"

"Yes—but how?" It wasn't as if she could hop on the back of a bald eagle—or could she?

"Not here, not now, but when you and I have some private time, I'll show you."

"Tease!" She put her lower lip out in a pout. "Not fair."

He shook his head. "It will be more than fair. I promise."

Emma placed a cold soda in Phoebe's hand, made the sign for eating, and pointed to a feast spread across the picnic table.

"I'm starving," Bert signed. "Let's see if the berry pudding you made is as good as it looks."

"Better," she taunted. "I tripled the sugar. Those berries were tart."

He gave a thumbs up and waited for her to go ahead of him. Bert told her what each dish was—bison burgers, bison chili, wheel bread, and fry bread sat alongside hot dogs, beans, and macaroni salad. Her berry pudding sat at the end of the table, a serving spoon in it standing at attention. Maybe she used a little too much sugar? *Hope it tastes okay.*

As the hours passed, the sky turned from blue to red and purple. Her stomach full, grateful the pudding was as good as Stephanie had promised it would be, Phoebe sighed, and leaned back in her chair. The

Blackfeather Clan had embraced Phoebe and her mother. No Inside-the-Beltway snobbery, no jockeying for favors, no demands for votes or support for pet projects and boondoggles. Just a grateful family sharing their joy and traditions with these two outsiders. Different in many ways, but alike in integrity, honor, and love. Family first wasn't just a campaign slogan for them. They lived and breathed their kinships. Like fry bread rising, they encompassed those lucky enough to be in their paths. The thought of going back to Washington dashed ice water on her warm thoughts. How did Bert do it? How did he get back on the plane and leave all *this* behind?

People liked to make fun of government employees. Politicians and citizens denigrated the efforts of civil servants, assuming they had no place else to go. What those fools didn't understand was the sacrifices people made to serve their country. Bert didn't wear a uniform, but he had, just as many others had. Each day he went to work to combat enemies of the United States, those who would seek to undermine, divide, and destroy our country with bombs or equally evil hateful rhetoric to incite violence. This man was a hero. And she for one, was damn glad to have him in her life.

Bert glanced up from a heated sign language conversation with Phoebe's mother about who would win the next baseball season. The senator was a Yankees fan, and Bert liked the Orioles. He caught her gaze and winked. She shook her head. Those two would be fighting at every family gathering. Her breath caught in her throat. *What am I thinking?* This isn't a wedding. It's just dinner with friends—and family.

The dogs leapt to their feet, and all heads swiveled toward the kitchen door. Grim faced, the sheriff came out, tipped his hat at Senator Wagner, and nodded at the rest of the party-goers. He strode over to Phoebe and Bert, his color ashen, his fingers running the rim of his hat.

"What's going on, Hal?" Bert signed.

The sheriff answered, and Bert blanched.

Phoebe tapped his arm. "Tell me."

The twinkle no longer in his eyes, he signed. "It's Sergei Kuznetsov, the Blacksmith. He killed the deputy escorting him to the detention center, stole the cruiser, and escaped."

Her vision blurred, and her breath came in little gasps. "No. Please tell me it's not true."

"He ditched the police car north of Billings and stole a pick-up truck. Hal says they think he's heading toward Canada, but he wanted us to know and to be on the lookout for him."

Phoebe put her face in her hands and wept. The Monster was on the loose.

Chapter Nineteen

Hotel LaBelle, Billings, Montana

Senator Wagner and her aide, Kyle, stood in the foyer of the Hotel LaBelle saying their good-byes. Bert, Hal, and her own security experts had urged the senator to return to Washington. The prospect of a sitting U.S. senator being kidnapped by a mercenary and being used to secure demands for a rogue nation meant she had to leave soon. The next flight out of Billings was in two hours, and she *had* to be on that plane. Bert admired how calm and collected she appeared to be despite the obvious urgency.

"Tallulah, Lucius, thank you for your hospitality." Senator Wagner tousled Miriam's hair. "I expect to hear amazing things about you, young lady."

"We're not far behind you, Senator," Tallulah said. "As soon as Hal told us the creep escaped, we decided to take our daughter back to her Choctaw roots. We're heading to Oklahoma and will stay there until we hear Kuznetsov is behind bars—and secure."

Tapping Bert's shoulder, Phoebe signed, "I see Bohpoli is glued to Miriam's side. I guess he'll be going with them to Oklahoma."

"You have an advantage over me. I can't see him."

"Trust me, he's there. What are they saying?"

Buying a little time, he rubbed Bisou's head. The

little dog hadn't left his lap all morning. He hesitated to repeat the last part of Tallulah's comments, but true to his integrity, he interpreted every word. He then added, "Please reconsider getting on the plane with your mother. The safest place for you is *away* from me."

Giving her head a violent shake, she snapped. "NO. Not going. If I run now, I will never stop running."

"There's no shame in protecting yourself."

She rolled her eyes. "I missed important signals in Mexico. An entire family—including the girl I was supposed to be helping—died on account of me."

"You were a researcher, helping deaf students get an education," Bert responded, puzzled. "What possible relationship could you have had to a girl's death?"

Phoebe waved him away and shook her head. "Not now. I'll tell you later, when we're alone."

Alone? When were they going to be alone? It seemed Phoebe was taking matters into her own hands. Not that he disliked the idea of her taking him into her hands, however, her safety was of paramount importance.

Before he could offer up his concerns, the dachshund leapt to the floor and followed her owner to her *grandmother*. Phoebe embraced her mother and signed, "Have a safe trip. I'll see you back in Washington in a week. I'm taking some unpaid leave. I have personal business to attend to."

Senator Wagner shot a glance at Bert, her eyebrow quirked in an unspoken question. He lifted his hands and shrugged, then signed, "I tried to convince her to go home with you."

The older woman's face softened, and she shook her head. "Please be safe. You're the only child I have."

Phoebe nodded, hugged her mother one last time, and waved and blew kisses as she left with Kyle at her elbow.

Phoebe returned to Bert's side and signed, "Glad she's going home. Safer for her."

He nodded and wondered what she could have possibly done wrong in Mexico. Her words made no sense. At the time she was a Fulbright scholar, a researcher, and an advocate for deaf children. What did she believe she could have done differently? *We've all had experiences we didn't feel good about.* It didn't mean she was responsible for someone's death. He wished he could wave Beautiful's medicine stick and make her feel better, but she had to do that for herself.

He was glad Tallulah and Lucius were leaving town. Hal was sending extra patrols out to the hotel, to keep an eye on the place. Toni would come in, clean, and do some food prep, but for now the hotel was closed. As for himself, Bert wasn't planning to leave Phoebe's side. This was an opportunity for them to get to know each other better. If they still liked each other at the end of the week, then they had some decisions to make. He was cautiously optimistic about the relationship, but didn't kid himself. Right now, maybe it was the novelty effect. Perhaps her apparent interest in him came from the fact they were *so different*. They were, to put it mildly, opposites.

Phoebe was white, lived on the east coast most of her life, and came from wealth and privilege. Bert was Native American, had traveled all over the world in various roles, and came from the great plains of the Crow Reservation where his roots ran deep. She was blonde, beautiful, and physically perfect. He was dark, scarred, and imperfect. The thought of being in bed with her, alone and naked sent shivers of desire—and stabs of fear—through him.

What if Phoebe found his injuries so hideous, so dreadful, and so disgusting, that she was not attracted but *repulsed* by him? He had worked hard to become a lawyer and had served his country, and continued to do so. But his professional stature had no bearing in the bedroom. She was an amazing woman with her own back story of difficulties and marginalization. Would her experience and her compassion bridge the divide between them? Time would tell, and they had only a week to find out before returning to Washington. Then what?

Tommy Otterlegs stomped into the lobby and announced, "I've been assigned to keep a special watch on Hotel LaBelle." He pointed at Tallulah and Lucius. "Your baby is in good hands."

He mentally slapped his forehead. Was there no end to the dilemma of dating Phoebe? Otterlegs, self-appointed busybody and the resident rez gossip, would tell everyone who would listen the senator's daughter was spending private time with him. Maybe he wouldn't find out?

"Wonderful, Tommy," Tallulah enthused. "Someone we know and trust is keeping an eye out. Plus Bert and Phoebe are staying here for the week, so between the three of you, I know everything will be fine."

So much for being under the radar.

The news would hit the Indian telegraph the minute Tommy walked out the door. A vision of all the women thrust upon him marched through his mind—and they all looked angry, especially the matchmakers. The rez gossip would pillory him. Not that inter-racial relationships were an oddity. There were many Native Americans who dated, and who were also married to whites on the rez and in the Billings area. The matchmakers, however, would not look kindly on this relationship. After all, they hadn't arranged it. How could she *possibly* be the right woman for him?

Phoebe plopped Bisou back on his lap. "Penny for your thoughts."

Bert signed. "I'm thinking I should take you for a drive to Kalispell and, get us out of town for a bit. We could get a couple of rooms at the historic hotel downtown and explore Whitefish, Flathead Lake, and Glacier National Park. Ready for a road trip?"

She furrowed her brow. "Isn't that on the other side of the state?"

He nodded. "And north. We share the park with Canada. It's a good day's drive. You haven't had much time to see Montana—outside of your adventures in the Pryor Mountains."

"I'm sure it's beautiful." She paused and looked around the hotel. "But I'm not sure I'm up for a long drive. The doctor said if I wasn't going back to D.C., he wanted to see me in his office in two days. I'd really like to get some rest." She locked eyes with him. "I thought we could stay here. Get to know each other better. What do you think?"

He grinned. "You don't want to know."

"Oh," she signed. "Intriguing. Were you thinking naughty things about me and you alone in this big, beautiful hotel?" She drew hearts on the back of his hand and favored him with a sideways look—and an impish smile.

Her touch took his breath away. Nearly paralyzed with desire warring with decorum, he fought to stay centered, not to heed all the images in his head of her naked—and welcoming his embrace. He shook his head to dispel the cloud of lust her proximity and scent created.

"Just gathering wool."

"You'd better be thinking about what we're going to do this week." She winked. "I expect you to show me a good time."

He nodded. "There's a great restaurant I'd like to take you to tonight. Very historic. It has a speakeasy in the basement. I'll ask the owner to show it to you."

She smiled. "Perfect."

****

Phoebe wanted to stomp her foot and pound a punching bag with frustration. Instead, she grabbed Bisou off his lap and strode out the front door, telling him the dog needed to go out. Fuming, she watched the little dog sniff the hummocks of grass and paw at interesting holes in the ground, and wondered what happened to the flirty man she'd spent time with at the baby naming. *Where did he go?* He promised her private time and flying lessons. What else could that mean but great sex?

Suddenly he'd become a pillar of rectitude. Didn't he understand she was here to get to know him, away from Washington, on her own time? Did she need to draw him a picture? The one from her high school sex education book showing a man and a woman in bed together—covered up, of course—leapt to her mind. Except the man in the bed was the sexy hunk back in the hotel and the woman was her—with a satisfied smile on her face.

She was going back in there and wasn't giving up. The man had gotten under her skin and she could not shake him off like she had the others. He was the *one*. Didn't he feel it, too? Mind made up, she was a woman on a mission. She picked Bisou up, headed back into the lobby, and released the dachshund on her own recognizance.

Bert sat by the door chatting with Lucius. Tallulah approached Phoebe nearly vibrating with tension. She took the hotel owner's cold hand while Bert translated. "We're going now. The SUV is packed to the brim, and Franny's playing tag with Bohpoli and Miriam. I hope the three of them sleep most of the way. Otherwise, it's going to be crazy."

Phoebe could only imagine a long car ride with a pug, an almost two-year old, and a supernatural being the size of a child with a mischievous streak. She released Tallulah's hand and signed while Bert translated. "Someday you'll look back at this and laugh."

The harried mother burst into tears and gave Phoebe a bear hug. "Without you, there wouldn't be a trip for us to go on. We'd be mourning our daughter. Thank you for saving her, for saving us."

She hugged Tallulah back and stepped away, her own eyes moist. "Safe travels. I'm so glad you have your baby back. I hope to see you again sometime."

Tallulah cocked her head and gave Phoebe a teary grin. "Of *course* you will. Everyone returns to Hotel LaBelle. That's the magic of this place—and the people."

Bert signed and spoke, "Tallulah, have you seen Beautiful lately? Is she here?"

"No, silly. She's watching over the twins. Never left after the party." She smirked. "You and Phoebe have the place all to yourselves." Tallulah gave a final glance around, blew them kisses, and walked out the door.

At least *somebody* was on her side, nudging this romance along. If only she could get Bert to see the light and not perceive it as an oncoming freight train. Well, dinner was a start. She'd take it slow. Shouldn't come across as a brazen hussy trying to get him into bed. Subtlety was required.

"What's the dress code for the restaurant?"

"Nice casual. We're in Montana, you'll rarely see someone in a suit and tie—unless they're going to court."

"Got it." She knew exactly what to wear. Not as form hugging as her riding clothes—and she'd seen the effect that outfit had had on him. A shiver ran down her spine as she remembered. The spark in his eye had been pure lust. And she had loved it. Stoking those flames would be her number one priority. But not all at once. He'd be the frog in the pot, and she'd turn the heat up a little at a time.

"In the meantime." She gave him her most come hither look. "Since we have the place all to ourselves, you could give me a tour of the hotel."

He frowned. "Haven't you seen it all?"

"I was in the kitchen and my room. The rest of the time—" she shuddered "—I was in the cabin."

"Come on. Let's start with the lobby and go from there."

Walking at his side, she admired the bulge of his back, shoulder, and arm muscles beneath a black T-shirt emphasizing the size of his biceps. When he wasn't out in the field, she thought, he must work out every day.

As they headed to the kitchen, Bert pointed out the long, smooth registration desk made of highly polished mahogany, and the intricately carved walls and ceiling of the same wood. "Back when the place was first built in the early 1900s, Lucius hired an artist who wanted to be another Frederic Remington. Every carving you see—deer, birds, fish, and waterways—was created by him."

She ran her hand over the walls, the tips of her fingers caressing each feather on a large goose. The detail was incredible. The artist was not only talented but patient. Wait. Early 1900s? Not possible. She turned to Bert. "You mean Lucius' grandfather built this place?"

"No." He shook his head. "Lucius, the man you just said good-bye to, is the original owner of Hotel LaBelle."

"You told me Lucius was a distant cousin who rejoined the Crow tribe."

Making the letter *a*, Bert tapped his thumb to his chin two times. "Family secrets."

"Please tell me before I die of curiosity."

"Almost four years ago Tallulah was invited to Billings to assist a hapless proprietor in getting the historic Hotel LaBelle back on her feet. She was working as a hotel inspector and consultant to distressed properties. You know she has powers, and her grandmother was a Choctaw Medicine woman, right?"

Phoebe nodded.

"The first night she was in the hotel, Tallulah met the original owner, *Love 'Em and Leave 'Em* Lucius Stewart. She thought he was a spirit, but he was neither dead nor alive. He was in limbo. Beautiful Blackfeather, the spirit you've met, blamed him for her daughter's death. She died in childbirth, but the baby survived. Tapping him with her medicine stick she said, 'You are cursed to stay in this dwelling you love more than my daughter. You are cursed to wander it alone until you find someone you love and who loves you back.'"

Mid-air, Phoebe grabbed his hand—and connected the dots with a flash of insight. She signed. "He's your ancestor? A great-great whatever?"

He nodded. "Grandfather."

"Holy shit. What happened? How did he come back to life?"

"When Beautiful realized he might never find someone, she decided she had been wrong to cast him into the world between worlds. She wanted to right the wrong, reverse the curse. Tallulah was the first person who was able to make Beautiful's medicine stick sing." He put his palms out and smiled. "You know the rest. They found their bliss, here at the Hotel LaBelle."

Will I find my happily ever after here, too? She needed to find out. Tonight.

He waved her over to the elevator. "One of the first in Montana." Phoebe admired the metal lattice work surrounding the elaborate cage elevator. "Emma will tell you she *personally* polished all the blackened brass and made it shine again."

"Pretty," she signed. "I haven't really had time to

226

appreciate it before today. I've been too busy."

"Busy fighting off bad guys." Bert grinned and gave her a look of pure admiration. "You kicked ass. You are a super hero."

Heat burned her face, and she ducked her head in embarrassment. If he found out about Mexico, he wouldn't think she was such a heroine. She had to tell him.

"I have to tell you about what happened in Mexico."

A puzzled expression crossed his face. "Now?"

"Yes. You need to know the truth about me. I screwed up." She took a deep breath and told Bert everything. "It started like a normal day. My client's family was running late, but with the traffic in Mexico City, that wasn't unusual." She had wandered out into the hallway to the reception area, hoping someone had simply forgotten to tell her the family was waiting. But the reception area had been empty.

She placed her hand on one garish orange seat and waited for the images to rush into her mind. Many people had been there, none of them from the Ramirez family. She repeated the process for each of the dozen seats in the room, narrowing the family's faded images present to the last three seats in the reception area. In her experience, her sharpest psychic images were less than forty-eight hours old. Past that time, her psychometric abilities faded, like a photo left in the sun, growing fainter with each passing day. Since their last visit had been two weeks ago, her psychic images of the Ramirez family would soon vanish.

Maria, a graduate student at the University of Mexico, stared at her computer monitor, engrossed in work. Phoebe tapped her on the shoulder.

Phoebe signed. "I've been expecting the Ramirez family for an hour. Have we received any messages from them?"

"Not that I know of," Maria signed back. "Let me check the TTY." Angela's family was barely able to afford their cell phone, much less a computer or Internet access, so the Institute had supplied them with a used TTY machine. Old technology, but it still worked. Maria came out of the back room, shaking her head. "Sorry, nothing there, either."

"So odd. We were going to finalize the school paperwork."

She turned to go to her office and stopped. Maybe something had happened to them? Perhaps something as simple as bad traffic? She tapped Maria again. "Anything on the news? Bus accident? Maybe delayed?"

"Let me check." Maria switched from her document to an Internet news site and searched the local news. No bus accidents, no traffic jams—well nothing more than the usual for a city of over twenty-one million people. Fingers flying, the graduate student searched several websites—then stopped—and pointed at the screen.

Phoebe leaned in. Her stomach dropped and her mouth went dry. Knees buckling, she gripped the edge of Maria's desk to keep from falling to the floor. If only she had focused on the whole family, instead of just the daughter, she could have stopped them from paying a coyote to smuggle them across the border and then leaving them to die in a tractor-trailer truck in the blazing sun.

Phoebe finished the story and wiped away tears. "I have gifts. I should have been able to save her."

Bert paused in front of a glass display case of intricate beadwork bearing price tags starting in the hundreds. "You know, Stephanie keeps this case full of Crow handiwork. Women on the rez create these and Stephanie gets them into showcases all over Billings."

"What does this have to do with me and my failure?"

"Once upon a time, Stephanie was Stephan. He was an MP at Camp Bullis in San Antonio. He said one day it occurred to him the whole time he was serving in the military, he was more at ease with the women than the men. He began to go to gay bars near the base. And met a Cree Two-Spirit woman who asked him why he wasn't being true to himself. He had rejected his spiritual nature to try to fit in. In essence, he killed his real self."

"And?" *What was he getting at?*

"Stephanie finished her hitch with the U.S. Army and vowed to return to her roots and herself. She re-connected with the women of the reservation and organized the artists' cooperative. Everything goes back to the artists and the rez. Stephanie doesn't keep a dime."

Phoebe's eyebrows shot up. "How does she survive?"

"She does just fine." He grinned. "She's part owner of the Garrett. Brought it back from the brink of bankruptcy when the original owners let it go downhill. She and Rod—you know, Elvis? They organized a group of LGBTQ investors to restore it to its former glory. It was Stephanie's idea to have the drag queen contests. Boom. National recognition."

The penny dropped and Phoebe nodded. "She found herself and in doing so, helped others and succeeded."

"Yes. Take this terrible event, this tragedy no one, no matter how gifted, could have predicted or prevented and use it to grow." He paused. "Don't do something because other people think it's the right thing for you. You owe it to yourself to dig in and remake your life in your own image—not your mother's."

She brushed a tear off her cheek and smiled. "My mother means well."

"I know. She wants the best for you. But at this point only you can say what you really want."

Shoulders back, she nodded. "You're right. I was lost, and my mother provided stability for me when I needed it. Time for me to take back my life."

"Good for you." He grinned. "Just don't toss me aside when you figure it out—okay?"

"You got it." She glanced around. "You know, I've seen the kitchen—and the sticky notes." Phoebe signed. "Why don't you show me the rooms?"

"Sure," he said. "Which one?"

"Let's start with yours." Standing in front of him, she grabbed the sides of his wheelchair, leaned in, and planted a passionate kiss on his lips. As he responded with equal heat, the image of feathers drifting in a breeze formed in her mind. He pulled her down onto his lap and wheeled them both into the open elevator cage.

Well, well, well, she thought. *The elevator's not the only thing going up.*

As she planted kisses on his neck and ears, his hand roamed under her blouse and found her bra, releasing her breasts from its confines. His strong, clever fingers stroked and pinched her nipples until they pebbled, and her breath came in short gasps. Head back, squirming on his lap, positioning herself for maximum contact, she welcomed his growing hardness and the excitement swelling her core. More, she wanted more, and she wanted it *now*.

He fumbled with the key to his room, then slammed the door open in his haste to get inside. As she worked her groin against his erection, she licked his shell shaped ear and nuzzled the spot at the base of his neck. She imagined performing a slow striptease for him, undressing herself one inch at a time, and tossing her clothes at him until she was naked. She'd wait for him to get into bed with her before kissing him from head to belly button—and below. After he begged for mercy, she would—

He placed a gentle hand on her shoulder while leaning back.

Frowning he held his phone up to his ear. Annoyance crossed his face, followed by concern. He pressed the end button. "One of my cousins, Jimmy Two-Toes, has been arrested. I have to go bail him out."

"Can't he wait?"

"He's pretty scared. He was so upset I barely could understand him. Says his mother's out of town, and he's mixed up in some drug thing. Said guys in the detention center think he squealed on them. They'll kill him." He shook his head and gave her a rueful look. "Talk about bad timing."

Disappointed and already missing him, she stood. "The sooner you go, the sooner you can get back here."

She twirled her hair. "While you're gone, I'll take a nap. I have a lot of plans for you, and I want to be rested and ready." Still tingling from his touch, Phoebe straightened her clothes and blew him a kiss. "Hurry back."

He grinned. "It's a deal. I'll be here before you know it."

Chapter Twenty

Hotel LaBelle, Billings, Montana

Once again mentally thanking Lucius and Tallulah for allowing him to leave his shadow black SUV at their hotel year-round, Bert pulled onto I-90, tires squealing. As he drove twenty miles over the speed limit, he fumed and thought of ways to scare the hell out of his idiot cousin. Jail was no place for a kid like him. Under his tough exterior Jimmy was a grandmother's child, spoiled rotten. He wouldn't last a minute inside. The goons in there would eat him alive. Between the Bloods, Crips, Nortenos, MT Front Working Class Skins, White Supremacists, and other less than savory elements, he'd be dead by midnight. Unlike Lucius, who'd had experience handling toughs back in the day, Jimmy had no fighting skill. *Knucklehead.* The second he got his hands on the kid, he was going to chew his ass out for being so stupid. Bad enough he drove like a maniac on his donor cycle, popping wheelies and riding without a helmet. Since when had the gear head turned into a druggie? If he weren't so fond of the kid, he'd have asked someone else to bail him out. But he was family. End of discussion. The city limit sign came into view and he put his blinker on for the exit to take to the Yellowstone County Detention Center.

He sighed. Jimmy's mother, Marjorie Longjaw, would have a heart attack when she found out. Where could she have gone? Her ailing mother lived with her, and Marjory took care of the older woman around the clock. Who was taking care of Jimmy's grandmother? Was that dumbass kid supposed to be looking after her? He gripped the steering wheel so hard, his knuckles turned white. Jimmy wasn't just going to be in trouble with the law. He was going to be in trouble with the tribe. The Crow didn't leave their frail elders to fend for themselves. Besides the kid adored his grandmother.

Something didn't smell right. He pulled out his cell phone, and violating the laws in the Billings Municipality, he searched for Marjorie's number in his phone. Did he have it under Two-Toes or Longjaw? Scrolling and glancing up to make sure he didn't rear end anyone, at last *Marjorie Talks Too Much* popped up in his contacts.

She picked up on the first ring. "Hello, who's this?"

"Marjorie, this is Bert Blackfeather. I'm checking in to see how you and your mother are doing."

"Oh, she's fine. She had some coffee and toast for breakfast. I try to tell her caffeine isn't good for her heart at this age, ya know, but she says she's ninety-six and she's going to eat whatever she wants. The doctor says she'll outlast me, ya know, he said she has good genes. Well, if she has good genes, and I have her genes, then wouldn't I have good genes, too? I mean, half of me came from her, so you'd think I'd have a good long life, wouldn't you?"

Bert ground his teeth and hurried to get a word in edgewise. "Absolutely, I agree. So Marjorie, are you home with your mother?"

"Yes, of course I am. Where else would I be? Silly me. I guess I could be at the grocery store, or running errands, or chasing after my crazy son, or working in the yard, or going down to the ladies' beadwork circle—"

"Marjorie," he barked. "Where is Jimmy?"

"You seem upset. Is there a problem? What happened? Is he in trouble?"

"He might be. Do you have any idea of where he is right now?"

"Yes, yes, I do. He's sitting in my living room playing video games with his best friend, Matthew. Do you need to talk with him?"

"Marjorie, has he been home with you all day?"

"Oh, my yes, last week he took a tumble on that damn motorcycle and broke his leg. Had to take him to St Vic's Emergency Room. Boy was it crowded. Full of sick kids and the police, lots of cops coming and going. The day Miriam was rescued by the senator's daughter, what's her name? Phoebe, that's right. Anyway, the ER was crazy busy, and it took forever for the docs to see Tommy, but ya know, it's okay, they had a lot going on, and he's just fine now. Just so ya know, he's not going anywhere. You need to talk to him? Want me to get him for you?"

Alarm bells blaring in his head, he mustered a calm, low voice. "If you don't mind, I'd like to ask him a couple of questions?"

"Sure thing, hold on, I have to take the phone to him. He isn't getting around very well, what with the leg, ya know. Jimmy, Bert Blackfeather's on the phone, wants to talk to you."

Marjorie ordered the boys to pause the game. The next voice was Jimmy's.

"Hey, what's shakin' bacon?"

Shit, shit, shit.

"Hi there, Jimmy, heard you broke your leg. How you holding up?"

"Pretty good, except I lost my wallet at the hospital. Had all my IDs, a few bucks, plus a bunch of business cards, like yours. Really pissed me off. I had tickets to see the Screaming Hyenas in there, too. Cost me a bundle."

"That stinks, Jimmy. Tell you what, I'll see if we can get you tickets for the Screeching whatevers, okay? A get well gift."

"*Awesome.* Thanks, Bert."

"I'll be in touch." Bert pressed end and spun his mental wheels. The call had been a ruse. Was the trap waiting for him in the detention parking lot? Or was the Blacksmith back at the hotel with Phoebe? He made a U-turn across the median, narrowly missing a sign. Driving like a man possessed, he speed dialed his high school friend. "Hal, this is Bert. Do you have any news about Kuznetsov?"

"Last news is he ditched the stolen car and disappeared off our radar. Maybe he's hitchhiking, maybe he met up with someone. He was heading north, so we figure he must be heading to Canada. We alerted the RCMP. We think he has confederates there, given it's where he was going to take Miriam and Phoebe."

Bert filled Hal in on his odd phone call and odder conversation with Marjorie and Jimmy.

Hal blew out a long breath. "That can't be good, Bert."

"I know. Tommy said he's supposed to keep an eye on the hotel, can you get him on the radio, see where he is."

"Hold on, let me get his fiancée on it." A muffled yell for Wanda followed. Bert glanced in his rearview mirror, half hoping to see a police cruiser. "Bert. We found Tommy, he's halfway to the rez, was going to talk to the Tribal Police Chief Jacob Graywolf about a missing Crow woman. I told him what's going on and ordered him to turn around and head to the LaBelle."

"Thanks, Hal."

The Blacksmith was coming to wreak his revenge.

The woman he cared for was alone and unprotected. He had to get there before anything happened to her, or he'd never forgive himself.

****

As Phoebe rolled over in bed and the room came into focus, she realized she had fallen asleep completely dressed, so exhausted she hadn't even removed her boots. She glanced at the area rug next to the bed and giggled. A Bisou sized lump under the middle of the material told her exactly where the little dog was. Badger hounds, she thought. They do love a good burrow and a good fight. Luckily no badgers threatened the immediate area, so the little dog was safe—and so was her owner.

She yawned, stretched, and glanced at the time. Bert had been gone only forty-five minutes, but it seemed like hours. She couldn't wait for him to get back so they could pick up where they left off. She smiled at the thought of the promised flying lessons. They could have dinner in the historic restaurant another night. Tonight was hers and they would be eating in. A shower was in order—along with a lacy nightgown she packed for the trip.

When she slid to the floor from the high bed, the lump under the rug bounced and moved to the edge. Bisou emerged from her tunnel panting. The little dog ran to Phoebe and jumped at her legs, digging at her as if she was a badger's warren. She lifted the dog and panic and fear flowed from Bisou to her. The dog was terrified. What was going on?

Heavy footsteps thumped in the hallway, shaking the floorboards.

The alarm in Bisou's mind was insistent, telling her to run, hide. Setting the dog down, Phoebe snatched the wooden chair out from under the desk and jammed the back under the door knob. Heart in her mouth, she grabbed her phone to call for help, praying the Billings police had text to 911 services. She pressed the on button, but the screen stayed black. The phone was dead. She couldn't even make an emergency call.

She ran to the window and threw the sash open, hoping Tommy Otterlegs was nearby—or anyone for that matter, other than the owner of the heavy footsteps coming closer. The room vibrated, the doorknob twisted, and the chair jiggled. With each vibration, the chair scooted back an inch. Muscles aching, she pushed the desk in front of the chair, hoping it would slow the monster down.

The Monster.

It had to be him. No one else would be kicking in the door. Only he would find a way to distract Bert, lure him away from the hotel, so he could get his filthy hands on her—and extract his revenge.

Bisou ran into the bathroom, and Phoebe followed.

Tears streaming down her face, she prayed for help, and locked the bathroom door with trembling hands. Once he got through the bedroom door, this one would be next. What could she use as a weapon? Look, woman, look.

The Monster is coming.

Her make-up, hair brush, and razor. *Useless.* A bottle of perfume. A can of hairspray. A pack of matches next to a candle. *Wait.* If she could light the hairspray on fire—surprise the bastard. Making sure Bisou wasn't in the way, she lit a match and a draft of air blew it out. So much for that. A lighter with a continuous flame would be more likely to work. She rubbed the elk tooth on her neck and it grew warmer. She tried to center herself, to concentrate on her strengths—in spite of her jelly legs and chattering teeth.

Focus, Phoebe, focus. I'm on my own. I have to take care of myself. What can I do?

The room vibrated and the bathroom boomed as the door knob jumped. Bisou dove under the bathmat. Heart beating like a hawk trapped in a net, her breath came in short gulps. The Monster was in her room. And he was going to kill her. Worse, he might be planning to do things to her that would make her pray for death before he did. Her gaze fell on the old fashioned toilet—and the heavy porcelain top. She hefted the lid, her arms cording with its weight, and sent a mental thank you to her personal trainer for forcing her to do her hated bench presses. Stepping next to the bathtub and behind the door, she clutched the lid to her chest, and waited.

A gauze covered fist punched through the thin wood and splinters flew into the room. The bandaged hand she had cleaned herself reached down to find the lock.

Time slowed down as if she was under water.

Phoebe raised the slab of porcelain to her shoulder.

The Monster's fingers searched for the lock, getting closer with every second.

Chopping downward with the cover, she smashed the hated hand and rejoiced at the sight of crimson ribbons dripping onto the floor. The surge of victory melted away when a foot kicked in the door—and the Monster followed. Just as he turned his head, she swung the lid like a baseball bat, aiming for his face, but hit his shoulder instead. Sobbing, Phoebe hefted the weaponized toilet part again, only to have it ripped out of her hands.

The Monster grinned and reached over to grab her with his good hand—and looked down, his face a mask of rage.

Attached to his leg was Bisou, her teeth dug in for dear life.

Using the distraction and blessing her little defender, Phoebe snatched up the aerosol can and hosed his face. Clawing at his eyes, shaking his leg, he tossed the little doxie into the side of the clawfoot tub. She fell at Phoebe's feet in a limp ball of red fur. The Monster snarled and grabbed at the air. In spite of the hairspray spewing into his eyes, he lunged forward. In his blind groping, he connected with Phoebe's arm. His eyes flew open, and he bared his teeth at her. Salient memories from his life, a thousand horrific acts of abuse and murder, all accompanied by his sadistic glee, surged into her mind.

Unable to stop the images and the emotions,

Phoebe instead focused on her own emotions and added them to his. Rage that this animal was still on the loose, at how he'd kidnapped Miriam and terrorized the child, at how he had lain in wait for her, just to get to Bert, and how he'd murdered a deputy and now her beloved Bisou—coursed through her body and came together in a knot of hatred. Holding the elk tooth in her other hand, she grabbed hold of her fury and sent it down her arm to his hand. A swirling cobalt cloud coiled around her wrist and pulsed, as if awaiting her command. Focusing her wrath on the Monster, she locked gazes with him—and a blue ball the size of a baseball flew from the tip of her finger, streaking up his arm, to his neck and igniting his face and hair in a burst of flames. He stumbled back out of the bathroom, beating at his head with his hands. The toilet lid, now shattered into jagged chunks, lay at her feet. She snatched up the largest and sharpest piece. Grief mixed with anger filled her legs with strength, and she stalked the predator— now her prey. Just as she raised the shard to stab him in the chest, an enormous eagle flew in through the open window and dove at the Monster.

Beak open, talons extended, the magnificent creature landed on the thug's still smoking head and dug his talons into the criminal's scalp. As the man whirled and beat at the bird, it dug in harder and pecked at the Monster's good eye. Stumbling, banging into furniture, blinded and desperate to escape the attack, the assailant, now the assaulted, didn't see the open window with the low windowsill.

As the Monster flailed at the air, the back of his legs connected hard with the windowsill. Had he been shorter, he would have fallen out the window. Instead, his head slammed into the upper pane and shattered the glass. Knees buckling, he fell forward and covered his face with his bloodied hands. Still attached to his scalp, the eagle tore at his ears with his razor-sharp beak. Footsteps thundered up the stairs and Wanda plus Tommy Otterlegs burst through the shattered door, guns extended.

Ceasing his savage pecking, the eagle loosened his talons and flew out the window.

Sparing a puzzled glance for the bird of prey, Tommy kicked the Monster's legs apart and Wanda cuffed him. After checking on Phoebe, they hauled him to his feet and shoved the bleeding, burned, and blinded man out of the room. Shaking like an aspen in a gale, Phoebe followed them down the hallway and clung to a wall as they went down in the elevator. As they dragged him out the front door, the red and white lights of an ambulance appeared. EMTs were coming to take care of the injured humans—even the Monster.

What about her dog? Was there no one to help her? Where was the emergency vet to treat her brave darling?

Bisou. My poor little baby.

The valiant little doxie had fought the Monster and had given her life for her mistress. Tears running down her face, she turned to go back into the bathroom, dreading what she would find. The little dog was where she had landed. Phoebe slid down to the floor, lifted the doxie onto her lap, and cradled her limp body. Rubbing the elk tooth, Phoebe recalled how she'd found Bisou at a dachshund rescue home and bonded with her when she first petted the little dog. The connection had been almost as powerful as the one she had with Bert. Her best friend, the dog had gone everywhere with her. School, work, even Mexico City. She'd been her mascot, confidant, and constant companion.

Bisou was so sweet, so good. She didn't deserve this.

The Monster *murdered* her. Her little friend was gone. Sobbing, shoulders shaking, she startled when a hand fell on her shoulder. She opened her eyes. It wasn't a hand. It was a huge wing. And the feathers brushed her cheek. She recognized those feathers, those feelings of strength and compassion. His act of comfort made her cry even harder.

The little bundle in her arms wriggled. Astonished, Phoebe gazed down at her tiny four-legged protector. She was alive! Bisou showered her arms with wet doggie kisses, and filled her heart with joy—and images bursting forth with her biting the Monster's ankle. The badger hound had lived up to her name. She turned to sign to Bert, to share her amazement and awe with the man she loved—no matter what form he was in. Instead of an eagle, an EMT stood at her side, an emergency kit in his hand, his face wreathed in concern. As the paramedic assisted her to her feet, her legs buckled, and she pitched forward. Stunned, still clutching Bisou, she stumbled out of the bathroom to the bed and plopped down.

It was over—*finally* over. Now she and Bert could get back to their lives.

Together.

Sharon Buchbinder

Chapter Twenty-One

Hotel LaBelle, Billings, Montana

Bert arrived as the paramedics were strapping the shackled and hand-cuffed Blacksmith to a gurney at the base of the steps of the hotel. Making haste, he parked his SUV, flipped the switch to open the door and slide the ramp out, and then sped out of the vehicle. He rolled out just in time to meet the EMTs, Otterlegs, Wanda, and the criminal at the ambulance. Bandages covered the Monster's eyes and arms, and curses streamed from his mouth in Russian and English.

Bert held a hand up, indicating the parade should stop. "Such a big man. Going after a deaf woman and her ten-pound dog. How low would you go to get revenge? Seems like you've bottomed out to me." He nodded at Otterlegs. "My friends tell me they have a nice secure federal cell waiting for you, separate from the other prisoners. You see, even criminals don't like people who abuse children and pets, so they're *trying* to keep you safe. Course there are no guarantees. Let's just hope your luck doesn't run out for the next one-hundred years." He slapped the man's wounded hand. Hard. The Monster howled. "You take care of yourself, Sergei. No one else will."

The paramedics rolled the screaming and cursing man into the back of the ambulance and Otterlegs hopped in.

"Tommy," Bert called. "Don't ever forget he's a trickster. Don't listen to a thing he says—or believe him if he says he's hurt."

"I won't take my eyes—or my weapon off him," Otterlegs responded. "This piece of garbage is going where it belongs."

"Be safe. Otherwise Wanda will never forgive you."

The redhead who'd been frowning the whole time gave Tommy a smile. "No matter what, you're not getting out of our wedding. Two months and you're mine forever. Don't you forget."

Grinning, Tommy waved until the EMT closed the back door.

Wanda turned to Bert. "I'm escorting them. Gotta run."

"Be safe. You don't want to trip and be on crutches on your wedding day."

Now. Where was Phoebe?

As if in answer to his thought, she appeared in the door of the hotel with a perky looking Bisou in her arms. Racing down the stairs, she nearly tripped, but righted herself at the last minute. She knelt in front of his chair, placed Bisou on his lap, and bowed her head. Shoulders shaking, huge sobs tore from her throat. Bert stroked her head and waited. At last she lifted her tear streaked face, leaned back on her heels, and gave him a crooked smile.

She signed. "What took you so long to get back here?"

Laughing, he responded, "I had to get back to my SUV and change. It would be hard to explain a naked man in your room."

"What if I want a naked man in my room? Like right now? Before any other disasters happen?"

His heart stuttered, and heat flushed his face. "You sure you're still ready to see me—in the *daylight*?"

She frowned and pursed her lips. "Do I look like someone afraid of taking on a challenge?"

"No. You look like a kick-ass heroine named Thunder Heart, and I would be honored and privileged to share your bed."

"You promised me flying lessons."

"And you shall have them. Now, where did we leave off?"

She stood, placed her hands on the sides of his chair, and leaned in for a long passionate kiss.

He closed his eyes and gave her a preview, taking her with him in his memories, soaring over the hotel, and then swirling and swooping down to the river to grab a fat flopping trout in his talons.

She pulled back, breaking the connection, blue eyes wide, her full red lips agape. "Amazing. I want more."

"Advanced flying lessons require both of us to be naked—and in bed, as close as two people can get."

Phoebe stood back. "What are you waiting for? Let's get going."

He chuckled. "Well, you are my boss. I don't want anyone to say you coerced me or I forced you. Do we need to put this in writing?"

She tilted her head and gave him a puzzled look.

"A legal document perhaps? I, Phoebe Wagner, hereby enter into consensual sex freely and without coercion with one Bert Blackfeather…"

She stomped her foot. "Give me your phone."

He handed her his cell.

Fingers flying, she smirked as she tapped. At last, she handed him the phone with a flourish.

"I Phoebe Wagner," he read, "being of sound mind and body, do hereby ask Bert Blackfeather to make wild and crazy love to me all day and all night, until we both fall asleep, are too sore to continue, or both. When we recover, I expect him to continue savaging me until I am a limp dishrag, totally satisfied and ruined for any other man."

"Okay," he signed. "That works."

Dodging a smack to his head, he raced her to the back door. As he rolled into the hotel, he wondered how he got so lucky and called out a plea to the Supreme Being.

Please make this the real thing. Please don't let this just be a fling for her. I don't think my heart can take it if she makes love to me and leaves me.

****

Phoebe paused outside the entry to the kitchen and turned to wait for Bert. "I need a shower," she signed. "The Monster—I can still feel him on my skin."

"You read my mind," Bert responded. "My face was all over his eye and ear."

"Since my room is taped off as a crime scene, I'm going to commandeer the one next to yours." She paused. "Tallulah will be okay with that, don't you think?"

"Yes, but what about Bisou?" He pointed at the doxie. "Is she okay?"

"I patted her all over and she kept wagging her tail. She kept replaying the image of her biting the shit out of the Monster." Phoebe grinned. "Extremely proud."

"Lived up to her fierce fighter reputation." He patted the little dog's head, and her tail swished back and forth. "If she's okay and you're okay, then I'm more than okay."

"Thirty minutes?" she asked. "Meet you in your room?"

"Perfect." He handed Bisou to her owner. "She's a hero, too."

Half an hour later, hair still damp, a fluffy white terry cloth robe wrapped around her, Phoebe stood at his hotel room door. Butterflies flew frantic circles in her belly threatening to fly up her throat and out of her dry mouth. Somewhere between her door and his, her knees had turned to rubber. What if he didn't find her attractive? What if she was lousy in bed? She was no virgin, but it had been awhile—like over two years with no man in her life. After Mexico, self-loathing and depression had robbed her of any sexual desire. Bert had aroused her sleeping tigress, but what if his libido didn't respond in similar strength? What if she scared the hell out of him? Men didn't like needy women. She needed him in the *best* possible way. In her heart. In her life. In her bed. She glanced at her watch. Forty minutes had passed. *Shit.* She was late to her own party. Fingers trembling, she turned the antique brass knob and inched the door open.

The setting sun seeped around the edges of the lowered shades, providing a soft backlight to the room. Pillows heaped behind his back, Bert sat upright in the four-poster bed with a white blanket pulled up to his waist. A broad smile wreathed his face and he signed, "I was beginning to worry I scared you away."

"Me afraid of you?" She laughed. "Never."

He craned his neck to look behind her. "Where's Bisou?"

"Sound asleep in her favorite place—under the area rug in my new room." She paused. "I didn't want her to get in the way of my flying lessons."

"You'll be a natural." He patted the bed. "Why don't you come over here and let me show you?"

She ran her fingers through her hair and shook her head, licking her lips and purposely allowing the robe to slide down one shoulder, exposing her cleavage. Smiling at his wide-eyed stare of appreciation, she caught the terrycloth just before it completely exposed her left breast. Working on a slow strip tease, she repeated the process with the other shoulder. His gaze glued to her chest, he licked his lips and his blanket began to tent. Intoxicated with her power to arouse him and her own pent up desires, she slid the rough material down her hardening nipples, exposing her areoles. Robe wrapped around her hips, she sashayed over to the side of the bed, leaned over, and planted a searing kiss on his waiting lips.

Responding with equal heat, his fingers feathered over her breasts, circling, circling, circling, but never touching her aching nipples. She pulled the fingers of his right hand over her pebbled nub and thrust a searching tongue deep into his mouth, tangling with his. A gentle hand slid beneath her robe, skimming her inner thighs and lower abdomen, gliding around, but never touching her moist core. She moaned and dropped the robe completely, and her naked breasts thrust against his upper body and sculpted muscles. Grabbing his wrist, she led him to her warm triangle,

249

mentally begging him to take her. A flash of blue sky caught her off guard and she pulled back.

He smiled and signed, "Afraid of flying?"

"No."

He slid the blanket down revealing his upper thighs—and his impressive erection. "Will this be a problem?"

Breathless, she shook her head and signed, "I may be walking funny tomorrow, my extra-large man."

He laughed and pulled her closer. She pulled away. "Condoms?"

"Of course." He pointed at a small foil package on the night stand. "Would you like to put it on for me?"

Nodding, Phoebe grabbed it, making quick work of opening the wrapper. Carefully she removed the condom, placed the latex on the head of his penis, and then unrolled it all the way down to the base of his thickened shaft with ever-so-slowly-dancing fingers. She spent extra time *adjusting* it, simply to watch the pleasure on his face.

He opened his eyes, grinned, and signed, "You surprise me."

"Why? Because I'm deaf, I shouldn't be good in bed?"

Bert shook his head. "Because you look like an angel—and tease me like a devil."

She tossed her hair over her shoulder and arched a brow at him. "More where that came from."

"Ready to take to the air?"

She nodded.

"Best way to fly with me is to ride me—like a horse."

My very own stallion. Smiling, Phoebe climbed

onto the bed and straddled his hips.

He grasped her by the waist and drew her down with care. The first touch of his rock-hard penis as he slid into her sent shudders of pleasure through her. She gasped.

Smiling, he signed, "Eyes closed."

As soon as her lids fell, he began a slow, rocking motion, and she responded in kind, her hands on his shoulders, her calves wrapped around his muscular thighs. The blast of the connection knocked the breath out of her and a cerulean sky grew into a large screen, a technicolor vision of the Montana plains. Wind tore at her face, and her arms transformed into large wings, and she tilted one way and then another. Suddenly she rose even higher into the sky, soaring on a thermal updraft, then plummeting downward. The ground raced up at terrifying speed, and her heart thundered in her chest. Mice ran in the long grasses. Trout jumped in the river. A rabbit quivered near its burrow. Instead of slicing through the air and snatching prey from hiding places, they bounced along on the gusts close to the land in a whirl of sky, earth, water, and wind. With each flip, each bump, each new sensation, she rose on her own updraft of arousal, climbing, climbing, climbing—

Back arched, a shudder of intense pleasure rippled through her like an earthquake—and she collapsed onto him, a quivering mass of aftershocks and jangling nerves. She caught her breath—his chest also heaved. Pushing herself up on her hands, she gazed down at him. His eyes opened, and he smiled and quirked an eyebrow, as if to say, "Well?"

She grinned and signed, "More flying lessons,

please."

"Anytime," he responded with a grin. "After I catch my breath. This was intense. You're the *only* woman who's ever taken flight with me." He stroked her hair, pushing it out of her eyes. "It was special. You're special."

"Good. Because, I want to see you naked." Dismounting her stallion, she began to pull the blanket back.

His hand shot out and grabbed her wrist. He shook his head. "No. Too ugly. Will make you sick. I'm not a whole man."

"The parts I see—and enjoyed—work just fine." Phoebe cocked her head. "I'm deaf. Do I disgust you?"

Shaking his head, he replied, "No, no, no. Perfect just the way you are."

"I ripped my soul out and handed it to you on a platter. I told you my dreadful secret. Yet, you still wanted me. Why do you think I wouldn't want you?"

"That's different."

"No, it's not." She paused. "Please, let me see all of you. Just the way you've seen all of me."

Jaw muscles twitching, he stared at the ceiling and flipped the blanket back. "There. Happy now?"

His strong, beautiful legs, each perfect thigh like marble covered in flesh, ended halfway down the calf. Scar tissue, smooth in some places, ragged jigsaw puzzles in others, covered the stumps where his legs and feet should have been. She reached out and stroked his leg, running her hand lightly down from his groin to the end of his leg. He shuddered and his penis jumped. She smiled. *He likes it. Good.* Climbing back onto the four-poster, she knelt at the foot and crawled toward the head of the bed, trailing butterfly kisses up both his legs. Every inch, every scar represented his sacrifice to his country. Every moment she was with him confirmed he was her mate. She'd known the first time they touched. There would never be another man like Bert in her life. She hoped the feelings were mutual. What if she was just a fling? A novel experience, or worse, bragging rights?

Her stomach plummeted at the thought. She had to know. *Now.*

Straddling his hips, she signed, "Are you happy?"

Bert signed, "Put your hand on my heart. Tell me what you feel."

Spreading her fingers, she placed her right palm on his chest, closed her eyes, and opened her mind. A rush of emotions rolled over her. Joy. Gratitude. Admiration. Amusement. Pride. Lust. Affection. Fear.

"Why are you afraid?"

"I don't want to lose you. I need to know. Will you forget about me once we get back to the East Coast? Am I just a Big Sky Country fling?"

"Never. And you? Am I just a bit of fun for you, a spree?"

By way of answer, Bert pulled her down to him, and branded her with a kiss.

Epilogue

Nine Months Later, Hotel LaBelle, Montana

Bert paced the gallery on the second floor, partly from anxiety and partly to ensure his prostheses still fit comfortably. Once he'd proposed to Phoebe—and wonder of wonders, she accepted—he'd yearned to walk down the aisle with her. He went back to Walter Reed and met with engineering students and prostheticians. They showed him state of the art prosthetics and introduced him to men and women amputees who wore them. Amazed at the range of sizes, shapes, colors, and new materials, he selected the design he thought would be most suitable. Two months later, they presented him with his new legs—and for the first time in a decade, he walked—albeit with assistance. After several more fittings, tweaks, and trials, Bert was satisfied his talons were safely tucked in and away from the titanium limbs. Most of the time, his wheelchair which was like an extension of his body, would be his preferred mode of mobility. But on formal occasions, in particular, he would wear his bionic legs. As he walked, the ebb and flow of conversation drifted up from below.

"The Honorable Ruth Wagner invites you to the wedding of her daughter, Phoebe and Mr. Bert Blackfeather—"

"We know what it says, Lucius," Senator Wagner called across the lobby. "We're here, just waiting for the guests to arrive."

"I knew they'd make a great couple," Lucius continued. "Just like I knew Bronco and Emma would get together, didn't I? I think summer weddings are the best. The gazebo and gardens are perfect for the outside seating. I'm glad Bert agreed to get the quartet from Montana State University. Even his old friend, Jamming Joe is here."

High heels clicked on the hardwood floor. "Where is the Justice of the Peace? Where's Stephanie? They should be here by now."

"There, there, you're not in Washington anymore, Senator," Lucius soothed. "We don't measure time by the nanoseconds. When everyone arrives, we'll start. Don't worry, Emma and Bronco's wedding was only thirty minutes past the time on the invite. We have another half-hour to go before anyone is officially late."

Amused Bert placed his hands on the railing and leaned over for a better view.

Out of uniform and looking handsome in a blazer and jeans, Hal entered the lobby and tipped his Stetson. "Senator Wagner. You look lovelier every time I see you. What's your secret?"

"Flattery will get you everywhere. Come over here and tell me why I shouldn't be losing my mind because the wedding planner slash Spiritual Leader slash auntie isn't here yet."

"Stephanie?" He chortled. "Don't worry. She likes to make a dramatic entrance. She'll be here. Let's find the bar, shall we?"

Hal took her elbow, threw a wink back at Lucius,

and led the blushing mother of the bride toward the back yard where a bar awaited customers.

Bert chuckled. *Another romance budding in Hotel LaBelle.*

Dressed in her finest pink party dress, Miriam pranced into the room ahead of Tallulah, a basket in her hand. "Do NOT toss those rose petals yet," Tallulah ordered.

Something tugged at Bert's heart, and he wondered if Phoebe would want to start a family soon. They both wanted children, and they'd had *plenty* of practice. It was time to get down to business.

Tallulah gave Lucius a peck on the cheek. "Hello, my love."

Her husband put his arms around her waist. "You need more kisses to keep the new baby happy." Leaning down, he kissed her belly. "Hello in there, little man."

"In your dreams. I know this is a girl."

"Wanna bet?"

Emma and Bronco arrived pushing a double stroller.

Tallulah waved and said, "Bohpoli returned to Billings with us, just giving you a heads up in case the twins start babbling at him. He's around here somewhere."

"What are we betting on?" Emma asked.

"I say it's a boy, and Tallulah says it's a girl," Lucius said.

Emma kissed Tallulah and Lucius and patted her relative's stomach. "I say it's a baby." She pointed at her own still flat belly. "And this one had better be a solo flyer, or I'm going to lose my mind. One set of twins with paranormal powers is *enough*."

Bronco laughed. "At least they'll all have lots of special teasing cousins to play with."

"Maybe one of them will put a *Kiss Me* sign on the other one's back, like they did to me when I was first introduced to the family," Lucius said shaking his head. "Took me all day to figure out why women and even a couple of men ran up, kissed me, and ran away laughing."

"Hmmm." Emma pointed at the teddy bear floating over Adam's side of the stroller and the dangling colored lights flashing on and off on Emily's side. "I suspect their practical jokes will be a bit more intense."

Bert wondered what kind of powers their children would have. An eagle-shifter and a Thunderbird might have some interesting offspring. Lordy, he hoped he and Phoebe could handle them.

Deep in conversation with Tommy Otterlegs, Jacob Graywolf, Chief of the Tribal Police, walked in the front door. Bert liked Jacob and was happy to see he'd been able to get time away from work to attend the wedding. Jacob and Tommy had been working together on a joint investigation into missing Native American women—and hitting dead ends. Nationally, no one knew how many Native American women were missing. And that was just the beginning of the difficulties of the investigation. He shook his head. The problem wouldn't be solved today. Time to take off his thinking cap and enjoy his special day.

Wanda Otterlegs entered the lobby and squeals of delight emerged from Emma and Tallulah. "Show us your tummy!"

Lucius shook his head. "There must be something in the water. Everyone's getting pregnant."

"Honey that is one thing you will *never* have to say about me." Stephanie swept into the room in a low cut, full-length turquoise gown complete with a train. Rod strode in behind her in full Elvis regalia. "Sweetheart, the band is outside. Why don't you run on out and go over your songs with them?"

"Heads up. Senator Wagner is having a heart attack," Lucius warned. "She thought you'd be here hours ago."

Stephanie snapped her fingers. "I have everything under control—even the weather. Look how perfect the day is. Not too hot, not humid, it's just like I ordered."

A petite blonde in a light gray suit appeared in the doorway and glanced around. "Is this the Blackfeather wedding?"

"Yes, and I'm Stephanie, I'll be doing the honors with you, Ms. Jeffers. I'm so glad you're here. Let's go out to the gazebo and talk about the ceremony. Would you like a drink?"

Lucius gave a low whistle. "She's a purdy little thing. Who woulda thunk, lady lawyers, lady judges, and lady justices of the peace?"

"You look at her that way one more time and you won't have *any* peace, mister," Tallulah snapped at him. "Beautiful—who is currently on the porch in a rocking chair, going at it like crazy—will make your life miserable if she even *thinks* you're working on your 'Love 'Em and Leave 'Em Lucius' title again."

Grabbing his wife by the waist, he swung her around. "I just love to see your eyes turn from blue to green, darlin'."

She punched his shoulder, and he planted a wet one on her lips.

"Where's the groom?" Emma asked. "He should be down here by now, don't you think?"

Bert called from the second floor. "I've been enjoying watching you guys. I think we could have a TV sit-com, maybe call it *All in the Hotel LaBelle Family*."

Emma looked up at him. "More like *The Addams Family Goes to Washington*."

"Oh-ho. Good one." Bert adjusted his war bonnet. "I'll be right down." He summoned the elevator and stepped out to oohs and ahhs.

"Looking good, bro'," Emma said and hugged him. "Great to see you back on your feet."

Lucius stage whispered to his wife, "Better get Senator Wagner. Tell her we're only going to be twenty minutes late."

Tallulah smothered a laugh. "Don't let word get out. Wouldn't want to set expectations for timeliness." She waved her hand at the rest of the group. "Come on people, let's go join the rest of the crowd."

Lucius gave Bert the once over. "I like the white suit. You look good for an old man getting hitched to a youngster."

"This from a man who's over a hundred and thirty years old?" Bert shook his head. "I'm not even forty, a baby by comparison to you."

"You're one lucky sonofabitch. Phoebe is gorgeous, smart, gifted—" he grinned. "—just like my wife. We're both lucky men."

Bert nodded. "Yes, we are."

"Let's get you out to the gazebo, pardner. It's hitching time."

****

Heart in her mouth, Phoebe waited in the office out of sight, clutching her bouquet. Her mother set her drink down and fussed over the veil making sure it was perfect.

"Mom, it's going to be okay." Phoebe signed. "No one will care if a pearl is missing."

"I care," her mother responded. "It was my wedding veil and each pearl on it came from your grandmother. It's something old—like me."

"You're not old," Phoebe signed. "You're young at heart, still beautiful—just ask the sheriff. I saw the way he looked at you outside. You're my heroine. I am so lucky to have you as my mother."

Her mother's eyes welled. "Stop. I'm going to ruin my makeup if I cry." She fanned her face. "I'm going to find Lucius, see if he's ready to walk you down the aisle with me."

Her mother returned with Lucius. He signed, "Beautiful," then spoke to her mother, who interpreted. "You are stunning. My mother was a dress maker, and she made many a fine wedding gown, but none this simple and elegant."

Phoebe's face heated under his scrutiny. "Thank you." The white sheath dress with a low scalloped collar edged in pearls had been her mother's idea.

"Something old—the veil. Something new—the dress," her mother signed. "Something borrowed—the pearl necklace belonging to Tallulah. And something blue—your beautiful blue eyes."

Lucius pointed at Bisou and her mother added, "Something red." The little dog pranced next to Phoebe's stiletto heels, a white ribbon adorning her neck.

Lucius put his elbow out to Phoebe, then grinned and nodded. Phoebe on the other hand, offered her free arm to her mother.

The trio walked onto the back porch, Lucius nodded at the band, and they began to play. As they walked down the white carpet behind Miriam and her rose petals and between the rows of white chairs filled with smiling family and friends, she reflected on the amazing turn of events in her life. In less than a year, this motley crew had become like family to Phoebe and her mother. What happened to the normally contained Wagner women? Something amazing had occurred at the Hotel LaBelle, a transformation of both women—and her life.

Right after returning to DC, Phoebe quit her job as Under Secretary at the Department of Homeland Defense and started a not for profit advocacy agency that hired those with paranormal powers who were, on the surface, disabled. Her group picked up where Bert's Anomaly Defense Division left off—taking on private cases, those not approved for government special agents. She and Bert had taken their time to get to know each other. After dating for six months in a town rife with gossip, no one believed they were *just friends*—nor did she. After a particularly athletic evening of lovemaking, she had taken the leap and told Bert she loved him. To her enormous relief and delight, he had responded enthusiastically with *I love you* and proposed to her. He wouldn't let her get out of bed until she said *Yes*—as if she would have said anything other than that. At last, she had found her passion at work and at home, much like Tallulah and Lucius and Bronco and Emma. Would she and Bert be blessed with little ones soon?

She couldn't wait to see what special abilities their children would have.

The trio arrived at the gazebo, and Lucius stepped off to the side. Bert, along with their future, stood waiting for her. Her mother, eyes sparkling with tears, leaned in for a kiss and then went to her seat next to Hal. Smiling, she wondered if the Hotel LaBelle was pushing the sheriff to her mother—or if it was pulling her mother to him? In any case, her beloved was waiting for her to begin their life of married bliss—and perhaps along with happiness, another adventure. Whatever happened, good times and bad, the people who loved them would be there for them.

If you haven't already, please check out the first two books in the Hotel LaBelle Series:

The Haunting of Hotel Labelle
and
Legacy of Evil

A word about the author...

After working in health care delivery for years, Sharon Buchbinder became an association executive, a health care researcher, and an academic in higher education. She had it all—a terrific, supportive husband, an amazing son, and a wonderful job. But that itch to write (some call it an obsession) kept beckoning her to "come on back" to writing fiction. Thanks to the kindness of family, friends, critique partners, and beta readers, she is now published in contemporary, erotic, paranormal, and romantic suspense. When not attempting to make students, colleagues, and babies laugh, she can be found herding cats, waiting on her dogs, fishing, dining with good friends, or writing. You can find her at http://www.sharonbuchbinder.com

~*~

RONE Finalist, 2018, Short Paranormal

~*~

Finalist, Florida Writers' Association, Royal Palm Literary Award, 2018

~*~

First Place: Series, Paranormal Romance Guild Reviewer's Choice Awards, Romance/Fantasy/Suspense/Time Travel/Historical Western, 2017

~*~

Second Place, Paranormal Novel, International Digital Awards (IDA) Contest from the Oklahoma Romance Writers of America, 2017

~*~

Finalist, Paranormal Romance, National Excellence in Romance Fiction Awards (NERFA), 2017

Thank you for purchasing
this publication of The Wild Rose Press, Inc.

For questions or more information
contact us at
info@thewildrosepress.com.

The Wild Rose Press, Inc.
www.thewildrosepress.com

To visit with authors of
The Wild Rose Press, Inc.
join our yahoo loop at
http://groups.yahoo.com/group/thewildrosepress/